THE END
of the
WORLD
as we
KNOW IT

THE END of the WORLD as we KNOW IT

IVA-MARIE PALMER

HOT
KEY
BOOKS

First published in Great Britain in 2014 by Hot Key Books
Northburgh House, 10 Northburgh Street, London EC1V 0AT

A CIP catalogue record for this book is available from the British Library.

ISBN: 978-1-4714-0253-1

1

This book is typeset in 10.5 Berling LT Std using Atomik ePublisher

Printed and bound by Clays Ltd, St Ives Plc

FSC

Hot Key Books supports the Forest Stewardship Council (FSC),
the leading international forest certification organisation, and is
committed to printing only on Greenpeace-approved FSC-certified paper.

www.hotkeybooks.com

Hot Key Books is part of the Bonnier Publishing Group
www.bonnierpublishing.com

This book is for Clark and Steve, without whom my place in the world wouldn't feel quite like mine.
And for you, Mom. I want to say so many things but none more important or true than that I miss you every day.

Have you ever had one of those life-changing days? "Oh, definitely," you say.

You're thinking: the night you got to second base; your first sip of Natty Light in that musty corner of your next-door neighbor's basement; that time at Taco Bell they gave you a chalupa instead of a gordita and you had a revelation about the menu that felt wise and universal—It's. All. The. Same. Shit.

Well, not to burst your burrito or anything, but you haven't had a life-changing day. Not really. Not in the deep-voiced, movie-trailer-narrator sense: "It was a day just like any other, until one event changed life as he knew it—forever."

Today is that day.

1

THE INVITE

Sarabeth Lewis, 6:49 P.M. Saturday,
Her Bedroom

Sarabeth Lewis was *bored.*

Not just bored with her bedroom, a pink-infused Martha Stewart project of her mom's that made her feel like she was about to be suffocated by cotton candy. Not just bored with the prospect of another Saturday night spent practicing her cello, which loomed in the corner like a massive ball and chain. Not just bored with looking up at the same old ceiling, wondering how a girl could be nearly done with high school without having made one real friend.

She was existentially bored. Bored to the core. Possibly bored in a way no one had ever been bored before. *At least I'm original,* she thought, rolling onto her stomach and heaving a sigh.

"Tonight's topic: three things I'll never be a part of," she said as she wrote the header across the top of her journal. Every topic she dreamed up lately contained the word *never*. Three places she'd never go. The three Interiors—as she called the popular kids who occupied the center of the cafeteria—who would never learn the difference between "their," "they're," and "there." Three supposedly hot guys she'd never go out with, even if they asked.

Pressing her pen to her lips she underlined *Three Things I'll Never Be a Part Of* and wrote: *a* Girls Gone Wild *video; my mother's annual Makeover Madness event*. The words poured onto the page in her loopy, A-plus penmanship. Sarabeth was the last teenager on Earth to give a crap about the Palmer Method. *The guest list for Teena McAuley's Casimir Pulaski Weekend party*.

Except she actually *was* on the guest list.

She flipped a few pages back in her journal and pulled out the red envelope that Teena's friend Dahlia Dovetail had handed her in the cafeteria yesterday. Across it was written the simple message: "You're in. Bring this invite to gain one admittance to Teena McAuley's Annual Casimir Pulaski Weekend Party." Once upon a time, Sarabeth and Teena had been friends, before Teena became a queen bee in eighth grade and left Sarabeth in her glitter-eye-shadow dust. But there was no way Teena had invited her out of fond distant memories. Sarabeth knew her twin brother, Cameron, was responsible. "It wouldn't kill you to get out once in a while," he'd told her on Monday, as she hovered over the stove, trying to master a crepe recipe by Julia Child. "Teena's big party is this weekend. Maybe I can get her to invite you." Cameron was nice, but he wasn't stupid. He had sway with Teena. Her crush on Cameron was as persistent and as obvious as Sarabeth's lack of a social life.

At the time, Sarabeth had thought it was just Cameron being nice and three-minutes-older big-brothery, expecting him to forget what he'd said. Cameron Oliver Orman Lewis—yes, his initials spelled COOL—was the rarest of Interiors. He played quarterback *and* skateboarded, was a drama-club leading man *and* edited the school paper, got good grades *and* went to all the best parties. Oh, and he was nice: Every freak, geek, and chic loved him. Sometimes it bugged Sarabeth that he was such a good guy; she couldn't even hate him for getting the popularity gene that she'd missed. Their mother, Olivia Lewis, had, postdivorce, risen to become the Chicagoland metropolitan area's most successful Gussy Me Up beauty franchisee. Now she often wondered aloud how Cameron had wound up so much more like her, while Sarabeth was like her absentee father. The ultimate insult.

Sarabeth ran her fingertips over the invitation, wishing she still felt as determined to go to the party as she had earlier today. She'd been so excited, she'd snuck a bottle of Chardonnay from her mom's wine rack, since even an outcast like Sarabeth knew you didn't go to Teena's without alcohol. Tinley didn't sell alcohol within its borders, and Sarabeth didn't have Cameron's college-friend connections to help her score liquor. Plus, she'd even ventured out to buy a new outfit. Sitting next to her on the bed was a shiny pink shopping bag from Charlie, one of the trendy stores in the mall she'd always been too scared to enter. Sarabeth dumped its contents onto her bedspread: the still-folded, wisp-thin green crepe sweater, the dark-rinse jeans, and Charlie's signature hot-pink tissue paper. The outfit was far from wild, except for the fact that Sarabeth usually stuck to shapeless black and gray sweaters and pants that didn't call attention to her five-foot-eleven frame.

Feeling the soft fabric of her sweater, Sarabeth instantly fell under its spell. She wanted to wear it. And not just for a date with her cello. She stared at the words on the invite and back at her reflection in the mirror. Maybe this was an I-want-to-get-into-your-brother's-pants invite—but so what? Why should the Interiors have all the fun? *Those kids could probably die tomorrow and feel like they've lived a great life*, Sarabeth thought, knowing she was being a little melodramatic. *And here I am, wondering if my life has even started*.

She pulled off her black T-shirt and slid the sweater on over her head. Even Gussy Me Up's number-one-selling lotion, Smooth Moves, couldn't duplicate the soft sensation.

And then she said the sentence no one should ever utter: "What's the worst that could happen?"

2

SHIRTS VS. SINS

Evan Brighton, 6:52 P.M. Saturday, Orland Ridge Mall

Evan Brighton couldn't decide whether to laugh or cry as he strolled through Orland Ridge Mall, tightly clutching an invitation to Teena McAuley's annual Casimir Pulaski Weekend bash, the knuckles of his left hand turning white. Coach would kill him for putting any strain on his star pitching hand, but Evan didn't care. This party was way more important than taking the Ermer Elephants to sectionals.

This was Teena McAuley.

Teena McAuley, astonishingly beautiful, impeccably dressed, and sexy as all hell—which was where Evan's impure thoughts would certainly send him, if the lessons of parent-enforced Bible study were true. Teena was more than just another girl. She was a dream come true.

Yesterday, Evan'd barely believed it when Teena sauntered up in last-period calculus and dropped the invitation onto his desk, winking one of her sparkly dark brown eyes at him as the envelope fell with a little whisper onto the gray desktop. The irony wasn't lost on Evan. Calculus was the class where he figured he'd blown any smidgen of a shot with Teena McAuley. A month ago, during an exam, she'd been leaning forward in her chair, right behind Evan. She smelled so good he'd stopped even bothering with the differential equation and just breathed deeply so he could smell her. Which sounded creepier than it was. Teena was just one of those people who smelled good. Anyone would be enticed by her flowery perfume as it mingled with a tinge of her sweet-smelling sweat, fresh from her eighth-period gym class. He could feel her breath on his neck, not to mention the threat of an erection growing in his pants.

Wholly unnerved by the idea that Teena might see him pop a boner, he'd croaked, "What are you doing?" His stupid exclamation had brought their teacher, Miss Holman, rushing over to seize Teena's exam and bust her for cheating. The one person in class he'd do anything for, and he'd gotten her suspended. Teena had barely looked at him since. Until now.

So here he was, scouring the mall, desperate for a miracle in the form of a wardrobe update to prove he was worth some kind of attention. It was one prong, the easiest prong, of his plan. He'd sized up the situation the same way he'd size up a batter, trying to take what he knew about a player and mingle it with what he felt in his gut.

What he knew was this:

1. Teena had liked him once. Okay, so it was back in kindergarten. She'd set a pan of plastic hot dogs on the play stove and grabbed Evan from the floor, where he'd been stacking alphabet blocks with future burnout Leo Starnick. "You're my husband," she said, kissing him quickly on the lips. Then she'd flitted away, leaving an awestruck Evan staring so long and so hard at the plastic wieners that the teacher had called his parents out of concern.

2. He was a good-enough-looking guy who, for all practical purposes, *should* have been able to get tail. Evan was the star pitcher of the Ermer Elephants, and girls who didn't know him did check him out. The problem came with girls who *did* know him: They also knew his stepdad was Godly Jim Gibson, head of the Soul Purpose Community Church, the mega-est of the megachurches, sitting at the outskirts of Tinley Hills. No girl wanted to be felt up by a guy whose stepdad's local cable show promised you'd "Watch and learn—or burn!" Unless you counted the chicks who attended the Find Your Soul Purpose teen workshops at the church. They were *easy*, with a creepy, culty center. He'd made out with one moonfaced girl at a church hayride, and she'd wanted to do it in the church "so God could watch." Even a practice round with someone like that seemed likely to put him on a path to obligatory marriage before age eighteen.

3. Teena always wanted what someone else had. Last year, she'd robbed her best friend, Nathalie Oliverio, of her football-stud boyfriend, Jason Keller, only to dump him when he sprained his wrist and was benched for the season.

Knowing all this, Evan decided he couldn't use a direct approach with Teena. He was going to throw her a curve. He absolutely had to publicly make out with someone tonight. He'd make sure to take advantage of the large quantities of available alcohol to find a willing girl who didn't make him too nervous. The girl had to be part of Teena's circle, cute enough to make Teena feel threatened, and not so drunk that she'd forget who Evan was by Monday at school. It was a long shot, but so was pitching more than one perfect game in a lifetime, and Evan had already pitched two.

Besides, you didn't just get invited to Teena McAuley's biggest party of the year. He had to be gaining some kind of social status just to merit an invite. He guessed it had something to do with the recent story in the student paper, the *Ermer Herald*. No one read the paper, true, but an extremely flattering photo of him pitching had recently appeared next to the headline THINGS LOOK "BRIGHTON" FOR ERMER ELEPHANTS. His hair was curling up in just the right way under the rim of his blue hat, his outstretched pitching arm looked ripped, and his normally wide eyes had taken on a semi-cool squint against the harsh glare of February's cold but blinding sun. Coach made Evan start practicing early, since Evan didn't play a winter sport. Playing varsity ball was about the only thing that made him feel normal and the only thing he could think of that might inspire Teena to think of him as an actual guy and not just a huge joke.

He'd been wandering the mall since blowing off Saturday practice at three thirty. He'd seen some of his classmates, mostly cute girls and all probably Teena invitees, at the mall, too. They'd all seemed surprised and confused to see Evan Brighton out doing anything remotely normal. When he wasn't at baseball practice, he maintained a steady and strictly enforced schedule of Bible study, churchgoing, and "supporting" his stepfather's mission by sitting in the front pew for televised fund-raising specials. He didn't usually hang out at the mall and had even heard one girl ask her friend, "Isn't he the one with the *church* dad?" The only person with less mall cred than him was Sarabeth Lewis, who he'd almost crashed into. She'd been clutching a distinctly pink shopping bag from Charlie, one of the nicer girls' stores in the mall, against her chest nervously. The smartest, most accomplished girl in their class was pretty much a loner, and if anything, she had seemed like she might be more uncomfortable at the mall than Evan was. His stomach growled, reminding him he'd been here for more than three hours and hadn't bought anything. Food first. Then he'd make a decision. He ambled past a mom pushing a double-wide stroller and brushed by the line of old men sitting alongside the gurgling water feature, all holding their wives' purses in their wrinkled laps.

The aromatic cocktail of the four most popular fast-food eateries collided together before he even made it past the Hat Hut. Cinnabon's hypnotically sweet odor rose up over the orange duck sauce from China Wok, dancing together with the spicy grease of Happy Gyro and the melted cheese and pungent garlic of Phat Phil's Pizza.

Evan spun left to get in line at Phil's, watching as Leo Starnick tossed a circle of dough in the air. An older girl in a tight CAMEO BEAUTY INSTITUTE tee studied Leo intently. Her talonlike nails gripped the top of the glass case filled with pasta salads and hot pizza slices as Leo worked in the open kitchen that faced the food court. Her eyes focused on Leo's sinewy arms, probably wishing Leo's gaze were directed at her instead of the dough.

If they were still friends, Evan might have asked Leo for help with his Teena predicament. Leo had a rep as a lady magnet, even if he did pull some trashy women. But they didn't exactly run in the same circles. Actually, if Evan thought about it, neither of them really belonged to *any* circle. Leo wasn't a full-on burnout, since he somehow played in the string ensemble and was rumored to be a near-genius, despite his GPA. And Evan might have played sports, but he was no jock. Every time he walked into the locker room, his teammates' conversation about tits, ass, and who was getting what abruptly stopped, as if Evan would be reporting back to his stepdad on their sins. It was hard to find a circle when everyone rated you about as much fun as a geriatric Walmart greeter.

Evan ordered two slices of pepperoni, and Leo walked over to ring him up. "It's one-fifty-two, man," Leo said with a grin.

Evan stared at Leo, bewildered. That was only enough to cover the Pepsi when his total should have been about seven or eight bucks. He pointed down at his slices. Leo shook his

17

head. It hit Evan that Leo had given him the slices for free. He pushed a few bills across the counter.

"Thanks, man." Evan dumped all his change in the tip jar, and Leo gave him a quick thumbs-up that would have looked dorky if someone else had done it, but somehow managed to look cool on Leo.

The simple fact that he hadn't paid for two slices gave Evan a boost. He devoured his pizza in a series of piggish gulps and washed everything down with his Pepsi. Now he could add Gluttony to his list of sins. Take that, Godly Jim Gibson.

Evan strode out of the food court toward King Clothing and stepped inside. The air felt cooler, and charged techno pulsed in his ears. The store was pretty empty, most shoppers not prone to picking up Saturday night's outfit on Saturday night. No sooner had Evan approached a display of jeans than a stocky guy he recognized as an outfielder from St. Albert's, one of the Catholic schools farther east, approached him. His silver name tag read DAVID.

"You checking out the Royals?" The guy gestured at the piles of jeans, pulling out a thirty-two-by-thirty-four, Evan's size. He unfolded them, draping the fabric carefully over one of his arms like he was showing Evan Jesus's shroud. "This is a good jean."

Evan reached out tentatively and felt the fabric of the "jean." It was soft and felt lived-in, nothing like the stiff denim his mom brought home from Kohl's, where she always bought Evan and Godly Jim matching khakis and polos. Evan peeked at the price tag on the waistband. Seventy-nine dollars.

"They're expensive," he commented, watching David's

expression change from cocky to annoyed.

"You're that dude who pitches for Ermer, aren't you?" he said with a fake smile. Evan could almost see the gears working in the guy's brain as he tried to make a sale. "Brighton, right? You're good. Look, you seem like a nice kid, but you're never going to get to second base in clothes like that."

Evan looked down at his glaring orange long-sleeved polo and compared its unflattering cut to the way David's tissue-thin T-shirt and V-neck sweater clung with the right tightness to his arms and abs. *That is so gay of me*, Evan thought. But it was like David had read his mind. He could afford the jeans, with money he'd saved from giving private pitching lessons. And they wouldn't do him any good with an old-man polo shirt. "And how much is that sweater in the window?" He pointed to a light gray sweater. He could practically hear Teena cooing, "Oooh, that's so *soft*."

David perked up a bit, a dimple appearing in his olive skin. "There's a sale on all slim-cut cashmere blends. Buy one, get one half off. You can get that and a backup for seventy-four ninety-nine."

It was a lot of money, but Evan had started to feel like he was taking the mound on a day when he knew he couldn't lose. "Okay, I'll take it all," he said decisively.

Twenty minutes later, Evan emerged from the store with the jeans, two sweaters, and two new soft tees like David's. The clothes in his bag symbolized Vanity, Greed, and probably Pride. *Not a bad Saturday night for a goody-goody*.

He looked up across the mall concourse, where the sin of Lust was taken care of by the window-filling posters of a platinum-blond Victoria's Secret model. As he stared a little too long into her deep cleavage, the model's face was replaced with Teena's. Evan gulped.

"What'd you buy, Evan?" he could almost hear poster-Teena saying. *"Something to make me think*, When did Evan Brighton get so doable?"

Evan felt blood rushing away from his face and arms and legs, like he was dying and coming to life simultaneously. An old lady clutching a tiny Hallmark bag tottered past him, muttering, "Pervert."

Evan sped toward the exit, his legs still wobbling. He was just feeling guilty. He'd spent a lot of money, and now he was going to lie to his mom and Jim to go to a party. But it was worth it, whatever happened tonight. *I need this*, he thought. Using a pitching tactic, he reminded himself that what mattered was the *game*, not the individual opponent. And tonight, he reminded himself, was not about Teena, even if it was about Teena.

He tossed his car keys up in the air, catching them on their way down. He had about an hour to find a safe place to change clothes and call one of the guys in his all-male, overnight Bible study to claim the flu and account for his absence. It wasn't the best of plans: Every Sunday, Evan always had to stand outside the church, flanked by his mom and stepdad, posing like a happy family as they sent worshippers on their way. He had to hope that none of his Bible study classmates would stop after church tomorrow to ask him if he was feeling better. Jim would probably love to end his world, Old Testament–style.

But for right now, he couldn't be bothered thinking about the future. The game was about to start, and he had to play.

3

SPECIAL DELIVERY

Leo Starnick, 7:29 P.M. Saturday, Phat Phil's Pizza, Orland Ridge Mall

Leo Starnick inhaled deeply, wondering if he could pop a blood vessel in his brain if he sucked in enough of the dank skunk weed he'd just spent last night's tip money on. His usual dealer, Tommy Philbin, had been busted by mall security for loitering outside the Hallmark store, where all the cute girls worked, so Leo had had to buy his stash off the zitty thirty-something dude who still hung out at City Arcade, aka Shitty Arcade, in the recesses of the mall basement.

He held in a cough until his eyes watered and stared past the mall Dumpsters up into space. Just as the vein in his temple started to pulse, he exhaled, the warm smoke from his lungs rising in white plumes against the cold, dark March sky. "No blood vessels were harmed during the making of this picture," he muttered to himself, watching the smoke vanish into whatever was beyond.

Leo leaned against the chain-link fence as a horsey blonde clip-clopped toward her car, chattering on her cell. "I just bought a totally boobalicious top for Teena's tonight. Adam is going to wish he never met that flat bitch he's with."

"She's a goner," he said, again to himself, with a roll of his eyes. It was a little game he liked to play while high, and bored, and not eager to return to his shit part-time job at Phat Phil's Pizza. He listened to mall patrons talking on their cells or to each other—and they always talked, pointlessly, endlessly, never shutting up—and decided who aliens would vanquish when they landed in Tinley Hills.

It was fucked-up fantasy gamer shit, he knew, but for some reason, Leo couldn't *not* think about aliens when he was alone with his thoughts and under the influence. They *had* to exist, and he had no doubt that—when they came in not-peace—they'd land here. It wasn't just stoner wish fulfillment. He'd really thought long and hard about this theory, and Tinley Hills was the place. With its 63,000-plus residents, it was just small enough for an alien race to overtake, but just big enough to be a worthwhile target. And the people made it easier. Most Tinley-ites thought that this nothing suburb was the center of the universe. Tinley Hills's motto was "Now this is the life," and tons of these morons believed it couldn't get better than this. Teena McAuley acted like just because Tinley wasn't Bumpkinville, she was two steps away from being "totally LA"—but better, because the crime rate was lower and everyone here had car insurance. Hell, when the aliens landed and told Teena's crowd anal probes were really hot in Hollywood, they'd line up to go first.

Leo would never be so dumb—low-quality marijuana or not. His brain was always going, even though everyone at S. H. Ermer High took him for nothing more than a garden-variety burnout. No matter that he played first-chair cello in the string ensemble, or that he'd gotten a near-perfect verbal on his SAT. His classmates focused on his other activities. Namely, getting stoned and sucking face with S. H. Ermer's sluttiest students (or, if things were going particularly well, the tramp-stamped, fake-baked, slightly older chicks who took classes at Cameo Beauty Institute in the mall). True, maybe he did think with his dick a good part of the time, but his dick was still smarter than the majority of Tinley Hills's residents.

Leo twirled the joint between his thumb and forefinger, watching as Evan Brighton exited the mall, clutching a black lacquered King Clothing bag and scanning the lot for his car. The kid looked lost in his own thoughts and seriously damaged, his eyes wide and his hair standing up in points. "Evan might make it," Leo said aloud. Back in grade school, they'd been friends. He was a good guy.

Leo pulled the joint up to his lips. Suddenly his pot was batted away, sending an arc of orange sparks into the air. Leo spun around on his faded black Doc Martens and found himself looking into the eyes of his boss, the aforementioned Phil, who was far more fat than phat. Phil's fleshy face glowed green under the lamplight, every pockmark and too-long nostril hair illuminated. His tiny eyes were engulfed in flesh. It was a wonder he could see.

"Talkin' to yourself again, Starnick?" he rasped. "And where's your hairnet?"

"Your mom's hair was in her face when she was servicing me last night," Leo deadpanned, running his hand over his messy mass of dark brown curls.

Phil's deep wheezy laugh went on for far too long. Phil loved "your mom" jokes, even if they were about his own mother. *Especially* if they were about his own mother.

"You've been requested," he said when he finally calmed down. "A Teena McAuley just ordered a dozen pies and specifically asked for you to deliver them."

Leo raised an eyebrow. In the middle of last summer, when the heat got so oppressive that the only place to get comfortable was the air-conditioned environs of the mall, Teena had succumbed to Leo's burnout charms. All he'd had to do was slide a free slice of Phil's veggie pie across the counter to her, smirk while glancing at the sheen of perspiration around her nose, and then turn his back on her. She'd stalked off, but returned later that night as Leo closed up, in a new outfit and makeup freshly applied by the professionals at Macy's. Leo had finished closing without speaking to her and then asked, "Wanna go somewhere?" to which Teena nodded with an irritated expression. They'd made it no farther than the parking lot of the Hot Cup Coffee Shop. Her friends didn't know: They'd all been vacationing or in the throes of their own summer flings. And her parents had been at their lakeside cabin in Traverse City, enjoying the spoils of Mike McAuley's still-thriving-against-all-odds real estate empire.

The sweaty affair had carried them all the way to the

beginning of September, even though Teena wasn't particularly nice to Leo and Leo thought she had all the layers of a cupcake. They kept off each other's nerves by making sure they seldom conversed. Leo put an end to it the week after school started, not picking up when she called, or heading out to the Dumpster whenever she approached Phil's counter. She'd have ditched him anyway, Leo figured, and they certainly weren't going to find out they were soul mates. Back at school, Teena seemed to have no trouble treating him like he didn't exist.

But now she wanted him to drop by. Her stubborn pride was less intense than he'd thought. He could give her one night of summer redux, Leo decided. Wouldn't Casimir Pulaski want it that way?

Phil lumbered behind him, breathing heavily. "I swear, Starnick, if this by-request business is you delivering weed on the side, I want my cut."

Fifteen minutes later, Leo was steering away from the mall toward Diamond Isle Estates, a subdivision next to the Ruby Shores Golf Course and Country Club. The smell of pepperoni, onions, and cheese permeated his car, mingling with the sweet, stale aroma of Leo's prework joints. He was driving his favorite stretch of LaGrange now, through the forest preserves, the only section of Tinley Hills not touched by a prefab McMansion or Applebee's. He rolled down the windows and let the crisp air whip against his skin as he inhaled the clean quiet.

He weaved down the curvy road, getting closer to Teena's house. He wondered how they were going to steal away from the crowd that had inevitably shown up for her annual Casimir

25

Pulaski Weekend bash. It was the biggest party of the year. Sad, considering only a handful of Ermer students even knew who the dead Polish dude was. Sadder still that, on that count, Leo couldn't even feel superior to his classmates. To him, Pulaski was just a street that ran through Lawn Grove, two towns over. But probably every school in Illinois had a long-weekend party like Teena's, so hopefully somewhere the Polack bastard was smiling.

Leo's phone vibrated. He looked at the screen. Teena.

"Wow, you really can't wait. Don't worry, I'm on my way," he said by way of a greeting.

"Whatever, Leo. The pizzas are for the party. And you're not invited," Teena sniped. She'd started handing out her invitations a few weeks in advance, so that the buzz would grow. She was the only teenage girl on Earth to handwrite summonses to her party instead of using a mass Facebook invite.

"So why'd you ask for me, then?" Leo said, turning down Emerald Cove Drive. Every street in Diamond Isle Estate was named for a precious gem.

"I just wanted to see you," Teena said, her voice picking up a breathiness that Leo couldn't resist. "But come to the back door."

"Back door?" Leo grinned before hanging up.

He took a left onto Sapphire Ridge Avenue, following it as it twisted onto Diamond Peak Lane, where Teena's house was the centerpiece of a cul-de-sac. It was the biggest house in the whole subdivision, sprawled across three lots like a Southern plantation, with ample parking. It had been specially designed by the developer for Teena's father. To Leo, it looked like someone was trying to overcompensate for a small dick with a lot of white columns.

Cars were lining the street, and people flowed into Teena's front door clutching bottles of hard lemonade and Goldschläger. It showed Teena's power over her followers. Tinley Hills was a dry town, and yet all her guests took the trouble to head outside the town borders to pay alcoholic tribute to her. That was part of why Teena's annual bash was such a big deal; it was guaranteed to be the drunkest Ermer party in Tinley Hills for the whole year.

Some Miley Cyrus song poured out the door, and a few already-drunk girls stripper-danced shoeless on the lawn, skipping between patches of grayed snow that still hadn't completely melted. It couldn't have been more than thirty degrees outside.

Leo pulled into the side drive, the brakes on his 1995 Honda Civic creaking like a door in a haunted house. He was a little annoyed with himself for following Teena's instructions but knew it probably killed her to have called him. He could play along.

He pulled out six pizzas from their red insulated case and walked up to the back door, which opened into the laundry room. He knocked and waited for a solid minute before Teena's face appeared in the window.

"I ordered twelve," she said when she opened the door, a touch of something strawberry and alcoholic on her breath. Her lean frame was displayed in a red halter dress that hit mid-thigh, baring what seemed like a mile of taut, tanned leg, an impressive feat considering she couldn't have been more than five-three. While she wasn't much in the chest department, her breasts filled the halter nicely, seeming to defy any need for extra support. Leo's eyes scrolled up toward her pillowy red lips, ski-jump nose, and wide-set dark brown eyes, curtained by soft, pale-blond waves. She took the pizzas from Leo and set them on top of the dryer.

"They're in the car. I was wondering, why *did* you order twelve?" Leo asked sarcastically, wondering if he was an idiot for being so easily seduced. But one look at Teena's lips and he accepted his fate. "You know, in pornos, the guy only brings one. It keeps things simple."

"You wish." She leaned her head out the door so they were almost nose-to-nose. Then she laid one hand on his chest and gave him a little shove backward toward his car.

"All twelve it is, then," Leo said, smirking, as he hopped down the concrete stairs. "If you're lucky, I'll give you a discount."

Teena extended her middle finger out the door, but Leo pretended not to see. He jogged to his car and grabbed the other sleeve of pizzas, looking up at the sky. "What am I thinking, right?" he said to no one. "Just vanquish me already."

Leo stepped into the laundry room. The first stack of pizzas and Teena were gone. He set down the next six pies and leaned against the cool metal of the dryer as he waited.

Teena sauntered back in a minute later, brushing by his body. Leo did his best not to react. He reminded himself that he wanted her, but he didn't like her. And he refused to treat Teena like a princess, like every other guy at Ermer did. He knew better.

She leaned against him and reached behind him, hefting up the pizza boxes with her toned arms. "I'll go put these in the other room for my invited guests," she said. "Why don't you meet me by the wine cellar?"

Leo's eyes widened. On one of those excruciating summer days, they'd sought the coolness of her dad's weird wine cellar and ended up having the hottest hookup known to man.

"You're not worried about being cold?" he asked as Teena tottered toward the door on her black high-heeled boots.

"Never with you," she said with a wink.

Leo wondered if tonight would surpass that sticky summer day. As soon as Teena was out of sight, he rushed out of the laundry room and down a narrow hallway to the big metal door that marked the entry to the wine cellar.

If you could call it that. Teena's dad hadn't just been thinking about his Beaujolais when he built the cellar; it was some end-of-the-world, protect-the-rich-dude shit. To access the door from the outside, your thumbprint had to register on the recognition pad. You also had to have a keycard—which Teena's dad reprogrammed each week—to get both in and back out again, which seemed intense and unnecessary to Leo. Beyond the racks of wine was a gun case, holding all of Mr. McAuley's totally-unnecessary-for-the-suburbs weaponry.

Teena's heels clicked down the hall, and Leo tried to put the Glocks and Uzis out of his mind; they were not exactly turn-ons in the moments before planned nudity with their owner's daughter. Especially if you were still a little high and a lot paranoid. Teena grinned and neared him, sipping from a fresh tumbler of some strawberry vodka girlie drink.

"Nothing for me?" Leo asked, closing the gap between them. She shook her head and pressed the thumbprint recognition pad, sliding her keycard into the metal slot. Leo watched as the door swung open with a groan, the light next to the slot turning from red to green. *It's go time.* She led him down the stairs.

"You won't need it," she said, turning to face him when they were at the bottom of the stairs. Leo's heart thumped, and he urged himself to calm down.

He took a piece of her hair and pushed it behind her shoulders, his fingers running under the halter dress strap, dancing along her collarbone. Teena backed away ever so slightly.

"You know what? I think I might go slip into something . . ."

"More comfortable? You're such a cliché," Leo said, even though he was excited by the prospect that Teena might have an outfit even sexier than what she was wearing.

Teena just grinned and backed up the stairs, holding eye contact with Leo the entire time. She slid her keycard into the door and stepped up out of the basement, her beautiful, flawless face peering around the edge of the door. Her pale hair sparkled in the low-lit room. "Leo?"

"Miss me already?" He looked up with a grin, but her eyes had gone from playful to icy cold.

"I'm blaming last summer on an extended case of sun poisoning," she said with the cool detachment of a hired assassin. "I would not go near you again if you were the last guy on Earth. How's that for cliché?"

Teena smirked one last time. And then she shut the heavy metal door in his face.

4

GETTING A LIFE

Sarabeth Lewis, 9:49 P.M. Saturday,
Diamond Isle Estates

Sarabeth pulled up to the curb two blocks from Teena's house in her mom's pink-and-ivory Gussy Me Up van. Cameron had to pick up his semi-skanky girlfriend from St. Christopher's in Lawn Grove, two towns over, so he'd taken their mom's new Escape hybrid SUV, while Sarabeth was stuck with the van. The vehicle was so obnoxious she might as well have been driving a giant cold sore.

A few girls Sarabeth recognized as dance squad members strutted down the sidewalk toward Teena's house, their shoulders bared in shimmery tanks and halters. As they passed, they shot looks at the van. Feeling ridiculous, Sarabeth ducked her head, pretending to look for something on the passenger seat.

After enough time had passed, she made her way up Teena's

walk, holding the chilly bottle of Chardonnay and feeling stupid. She rang the bell, even though the front door was still partially open. Karen Walsh, who presided over all of Ermer's anti-drinking programs, opened it the rest of the way, looking tipsy. Sarabeth handed her the invitation and the wine. Karen made a weird face at the wine and the invite, then slur-yelled, "Teeeeennna, I don't know this girl."

Sarabeth leaned against the railing alongside the stairs, feeling suddenly small. It was hard enough psyching herself up to go to an Interior party. At the very least, she wanted to get in.

Teena materialized in the living room, sauntering up to the door. "Karen, you didn't have to yell. Sarabeth!" Teena cooed shrilly. "I'm so glad you could make it."

She stepped backward into her house and gestured for Sarabeth to come inside. The house was much bigger than the one Teena had lived in when they were friends, and Sarabeth tentatively entered the foyer. It was a wide, high-ceilinged space situated between a massive living room, where most of the furniture had been cleared out and guests danced or gathered around a low china-cabinet-turned-makeshift-bar, and an equally large dining room, where three kegs were lined up next to an oak staircase. Sarabeth recognized some of Cameron's football teammates playing beer pong on the polished mahogany table.

She unbuttoned her pea coat and slid out of it, leaving just a thin sweater between herself and a room full of people. She suddenly felt naked, even though her sweater was practically a burka compared with the low-cut tops every other girl wore. From an evolutionary standpoint, none of the guys here would

32

notice a girl in a long-sleeved, modestly cut sweater. *I have nothing to show off*, she thought, pushing up her sleeves. Wrists would have to do.

"I thought you'd show up with your brother, though," Teena said to Sarabeth with a blindingly white smile. "Where is Cameron?"

Sarabeth rolled her eyes nonchalantly, like she and Teena constantly had conversations about Cameron. "He's picking up his girlfriend, Nina. She goes to St. Christopher's in Lawn Grove. God only knows why they got back together."

Teena's face fell, and in that instant Sarabeth knew she'd been right: Teena had only invited her to get to Cameron. Cameron and Nina *had* broken things off just after Valentine's Day; maybe Cameron hadn't put the word out that they'd reunited on Nina's birthday last week.

"Yeah, I don't get why your brother is with her, either," Teena said in a clipped tone very different from the one she'd used to greet Sarabeth. She clapped her hands together. "Well, why don't I give you a quick walk-through and show you where to put that?" She pointed at the pea coat draped over Sarabeth's arms like it was a dead animal.

Teena turned on her high heels and wove expertly around Faith Miller and three of her friends, who were grinding messily with each other. They passed a couple making out and two jocks engaging in a chugging contest. *This isn't a party, it's an obstacle course*, Sarabeth thought, feeling disheartened. Who was she going to talk to?

Teena turned down a long dim hallway that led past a laundry room and toward a big metal door. "I'm having everyone put their coats in the basement," she explained. She walked ahead of Sarabeth, accessing the door with a thumbprint pad and a keycard like something out of a spy movie.

Sarabeth debated saying she didn't feel well and just leaving. She could even go get a coffee somewhere so her mom wouldn't question her early return. But then she reminded herself that the hardest part had to be walking through the door in the first place. She would give it an hour.

Teena was waiting with an impatient look etched on her pretty face. "Head down the stairs, and on your left, you'll see a rack of coats where you can hang yours, 'kay?"

Sarabeth forced a smile, wondering how she and Teena had ever been friends. She stepped onto the dimly lit staircase, and cool, dry air hit her skin. At the bottom of the staircase, Sarabeth looked left for the rack Teena had mentioned, but there was nothing in sight. No coats to the right, either. Teena's light giggle descended from the top of the stairs, and a chill crept up Sarabeth's spine. She looked back toward the big metal door just as it closed, in a solid, heavy, airtight kind of way.

Sarabeth ran to the top of the staircase, pushing against the door. It had no knob. No discernible handle on the inside. There was a keycard slit and another thumbprint pad, and that was it. Her stomach instantly tied itself in dozens of painful little knots. How long would she be down here? Why had she trusted Teena to send her down a dark, cold staircase? Why on earth, when she'd wondered about the worst thing that could happen, hadn't she thought of *this*? And why did she have the sinking feeling the worst was still to come?

5

IT'S MY PARTY AND I'LL CRY IF I WANT TO

Teena McAuley, 10:08 P.M. Saturday, Diamond Isle Estates

"Teena, did you invite Evan Brighton?" Karen Walsh's shrill voice came through the intercom in Teena's room. "He has an invitation, but I don't know why."

If you wanted something done right, you didn't ask a drunk girl to do it. She'd told Karen she was taking a little break—after learning Cameron was going to bring that non-Virgin Mary, Nina, she needed a breather—but to let her know when Evan Brighton got there. Teena should have given the assignment to someone who hadn't been mainlining Jell-O shots all night.

"I'll be right down," Teena sighed, letting go of the speaker button on her nightstand. "Subtle, Karen," she mumbled to herself as she sprang up from her oak four-poster bed.

Teena had about given up on the loser, figuring he'd chickened out.

She wove past a group of her girlfriends, all wasted and comparing hair textures. "My hair is so fine," whined Nathalie Oliverio, clutching her straight caramel strands. "I can't do anything with it. Look at Teena's hair. It's so thick."

Teena smiled tightly. Locking up Nathalie for the night would be great. Actually, she was kind of sick of *all* the guests who she wasn't locking in the wine cellar, aka the Loser Dungeon. She used to like hosting the most exclusive party at Ermer High—her freshman year, even seniors had begged her for invitations—but now that she was a senior, throwing the year's biggest bash had lost its luster.

In the living room, defensive lineman Dave Brandt was performing yet another keg stand, with three other football players holding up his massive, jiggly frame. As he chugged upside down, his Ermer Elephants shirt slid down, exposing his pasty belly. *Nasty.*

"Thanks, Karen, I'll take it from here." Teena patted Karen's bony shoulder, exposed in an all-wrong off-the-shoulder sweater. Teena greeted Evan with a thousand-watt smile.

She was surprised to see him looking so . . . good. She knew he had the basics: a lithe, athletic frame; a decent face; and thick, sandy-blond hair. And here, on her doorstep, he'd encased his basics in a cashmere sweater that cut close to his lean abdomen and a pair of dark jeans that hinted at muscular legs and showed off a very cute butt, Teena's boy weakness. Evan Brighton was supposed to show up at her party in an ugly polo shirt still creased by store folds and a pair of Dockers that Mommy had ironed for Sunday's sermon.

"Hi, uh, Teena," he said, picking up a Jewel bag at his feet and handing it to her. "I, uh, brought some chips and dip."

Okay, here was the loser she knew and didn't love. Who brought chips and dip to her party? Would he pull out Scattergories next? Teena forced herself not to laugh, instead taking Evan by the arm.

"You're so thoughtful! Thank you," she said sweetly, steering Evan into the living room. "I think there's a bowl downstairs that needs refilling. Do you want to come with me?"

Evan's ruddy cheeks turned redder. "Um, sure," he said, smiling widely.

This was just too easy. She probably could have just asked Evan outright, "Hey, I'm going to lock you underground for several hours, maybe all night, okay?"

"Come on." She brushed past Karen, Nathalie, and several other girls. They watched her, bewildered either by Evan's new look or by the fact that Teena was talking to him. She had her reasons, though. Evan had to pay for getting her busted in calculus. And while Teena could take an occasional detention for using her cell phone in class or showing up late for first-period French without a note, she'd never in her life been suspended before. She'd had to give up her red Honda Pilot for a full week, and her dad had started imposing limits on her Visa card.

As for Leo, she should have left him down in the cellar to rot the same day they'd hooked up there. She hated that *he'd* been the one to stop calling *her*. And even in the middle of their fling, or whatever it had been, he'd treated her like a piece of meat. Like he was so deep and thoughtful and intellectual, and *she* was the moron who looked good naked. She grinned to herself, thinking of Leo's face as she shut the door on him. Who was the moron now?

She'd really only intended to exact revenge on Leo and Evan. Sarabeth had been a crime of passion. It was true—she'd never have invited her to the party if she could help it. But Cameron could make her act not like herself at all. He'd hinted that it would be nice of her to throw an invite his sister's way. So finally, on Friday, at school, she'd casually said, "I have a few extra invites for my party tonight. Do you think your sister would still want to go?" Cameron had raised an eyebrow and looked at her skeptically, but she'd been sincere. Sure, she didn't *want* losers at her party, but a girl had to do what a girl had to do to get the guy she wanted to do.

Teena turned to look back at Evan, who was walking goggle-eyed through the kitchen, where things had gotten even rowdier as more liquor was consumed. Dahlia Dovetail was sitting on the counter with her legs wrapped around Brad Michner, her ever-present elf boots pressed into his back. Brad's hands were shoved up her shirt, clumsily fumbling with her breasts.

"Only a little farther," she purred, watching the blush return to Evan's face. He really would be cute if it weren't for his wide-eyed Jesus-freak stare. What girl wanted to date a guy whose stepfather could banish them to hell?

She slowed her steps and took his arm. "You're not nervous, are you?" She lowered her eyelids, looking up at him through her lashes.

"No," he said, sounding as nervous as if Teena had started to unbutton his pants. She thumbed the fingerprint pad, slid in the keycard, and opened the door. And there was Leo in the middle of the stairs. Sarabeth stood on the steps behind him, her hands on her hips in a display of attitude Teena would never have imagined possible.

"Is it okay if we open this?" Leo asked, holding up the bottle of Opus One wine that Teena's dad had bought himself the day he golfed a three-over-par at Goose's Landing Country Club. The certificate of its authenticity was framed, while Teena's own birth certificate was stuffed in a box somewhere. Leo knew all of this, because in a weakened state, Teena had entrusted him with a rant about her father and how he cared more about his booze and guns than his own family.

"No!" she shouted, running down the stairs and pulling Evan with her. Her heart beat wildly. Trashing her parents' house was hardly a big deal—that's what housekeepers were for—but the demise of Mr. McAuley's Opus One would be the death of her.

She reached Leo and grabbed for the bottle of wine, her left shoe nearly coming off in the process. Leo waved the bottle tauntingly, holding it hostage over his head.

"It's yours, if you let us out," Sarabeth said quietly, a flush in her cheeks. Teena paused. Who did Sarabeth think she was?

"Okay, fine," Teena said through gritted teeth, hating that she had to give in to these losers. "But you can't stay for the party."

"Oh, what a letdown," Leo said sarcastically.

Teena dug into her pocket for her keycard and realized with a jolt that it wasn't there. In her rush to grab the bottle from Leo, she'd left it in its slot. On the other side of the entryway.

Her eyes darted up. The door was still open a crack, thank God. She lunged toward it, stumbling forward. Her body connected with the cool metal just as it closed completely, the whooshing, suctioning noise practically slapping her in the face.

Sprawled on the steps, Teena looked up at the top of the stairs helplessly. Now she was trapped, too.

6

CORKSCREWED

Evan Brighton, 10:13 P.M. Saturday,
Teena McAuley's Basement

For a second, for a split, pure-perfection second, Evan had believed that Teena was taking him to a secluded area to make out. In that second, he'd managed to thank God for the fact that he'd blown money on a sweater that Teena had already touched twice and that he'd had money left over to stop and buy the chips and dip. He'd also managed to put God far, far out of his thoughts as his brain took in every inch of Teena in her tiny red dress.

But that split second was way over. Evan might have been naive, but he wasn't stupid. As soon as he saw the unlikely duo of Leo Starnick and Sarabeth Lewis standing on the stairs waiting for Teena to open the big metal door, he knew she was planning to lock him down here. *Effing calculus*, he'd thought, not yet able to think profanity, even if he'd already been thinking profanely.

That second, that door-opening second, was over for everyone. Because now it wasn't just Teena's hand-selected crop of punishees locked down here. Teena herself was trapped, too. She was frantic, her eyes darting back and forth around the low-lit space, pacing on her heels, each click sounding like gunfire. She was either looking for a key or having a fit. She scanned the highest parts of the room, as if seeking answers from above, or hoping someone at the party overhead would sense that their hostess was trapped underground.

Sarabeth Lewis was the opposite. Still and calm, she simply sat on the bottom step, as if resigned to this new fact of her life. She pulled out her cell phone and stared at the screen. "No signal," she said plainly, even though no one seemed to hear her.

Leo Starnick just wore an amused grin, enjoying the strangeness of the moment. Still standing on the staircase, he looked down at the rest of them as if deciding what to do with them.

Evan wondered what his own face looked like at that moment. If Teena's parents were away for the long weekend, and Teena's key was on the other side of the door, then they were trapped down here until Monday. Monday, so he'd miss Sunday services. He'd be caught in his lie for sure. On the bright side, he was trapped with Teena. For tonight, Sunday, and part of Monday, at least. That was true get-to-know-you time. But . . . shit. He was trapped. *With. Teena.* What if he fell asleep and had a dream about her and talked in his sleep? What if he farted? Or woke up with morning breath? Or had a wet dream? In front of Teena? In his brand-new overpriced jeans?

"Is there another way out of here?" Sarabeth directed a hostile look at Teena before averting her eyes.

Teena dragged a stool over to a cabinet filled with canned goods. She stepped on it, wobbling slightly in her heels, and began feeling around on the top shelf.

"Let me do it," Evan said, standing up and glad for the chance to do something. "What are you looking for?"

Teena rolled her eyes as she stepped down, clattering past him. She violently pulled a bottle of wine from one of the lower racks and sat down on the stairs next to Sarabeth. "Nothing. I'm already done. I thought my dad might have an emergency keycard there."

Leo, who was still holding the bottle of expensive wine, shrugged. "You're all too worried," he said. He hopped down the last few stairs and ducked into the room to the right of the staircase, opposite the wine cellar. Evan followed him in. Inside were a set of brown couches, a flat-screen TV with a built-in DVD player, a coffee table, and a tall bookshelf containing an assortment of board games, several rows of DVDs and CDs, and a meager selection of books that Godly Jim would be happy to see contained a copy of the Holy Bible. A massive generator stood in the far corner, apparently to power all this equipment if ever the need should arise.

Leo flopped on a couch with the wine and closed his eyes. Evan tentatively took a seat, too, still holding the chips and dip. The girls soon followed, until everyone was seated around the coffee table, like they were all friends hanging out at some ski lodge, waiting for hot chocolate—rather than completely mismatched classmates trapped in a basement.

"Teena, won't one of your friends figure out that you're not there anymore?" Evan put the snacks on the table and opened a bag of corn chips.

Teena put her head in her hands and laughed. "You bring chips and dip to a party where the only thing on anyone's mind is beer and shots, and you seriously think anyone cares if I disappear? My being gone just means they can burn the place down. My parents are going to kill me."

Sarabeth spoke up. "No one is going to mess up your house any more than you'd already let them."

"You're lucky you're even invited," Teena shot back.

"Oh, yes, thank you, Teena, for inviting us to a party so you can trap us in a bomb shelter for an entire long weekend," Leo said sarcastically. He stood up and held the bottle of wine like a gavel. "I want payback. So I say we open this bottle of wine and try to make the most of tonight. For a toast, we're going to clink glasses and say, 'Fuck you, Teena.' Corkscrew's in here, I'm guessing?" He stopped near a glass-front cabinet holding wine glasses and various implements.

Teena sprang up from the couch and had Leo's arm in a tight grip within seconds. "You're not opening that bottle," she said gravely. "Put it back, Leo."

"What do you mean? If we try it and don't like it, there are dozens more bottles to choose from. Don't be a party pooper, Teena." He held up the bottle with his other arm and examined the wrapping on the neck. Teena pulled at his elbow.

"I like Leo's idea," Sarabeth said calmly. "I could use a drink."

"Not from this bottle," Teena protested, yanking Leo's arm

with both hands.

"I think you've given up your right to play sommelier," Leo said, trying to pull his arm away from Teena.

"Give it back!" Teena squealed.

Evan debated whether he should step in and take the bottle from Leo. But Leo had given him free pizza at the mall. And even if he wasn't that mad about being locked down here, Teena's insult had stung. So what if he'd brought chips and dip? It was *thoughtful*.

On the other side of the coffee table, Teena managed to wrap her hand around the bottle's neck. Leo held on with both hands. Evan and Sarabeth watched the tug-of-war. Leo smirked as Teena strained.

"Just give it to me!" Teena finally yelled, putting her whole body into giving the bottle a single, solid yank.

It flew up in the air and seemed to hang, suspended, above their heads. Everyone watched as it turned three-hundred-sixty degrees in slo-mo, before beginning its long descent to the cold concrete floor. The bottle collided with the ground, and there was a huge crash. Everything shook.

And then, an explosion ripped through the room, louder than any kind of wrath-of-God shit Evan's stepdad preached about. Timber snapped above them, and the floor shook below them. The staircase to the cellar cracked in half, like something had unzipped it down the middle.

Evan felt himself lift from the couch, the bag of chips still in his hand, and crash to the floor. He hit his head, hard, and felt the cool concrete under his cheek. He couldn't move as he watched a torrent of debris from the house above come down the stairs in a tidal wave. He closed his eyes as particles of dust flew at them. From the next room he heard a symphony of wine bottles bursting.

Evan tried to push up from the floor, but another crash rocked the room, forcing him back down. The world felt like a capsizing boat as it swayed beneath him. He kept his eyes closed as it rumbled again, less violently, then swayed gently, almost like it was trying to rock him to sleep.

Then, nothing. Everything was still. Evan opened his eyes.

Sarabeth was on the floor across from him, rubbing her head. Her green sweater was coated with gray dust and had a hole torn in the elbow, a large red scratch appearing in the gap. Teena was stomach-down on the floor. She lifted her head, her blond hair caked with ash. Leo was on his back at the center of the couches, staring blankly upward. *Was he dead?* Evan wondered. Then he saw Leo's chest rise and fall as he took a breath.

This reminded Evan to breathe, a cloud of dust finding its way into his lungs. He coughed, feeling aches all over his body from the fall. Next to him, Leo was sitting up, intensely staring into the sky. Evan followed Leo's gaze upward. The others did the same.

All they could see—all that was left—was the night sky above.

Teena's house had been ripped from its foundation. More than half was completely gone. Only the kitchen and part of the upstairs remained. A keg rolled back and forth. A chunk of countertop lay on its side.

Evan's eyes fell on Dahlia Dovetail's trademark elf boots, the ones he'd seen clasped against Brad Michner's back on the way in. He followed the boots up to her legs, still wrapped tightly around Brad.

But her top half was gone.

Evan struggled to get to his feet, his legs like rubber bands. He took two woozy steps backward, reeling as he tasted Phat Phil's pepperoni return to his mouth. He couldn't tear his eyes away from Dahlia's intestines, dangling like giant strands of spaghetti.

He looked into the open bag of corn chips still clutched in his sweaty hands and vomited into it.

7

ALIENS AND OTHER PARTY FOULS

*Leo Starnick, 10:31 P.M. Saturday,
Teena McAuley's Basement*

Leo had pictured the world ending differently. He'd always figured he'd be doing something cool, like playing a guitar solo on top of a mountain somewhere, watching as everything turned to rubble. Or being a hero, carrying some hot chick away from flowing lava. Maybe diving off some cliff into the ocean as flames licked his feet. Big movie shit.

Instead, he was in a basement, with a splotch of expensive wine on his Phat Phil's Pizza polo shirt.

For seven full minutes, he, Evan, Teena, and Sarabeth stood in silence, looking up through the giant gash in the ceiling at the night sky that was just hovering there, still and starry, like nothing had happened. Like they couldn't all look left and see the half-a-body of Dahlia Dovetail or the grayed, still form of Brad Michner.

Maybe the damage had been isolated to Teena's house. Maybe it wasn't an apocalypse scenario. Maybe it was a gas line explosion or a giant Midwestern earthquake.

Still, Leo had a feeling. He breathed in, and a charred meaty scent filled his nostrils. He winced. He'd smelled burnt flesh once before, when Phat Phil had put his arm too far in the pizza oven, singeing all the hairs and causing his hand to instantly blister. This smell was stronger. And unlike Phil's incident, there were no cries of pain. Just deafening silence.

He looked up at the sky again, calm and quiet—everything so quiet—and realized that it had tricked him earlier. It wasn't the same sky it had been when the night began. The twinkling stars, so innocent before, looked dulled and tainted. A deep purple light hung along the horizon, and Leo blinked, suddenly understanding. They'd landed.

Aliens had landed. *It actually happened.* He couldn't tell the others, not yet. He'd always said aliens would hit Tinley Hills, and now they had. He'd thought most of the people upstairs at the party were idiots, and that the world would be better without them, but he realized now he hadn't meant it. He never wanted to do them real harm.

He didn't get how he'd been spared. How *they'd* been spared. Sarabeth had a minor elbow scrape, and even Teena, who fell near the glass, had sustained only the tiniest of cuts on her hand. All four of them were okay. At least, physically speaking. But what did that mean? And how long did they have before they weren't okay?

"Anyone up for Spin the Bottle?" Leo heard himself say. He

tried to never talk just to fill up the silence, but it felt good to hear his own voice.

"Is anyone hurt? I mean, down here," Sarabeth said. Leo couldn't help noticing how pretty her green eyes looked in the near-dark, even though they were scared and watering. He'd always had a little thing for Sarabeth, and yet she was the only girl he couldn't nail down.

"I'm . . . cold." Teena stood up, her lips quivering and tears dripping silently from her eyes. She wiped them away with the backs of her hands. "And I want to know what happened to my house. And my friends." She choked on a sob.

Evan took off his jacket and draped it over Teena's bare shoulders. Teena smiled faintly, and Evan blushed, all of which made Leo feel better about his own Sarabeth musings. Maybe that's what male hormones told you to do in crisis mode. Made sense from a survival-of-the-species standpoint.

Sarabeth, who'd taken a seat on the couch, spoke in a whisper. "Do you think we need to go see what happened? If anyone needs help?"

"Probably." Leo stood and smoothed down his polo shirt, like he was making a delivery. It wasn't that he wanted to see any more destruction, but he wanted to know if he was right. "Not to be sexist, but I'll go first, and Evan should be on the other side of you two." He gestured to Sarabeth and Teena.

Sarabeth unfolded herself and stood behind Leo. "I'm okay with that," she said, sounding surprised by her own admission. Teena fell into place behind her, followed by Evan. This leader shit was new, scary territory.

"The stairs are messed up," Leo said, picking up a flashlight that had fallen from one of the shelves to the floor. The chasm between the top stair and the kitchen floor was almost four feet wide. The drop down was only about ten feet, but the basement beneath was a dangerous mess of broken glass and debris from upstairs.

"Teena, you should take off your shoes. You can't walk up the stairs in those." Leo pointed at Teena's sky-high boots.

Teena scowled at him. "And go barefoot? I'll keep the shoes on."

"Fine," he said. They'd all fought enough. "Everyone, hold onto the shoulder of the person in front of you. Let's go." At the top, he could just cover the gap, even if it felt like his groin was going to rip in half as his legs stretched across the opening.

"One small step for mankind," he muttered, grabbing onto the destroyed countertop and pulling his other leg across. Once on solid-ish ground, he anchored one arm to the counter and reached for Sarabeth with his other one.

Sarabeth clutched Leo's arm, making every movement a slow, cautious one. Leo didn't mind as she grasped his arm tightly, allowing him to bear some of her weight. She exhaled as she landed behind him, keeping a hand on his shoulder as she watched the others nervously.

Teena came next, a look of determination on her face as she clung to Evan with her left hand. The splintered stairs weren't exactly sturdy, and Teena's boots weren't helping. Leo scooted forward and stretched his arm further.

Teena locked her right hand around Leo's arm, then stepped without looking. A splintered board cracked under her foot, wood dropping into the chasm. She yelped as she started to fall, but Evan and Leo both had good grips on her arms, and she floated above the hole.

Panic registered on Evan's face as he looked down to the floor, his eyes landing on a huge pane of broken glass that must have been from one of the kitchen cabinets.

"Don't look down," Evan said, his voice a croak.

"I wasn't looking down," Teena snapped back, suddenly taking a peek at the sharp-edged debris below.

"It's going to be fine," Evan told Teena, cautiously taking her by the waist and lifting her so that Leo could get a better grip under her arms. Leo tugged backward, and he and Teena crashed to the kitchen floor, just inches from Dahlia's innards. Teena gagged, putting her hand over her mouth and nose, and scrambled to her feet.

Evan crossed easily. "Everyone okay?" he asked, looking right at Teena, who nodded.

Sarabeth dropped her hand from Leo's shoulder and sighed, like a suspenseful movie scene had just ended. "I think so," she said. Leo shot Evan a thumbs-up. The four of them were now standing in a circle, relief bopping around between them like an invisible hacky sack.

But the relief was temporary. Leo stepped away from the circle to see what surrounded them. What he saw looked like when he delivered an everything pie, took a left turn too fast, and sent all the toppings to the middle of the pizza. They weren't standing in the kitchen. They were standing in an epicenter of destruction. The only light came from the moon above, but it was bright enough to see more than anyone wanted to.

Charred furniture lay everywhere, like a fire had crackled

quick and hot but never quite caught. Beyond Dahlia and Brad were more bodies, some of them still intact, others rendered unrecognizable. Guts spilled out into a rainbow puddle of condiments from the toppled fridge. Muscles and tendons coated the floor like the road kill on LaGrange that didn't get picked up for several days. Leo tasted his puke as he swallowed it down.

The people Leo recognized were the worst to see. Nathalie Oliverio's face was still pretty, even though her hair had burned off and her arm was detached and lying across her body. Karen Walsh had a gruesome, openmouthed smile, and her stomach was ripped open.

"Ohmygodohmygodohmygodohmygod," Teena spewed, the pace of her words matching Leo's own heartbeat. "They're all dead. Everyone is dead. Why did this happen?"

"Who else is dead? Where's Cameron?" Sarabeth's quavering voice layered on top of Teena's continued freak-out. She grasped her upper arms, her fingers digging into her skin so deeply Leo was afraid she'd draw blood.

"What did this?" Evan said, adding to the chorus of panic. He looked around at the destruction with wide, fearful eyes. "This is the end of days, isn't it? On the one night I lied to get out of Bible study?" He looked up at the sky, like he half expected to see God glaring down like an angry detention monitor.

The cacophony grew and grew, the whos and whats and whys and hows and whens of the deaths piling up in the air like dirt filling in an open grave.

This is what it's like to be buried alive, Leo thought. Then, three words pressed against his lips, and didn't ask permission to come out.

"It was aliens," he blurted.

Everyone shut up. Three faces turned on him, like he'd just said something more insane than Evan had. Seriously? They believed in God murdering the shit out of a party full of people, but not in angry life from other planets?

"Little men from outer space? Sure." Teena rolled her eyes as if his comment had pressed her reset button. "Great. Everyone's dead and you're batshit crazy. Why aliens? Why not a nuclear spill?"

"Teena, the nearest nuclear power plant is in the Quad Cities," Leo said, drawing himself up to his full height as he closed the gap between them. "You've gotta believe me."

Teena backed away from him, sidestepping an arm on the floor still sheathed in an Ermer Elephants letterman jacket sleeve. "Um, could you not get so close to me?"

Whatever. Teena would never say he was right about anything. But Evan was still staring at him weirdly, too, as if trying to decide whether Leo would turn into the devil to claim Evan's soul. Maybe it had been too soon to break out his theory.

Leo made his way a little farther into the debris. Dave Brandt had died mid-keg stand, his flabby stomach exposed. His entire lower body had twisted so his ass crack, peeking out from his Levi's, was on his front.

"It's like his middle name was Dignity," Leo said in a reverent tone, directing the comment at Evan.

Evan's terror-mask face faded as he chuckled lightly, then looked ashamed for doing so.

"I thought maybe it was too soon," Leo said, trying to ease Evan's guilt. "But then I figured, it's always going to be too soon. They're dead, we're alive. Savor the little things, right?"

He looked at Sarabeth last. He hated the idea of her thinking he was a lunatic. In string ensemble, she gave him shit, and he kind of liked it. But this was different. Her wide eyes searched his, and he felt hopeful. His ally at last.

"What do you think we should do?" she asked, surprising him.

"You believe me?" He tried not to look too ecstatic.

She shook her head and, with a laugh, said, "About the aliens? No way."

She shrugged, her gemlike eyes glittering above the flashlight's beam. "But at least you saying something as crazy as aliens shut up the horrible thoughts in my brain. I guess I find you mysteriously reassuring."

Mysteriously reassuring. Leo liked the sound of that. His mind wandered, again, to a place where they were alone. *You are so fucked-up, man,* he scolded himself. But Sarabeth was right in one respect: If nothing else, he knew how to calm people down.

He pulled out the bag of weed he'd bought earlier at Shitty Arcade. It was hardly of the quality you wanted to smoke at the end of the world, but it would have to do. He packed some into the bowl he always kept in his jeans pocket and held it aloft.

"Everyone, calm down. I think we all deserve a little something to numb the effects of this evening." He held his lighter to the pot and inhaled, feeling the knot in his stomach start to loosen. He exhaled, slowly. "And then Teena's going to show us her daddy's gun collection."

You're thinking it's odd—maybe even a little psychotic—that these four people can be victims of a totally heinous attack and yet still be cracking jokes and checking each other out. But until you're in their shoes, try not to form an opinion about them.

Fear works in mysterious ways. Nervous joke-cracking, awkward flirting, even some irritated arguments are not out of the norm, especially when you're a high school student and not a world leader or a decorated general. Without some hyperactive hormones to remind them there are pleasures to being alive, Leo, Sarabeth, Evan, and Teena might never even have tried to leave the basement. And then our story would end here while the four of them clustered in a corner, silent and cowering, trying to survive off Napa Valley wines and jars of olives.

And no one wants that, right?

8

PLEASE, BE A DEER

Sarabeth Lewis, 11:47 P.M. Saturday, Diamond Peak Lane

Sarabeth could start a new "never" topic in her journal: *Things I Never Thought I'd Do But Did.*

Like smoke pot. Yesterday, the idea she might one day hold a joint to her lips had never occurred to her. Yet here she was, stepping out onto Teena's demolished front lawn, her brain feeling like it was covered with a not-unpleasant layer of peach fuzz.

Or hold a gun. Normally, just catching a glimpse of gun hilts in the Tinley Hills police officers' holsters was enough to make her shudder. But somehow, she held a tiny Smith & Wesson .38 Special in her hand. A "lady gun," as Leo termed it. She was suddenly a party-going, drug-doing, gun-toting teenager.

She wished she could go back to being bored.

Sarabeth, Leo, Evan, and Teena were standing on the remarkably still-intact front stoop of Teena's house. The house may as well have been made of Play-Doh, the way it had smushed to one side, the contents spilling together like guts. Or, in the case of the dead people inside, actual guts. Sarabeth closed her eyes tight, shaking away images of her mauled classmates. She almost wanted to thank Leo for providing a means to take the edge off. Almost.

Her eyes began to adjust to the total dark. The power was out as far as Sarabeth could see, but even without light, she could tell that the silhouettes of the massive houses on Diamond Peak Lane had changed. Roofs had been ripped off or whole top floors taken away, leaving black, shadowy structures standing against the sky like a row of jagged, uneven teeth. Some of the streetlamps had been snapped in half, while others stood dead and lightless, like extinguished birthday candles. Whole chunks of the street had been ripped or suctioned up from the surface, like pieces of an apocalyptic Whack-A-Mole game. Cars lay on their sides as if they were useless, broken toys. With all the houses on the street blacked out, there was no suburban light pollution, and every star in the sky strutted its stuff above, almost mockingly. The only source of movement in the cold air was their own visible breaths.

"My whole street is gone," Teena said, a quiver in her voice. She walked ahead of them, the first to step off her porch. When she'd discovered that most of her closet had fallen from the top floor into the first-floor living room, Teena had put on a tight-fitting USC hoodie and a pair of her Paige skinny jeans, but insisted on keeping her stiletto boots on. So she struck an

58

incongruous pose amid the wreckage as she expertly tottered across the uneven ground that was formerly her front yard. Deck chairs, grills, and kids' Big Wheels littered the area. Teena stood at the curb with her hands on her hips, looking out over the destroyed block.

"What's that thing?" Teena pointed to a huge dark gray metal orb with strips of lighter silver metal coiled around it. Bursts of steam rose from the hundreds of tiny holes that dotted the sphere, like a giant space-age golf ball. Teena approached it, stepping back quickly when she got close. "It's giving off crazy heat."

Sarabeth went to stand next to her, careful not to trip over the debris. The hunk of metal didn't look like a recognizable part of anything. She glanced sideways at Leo, who was crouching near the orb. He probably thought it was some alien artifact. He was so convinced that aliens had attacked that Sarabeth almost wanted to believe him. Almost. It wasn't so much that she didn't believe in life from other planets, it was that she never believed that life would want to do humankind harm. She'd watched *E.T.* one too many times.

"Maybe it's a piece of a satellite," Sarabeth said. "One could have crashed to Earth."

Leo looked up at her. "I don't think a satellite could wipe out the whole block like this."

"Or part of the space station," Evan volunteered, seeming less panicked than when he proposed God as the perpetrator. "That's still around, right?"

"I think so," Teena said, starting to back away from the thing as if a thought had crossed her mind. "Or it could be some kind of bomb." She looked at them all with a serious expression, her hand on her gun like she half expected the culprits to emerge from behind the piles of debris. She toted a semi-automatic pistol and wore an Uzi submachine gun across her back.

They all paused, considering her theory. A bomb seemed plausible, Sarabeth thought as she eyed the ragged, dormant houses left behind. Or maybe it really was a huge piece of space junk. From aliens, like Leo thought.

"There's my car," Evan said, breaking the silence. He pointed a flashlight at half of a champagne-colored Ford Taurus that stuck up out of a chasm in the street. The license plate holder read, JOIN THE CRUISE-ADES! SOUL PURPOSE CHURCH CAR SHOW '04. He had a small .45 shoved in the waistband of his jeans, but seemed more comfortable with the baseball bat he'd found on the lawn.

They'd decided to go to the authorities, to report the deaths at Teena's house. Oddly enough, going to the police had come up while they'd passed around Leo's pipe. Now it looked like they had more to report. While the idea of talking to the police high on drugs made Sarabeth shakily paranoid, reporting the tragedy made sense.

Leo hopped off the stoop and trod over the grayish-brown winter-crusted lawn. He peered around the side of the house, or where the side of the house had been.

"My car's too small for all of us," Leo declared, looking at the mess. "And, actually, too small to find."

Teena crossed her arms over her chest. "Don't look at me," she said. "No way am I driving. I've been through enough."

Sarabeth couldn't believe Teena would be a bitch even at

a moment like this. "I can drive." Sarabeth pointed into the distance.

Two blocks away, exactly where Sarabeth had parked it, sat her mother's Pepto-pink Gussy Me Up van, obnoxiously proud and pristine under a strip of moonlight that shone down through the trees. She wondered if it was a sign. The van had survived, and she had a feeling Cameron had, too. For the first time in her life, she had one of those twin-connection moments, and she just *knew* Cameron was okay. She still didn't know what or who had done this, or how far the damage extended. But if her instincts were right and Cameron was alive, maybe there were other survivors, too.

"That's a badass vehicle, SB," Leo said, knocking her lightly on the shoulder as he passed. Her nose wrinkled automatically at the "SB" nickname she hated, but her arm tingled from his touch. The effects of drugs and nerves, Sarabeth told herself. Leo Starnick making her tingle was most definitely on the "never" list.

Leo started toward the van, motioning for everyone to follow. He carried an Uzi from Teena's dad's arsenal and had tucked a Glock pistol down the back of his jeans. It made his polo shirt ride up, exposing a smooth patch of olive skin.

The group followed him in silence. Sarabeth imagined her mom's social advice in this scenario: "Possibly being the last people on Earth is not an appropriate conversation topic in mixed company."

Sarabeth winced and tried not to think about her mom. She'd been so mad at having to take the embarrassing pink van to her first high school party, while Cameron had gotten the Ford Escape. Sarabeth's last interaction with her mom had been a dirty look. And now they both might be . . .

She pushed the thought away as they approached the van. Sarabeth pressed the UNLOCK button, and the doors responded as they always did, the little bullet-shaped locks popping up out of their slots. It was so bizarrely normal on a night that had been anything but. She pulled open the driver's-side door.

"I'll drive," Leo volunteered, stepping up next to her and reaching for the keys.

Sarabeth yanked her hand away, surprising herself. "My van, I drive," she said, even though she really didn't want to. Her hands and fingers felt disconnected from her elbows, and those barely seemed to coordinate with her arms. She might as well have been a brain and a stomach bobbing along. But Leo's cockiness brought her right back to the string ensemble room, where he exasperated her daily. So she brushed past him and climbed into the driver's seat.

Teena automatically took the front passenger seat, while Evan and Leo slid across the bench seat in back. Leo moved fluidly, like he'd barely been affected by the pot. Evan, a fellow first-timer, tripped trying to climb into the backseat. Sarabeth opened the center console and offered the group Clif Bars, feeling self-conscious for being hungry at a time like this. But everyone greedily grabbed one.

The van was quiet, save for the sound of wrappers crinkling. Biting into the chalky energy bar, Sarabeth shoved the keys into the ignition, and the van hummed to life. She pulled away from the curb slowly so the van wouldn't slip into the gap that split the road in two.

She gripped the wheel tightly and her eyes trained on the path of light cut by her brights. She maneuvered the van through the obstacle course formed by the detritus of Teena's subdivision. A flat-screen TV was impaled on a front yard flagpole. A red washing machine half-embedded in the pavement looked like a jagged, bloody tooth. A three-foot-high plastic Santa—a Christmas leftover someone had been too lazy to take off their lawn—looked at Sarabeth with dead eyes. She shuddered. One less thing on that family's to-do list.

Sarabeth turned right onto Emerald Cove Drive, where the street was barely disrupted. The lights were out, and all the homes seemed asleep, like it was much later at night and no one had heard a thing. But aside from that eerieness, the street looked almost normal. It was hard to believe that she'd come this way just hours ago, when her worst fear was saying something stupid or being one of the only people at the party not drinking. Sarabeth gave the van a little gas, now eager to get to the police.

Out of the corner of her eye, she saw a flicker. She focused in on it but could see only shadows in the intruding dark.

"Sarabeth, do you brake for animals?" Teena said next to her.

The question came out of nowhere, just like the deer that had stepped out in front of the car. Deer had always looked alien to Sarabeth, with their triangular, expressionless faces and deep, hollow eyes. Now, as the animal walked out into the middle of the road on its skinny, wobbly legs, Sarabeth felt like it was her kindred spirit.

Sarabeth pressed down on what she thought was the brake.

The van picked up speed instantly.

She'd hit the gas.

"What are you doing?" Teena screamed, clutching her armrests in terror.

"I don't know!" Sarabeth screamed back, her foot fumbling to find the brake. By accident, she floored the gas again. A wail escaped from her just as Leo reached up from the backseat and put his hands on the wheel, wrenching the van to the right. It sped up onto the curb at sixty miles per hour.

The deer sprinted away into the darkness. It was safe. She didn't have to see anything else die tonight.

Relief flooding her, Sarabeth felt her foot finally close in on the brake, pushing as hard as she could. Sarabeth and Teena slammed against their seats. Leo's grip didn't hold, and he was wrenched into the backseat again, sliding sideways and pushing Evan into the window.

But then a sickeningly loud thud sounded throughout the van, shaking it from side to side as it abruptly stopped. *There must have been another deer*, Sarabeth thought.

Tears sprang to her eyes. Automatically, she jumped out of the car to see if there was any hope for the animal. Or what if she'd hit a person? A sob choked its way from the back of her throat.

"Sarabeth, don't," Leo said, sliding open his door and following her to the front of the van. "You don't know what's out there."

She skidded to a stop inches from a thing she couldn't bring herself to call by name. Her toes curled in her shoes to avoid contact with the thing collapsed against the van's grill. The thing had grayish-purple wrinkly flesh under a violet membrane of slime, some of which stretched from the bumper like gum that had been stepped in. Giant, cookie-sized eyes, black and pupil-less, and netted like a fly's. Flared, cavernous nostrils, but no mouth. Legs and arms that had to be four feet long, and wrinkly hands that bore six knotty fingers tipped with pointed, daggerlike claws. And on the hands, if you could call them that, humanoid opposable thumbs—gray, long, and clawless.

Leo had been right. And there was no way this thing was pals with E.T. The only comforting thing about the creature was that it was dead.

Leo exhaled heavily, reminding Sarabeth he was standing there, too. She looked up to find him studying her. "Okay, is it just me, or does this thing smell like really good coffee?" Leo said. His lips went up in a half smirk, but Sarabeth noted the anxiety in his eyes.

She allowed herself to inhale. It *did* kind of smell like her mom's favorite Kona blend.

The others had emerged from the van, gathering behind them. Teena got as close as she could without touching any of the goo trail coming off the thing's scary, muscular form. She stared at the being, her brown eyes wide, stopping just short of poking the alien with a stick.

"That's not a little green man," Evan said flatly. He took a deep breath. "And it probably hasn't been working alone."

"Yeah, which makes me wonder why we're all standing here and not driving away as fast as we can," Teena said.

"Sarabeth killed it," Leo said. "We're safe."

"*Killed* and *safe* might be stretching it," Teena said, pointing to the creature on the ground. The alien's arms and legs made squishy sounds as they lifted off the pavement.

Teena backed away slowly, crawling into the van. Evan crept toward the doors, too. But Sarabeth couldn't move. Chocolate chip Clif Bar dust whirled in her throat.

No sudden movements, Sarabeth thought. She stepped backward, her hands shaking.

Suddenly, the alien extended one arm, swiping the air with its claws.

"Kill it!" Teena screeched from inside the van. But Sarabeth was still frozen. Leo fumbled with his Uzi, consternation and fear on his face.

Leo pulled on the trigger, but nothing happened. The tall alien was rising to its feet just steps away from them. Its hammer-shaped head stood atop a long neck where—instead of the grayish-purple wrinkled skin—the alien had smooth silvery panels, almost like a fish's scales. It was like they'd woken an uglier, less cuddly grizzly bear.

"There must be a safety or something. I don't know how to shoot a fucking Uzi!" he yelped nervously. "Where's your gun?"

With shaky hands, Sarabeth pulled the .38 from the waistband of her jeans and pointed it at the beast. Then she froze, completely unable to pull the trigger. She looked at Leo, panicked.

The alien reached out for her, its claws coming centimeters from her stomach. Sarabeth screamed.

Leo came up behind her and pressed his chest to her back. He took her hand under his, his index finger over hers on the trigger, like he was teaching her how to play pool. He cocked

66

the hammer of the gun and then pulled the trigger, shooting the alien in the chest. Together, they shot a second time, the bullet hitting right next to the first wound.

The moment replayed itself for Sarabeth even as it was happening. Making full-body contact with Leo Starnick. Firing a gun. At an alien she'd hit with her mother's pink van. All worthy entries for the *Never Thought I'd* list.

They might have been her last entries. The bullets didn't seem to be penetrating very far, and the alien just seemed angry.

They cocked the hammer back a third time, but Teena jumped from the van and pushed them out of the way.

"You're too slow," she said, and efficiently unloaded five straight shots into the alien's head and another right into its chest, where the bullet made a satisfying splat. Its body drooped and fell to the ground, hard. Sarabeth and Leo stared at Teena, shocked.

She glared at them. "What?" she said. "So I know how to fire a gun. And I don't need a boy to help me." Evan, who'd emerged from the van during the skirmish and was holding his baseball bat aloft, like he was guarding Teena, backed away.

Sarabeth realized that Leo's hand was still wrapped around hers, and that she was leaning into his back. They sprang apart.

She looked at Teena admiringly, suddenly grateful to her, bitch or not. "Thank you."

"Yeah, what Sarabeth said." Leo picked up his Uzi, which had fallen to the ground.

"It's like you're the only guy in the world who's never played a video game." Teena loaded another clip into her gun with a definitive click.

"Should we take the alien's body with us?" Evan said. "To show the police?"

"Dude," Leo said, "I don't want to ride with that thing."

"Maybe we can drag it," Evan suggested.

"Evan's probably right," Sarabeth said. "The police will never believe us without proof."

"Fine, you guys tie it to the hood. There's not enough Purell in the world," Teena said.

Evan took a few tentative steps onto the property of a two-story Tudor-style home and peered down the long driveway. A boat wearing its winter tarp stood outside the garage. "There might be an easier way to do this."

"We're going to steal a boat?" Leo said. "Seriously, Evan?"

"Well, it seems easier than getting him on top of the van," Evan said nervously.

"Man, that's awesome. I'm in!" Leo happily ran down the driveway, with Evan following. Teena rolled her eyes.

"Boys," she muttered to herself, tucking her gun back into her jeans. To Sarabeth, she said, "Back up the van to the boat so we can pull up to the alien. Like I said, not touching this."

Relieved to have something to do besides tremor in fear, Sarabeth got in the driver's seat and reversed the van as Teena stood off to the side, directing her.

"You're up on the curb again," she scolded. Sarabeth turned the wheel. "Now you're going to kill the mailbox. Did they just let you pass driver's ed because you're good at math?"

Sarabeth ignored the remark and secretly hoped maybe they'd be caught stealing the boat. She had come to terms with the fact that aliens had landed but was disturbed that even on this block where the homes were intact, no one was emerging to see what had caused the explosion. No one came to the window of the Tudor to yell at them. No one stepped off the back porch as Leo and Evan pulled the cover off the boat.

"Holy shit, look at this monster!" Leo shouted, a wild grin taking over his face.

The boat was named the *Big Ditka*, after the former Chicago Bears coach. The hull was painted in the team's colors, orange and blue, but in a nonsensical zebra-stripe pattern, and mounted on the helm was a fiberglass bear head wearing a football helmet.

"It's so weird that people act like Ditka is still the coach," Evan said.

"It's so much weirder that you're talking about sports when we're about to put a dead alien in a boat," Teena said.

Leo attached the boat to the hitch at the back of the van, and Sarabeth steered the van down the driveway to where the big grayish-purple alien lay dead. As she got out of the car, Sarabeth reached in back, grabbing some of the thick plastic Gussy Me Up bags her mom used for delivering orders. "Put these on your hands, so we don't touch it directly," she said, passing out the bags and ignoring Teena's annoyed look.

Evan and Teena took the head side, and Leo and Sarabeth the legs. Evan counted to three, and everyone lifted.

"Gross," Leo said, turning his face away from the creature.

"I can't do this," Teena squealed, dropping her section to the ground and shaking the bags off her hands and onto the lawn. With a nauseated look, Evan picked up her slack and hefted the alien up under its shoulders.

Sarabeth rolled her eyes. The alien's skin was squishy, sure. But for some reason, this wasn't as gross to her as dissecting a pig had been in biology. Maybe because she'd felt bad for the pig.

The alien was aloft, and heavier than its long, narrow limbs made it look, with a density to its shiny skin that Sarabeth hadn't been expecting. With Teena watching uselessly, they tossed it into the back of the boat, where it landed with a thud. Sarabeth pulled an orange-and-blue plaid blanket from under the captain's seat and placed it over the body.

Leo smirked.

"What? It's a dead body."

Teena was already getting back into the van. "Come on, people. Let's move."

They took the seats they had before—girls in front, guys in back—and Sarabeth drove slowly down the street. The van swerved from side to side as she tried to steer it and the boat.

They made it no farther than the first stop sign leading out of the subdivision when they heard a thumping noise behind them. Sarabeth sped up a little, and another thump rattled the van.

"What is that?" Evan asked.

"Guys, this isn't good," Teena said, staring wide-eyed in her side mirror.

"Yeah, in general, things are pretty shitty," Leo said. "But at least we're still alive."

"No, I mean *that*," she said, pointing behind them.

Illuminated by the taillights, the alien was standing up in the boat, the blanket hanging around it like a cape. It could have been sailing the high seas, the way it clung to the ship's steering wheel.

"I-I sh-shot that thing," Teena stammered. "It was dead."

"They can come back to life?" Evan yelped, with panic rising in his voice again.

"Can it get in?" Sarabeth asked, her heart bouncing wildly in her chest. "What should I do?"

"Go as fast as you can!" Leo shouted. Sarabeth hit the gas, the odometer hitting fifty, then sixty. The van rattled with the weight of the boat behind it. In the rearview mirror, both the alien and the *Big Ditka* vibrated with the speed. She'd never ridden a roller coaster, but Sarabeth imagined it felt like this.

"Hard right, right here!" Leo cried as they approached a side street. Sarabeth flung all her weight against the wheel, and the van lifted half off the ground on her side. With a crash, the boat broke free of the vehicle and careened away, the alien falling onto the pavement as the *Big Ditka* clattered away.

Sarabeth checked the rearview mirror. The alien pulled itself up off the ground. Its movements were slow, but it didn't limp or wobble as it dusted itself off and disappeared into the night. Sarabeth pulled to the side of the road, leaning her head against the steering wheel and breathing in short bursts.

A fresh wave of grim panic washed over the van.

"I hate tonight. I hate it." Teena, shaking, was talking more to herself than to the rest of them. "This means it's still out there. There might be more. I'm going to die."

"We're all g-going to d-die," Evan stammered, his face such a perfect expression of terror that actors could learn from it.

"They can't be killed." Sarabeth felt like she was talking

71

in someone else's voice. "What kind of thing can't be killed? They're impervious."

"I love it when you talk dirty," Leo joked.

Teena sighed in annoyance. Evan blushed. Sarabeth realized Leo's joke had snapped them out of their fear spiral once again. Sarabeth glared back at him, even though she could still feel the warmth of his hand closing over hers. "That is so not happening."

Leo shrugged, grinning. "Never say never."

9

NOBODY'S HOME

Leo Starnick, 12:39 A.M. Sunday, Emerald Cove Drive

"Not to ruin what may possibly be the only moment of male attention you enjoy in your life, Sarabeth, but the bloodthirsty fuckhead from outer space—you know, the one we littered with bullets?—is on the loose out there." Teena, who'd been freaking out moments ago, suddenly looked pissed off. "We need to move. What if that guy is coming back with friends?"

Sarabeth nodded, all businesslike. Cute businesslike. "You're right," she said. "Let's get to the police."

Leo wondered how he and Evan had wound up sitting bitch in the backseat while Sarabeth steered them from danger and Teena rode shotgun—in the literal sense. All those studies about chicks being more academically successful than guys could be recalibrated to also include superior survival skills.

She turned out onto LaGrange, the street Leo had taken just hours before, when he'd thought tonight's excitement would come from some Teena hate-sex. He looked out the window, and from the stillness outside, he knew what to expect. The world was eerily empty. And dark. The police station was on the left-hand side, a cobblestone brick building surrounded by thin white birch trees, designed to match the look of Teena's subdivision. To Leo, it looked like a satellite office for Santa Claus, not a place for cops. He could see from the street there were no lights on, and no squad cars in the parking lot. Sarabeth turned into the entrance anyway, stopping the van alongside the handicapped ramp. The lampposts that ran up the walkway to the station were all out.

"We should check inside, right?" Evan asked. "Maybe the power's just out."

"Don't get your hopes up," Leo said. "It doesn't look like anyone's home."

"Yeah, and there could be a trap inside," Teena added, folding her arms over her chest and looking like she hated them all.

"Why would you say that?" Sarabeth looked sideways at her with an odd expression.

"There's always a trap inside. See a movie."

"Perfect, that's just what we all need to feel supergreat about going up to the dark, spooky door," Sarabeth said, but hopped out anyway. Leo was right behind her with Evan, and after a few seconds' pause, and probably the realization she'd be all alone in the empty parking lot, Teena eventually hopped out, too.

Sarabeth marched up to the glass door and opened it. Leo felt like a jerk for letting her go in first. He could see her face

74

grow pale even in the darkness. Beside him, Teena hugged her hoodie tighter, and Evan sucked in a sharp breath.

It was as empty as Leo had figured it would be. Nothing indicated there'd been a struggle. Papers were scattered on desks, and some phones were left off their receivers, like people just stopped what they were doing and left.

"This gives me the creeps," Evan said.

"Yeah, it's almost as bad as my house," Teena seconded.

Leo watched Sarabeth's face for signs of what she was feeling, but she gave nothing away. "Let's go back to the van. Now."

No one argued, and they all filed out quickly, not speaking again until they were safely in their seats.

"There was something wrong there, but I can't put my finger on it," Sarabeth said. "It was like I felt a presence, even if I didn't see anything. See *them*."

At the mention of *them*, the van's metal bones creaked, and they all jumped.

Leo breathed through his teeth, to slow down his wild heartbeat. "What should we do next?"

"Maybe we should get supplies," Evan said, nervous.

"Oh, like some chips and dip?" Teena shot back. Cruelly, Leo thought. Evan needed to work on his game, but he'd been nothing but nice to Teena. "What good will supplies do? Guns don't even work."

"And you hate us all and blah, blah, blah," Sarabeth said through gritted teeth. Leo had never seen her angry before. "And the aliens should have killed us, not your friends and ..."

Smash!

The back passenger window rained glass onto the pavement.

75

Evan sat with his jaw set and his baseball bat hanging halfway out the window, which was now nothing more than a glass-shard frame.

"What happened?" Sarabeth sounded like she'd been holding her breath. "Did *you* bust the window, Evan?"

"I'm sorry," Evan said sheepishly. "I just . . . I don't think it's good to be arguing."

"Dude. You smashed a window. With a bat," Leo said, shaking his head and wondering if Evan had more game than he'd thought. "I should give you props. Or kick your ass. Not sure which."

"Evan, suppress rage much?" Teena eyeballed Evan with what Leo swore was a glimmer of interest. "You might as well just ask the aliens if they want fries with us."

Sarabeth seemed to agree as she drove back onto LaGrange, keeping them moving.

"Sorry, I'm a little tense," Evan croaked out, the bat now hanging limply in his hand. Teena spun around, Evan's pussy-sounding answer probably putting an end to any tingling sensations she'd been experiencing.

Leo wondered why Brighton didn't just man-up and tell Teena off. She'd go for that. But maybe it was better that Evan was crap with girls. Being one of two guys on the run with two very capable females put Leo under some pressure. Evan already had the athlete thing going. If he mastered chicks, too, what would Leo bring to the table?

"We should probably check on our families," Evan said a little shakily, looking at the tree branches ripple by. "Make the rounds and stuff."

"He's right," Sarabeth agreed. "Whose house is closest?"

"Mine, probably," Leo said. Sarabeth looked at Leo, kind of incredulously, he thought. Like a guy who delivered pizzas couldn't reside within a five-mile radius of Teena. "I'm in the Oaks," he said. "It's not We-Shit-Diamonds Land, but I'm sure we can find a car-window-sized piece of plastic wrap and some duct tape."

Without a word, Sarabeth swung a sloppy U-turn. Taking Leo's directions, she made a quick right at a street just a few blocks down from Teena's. The Oaks were Tinley Hills's first subdivision, but unlike Diamond Isle Estates, the Oaks dated back to post-World War II and hadn't been built for the nouveau riche, or the nouveau anything. What were probably bright shiny homes back in the fifties were now shingled dens of pity.

The Oaks houses were unharmed, but as deathly quiet as the Diamond Isle homes had been. The always-on TV that flickered through the O'Malleys' graying curtains was off. Old Smoking Man, a quiet guy who'd moved in onto Leo's street, wasn't out on his porch in his Hanes undershirt, ashing his cigarettes into an old Hills Bros. can. Even the Tower, a party house at the end of the street where Leo sometimes hung out with a bunch of junior-college dropouts, didn't have its usual assortment of stoners on the porch.

The neighborhood was dead but without the bodies. Beyond the humble houses of the Oaks, a dust-and-smoke cloud still rose from Teena's house at Diamond Isle. Had the aliens zapped it on purpose, or just made a destructive landing? Was the weird sphere thing a weapon or a piece of their ship? That Teena's house was either a target or the first landmark the aliens saw made sense to Leo. He'd always believed aliens would go for the best real estate, not for the trailer parks, like all the *Weekly World News* types thought. Why would anyone travel, like, light-years to check out rows of double-wides and some rusty playground equipment, or in the case of the Oaks, rows of shoe-box houses, all without premium cable?

Leo instructed Sarabeth to park in front of his house at the end of the block, suddenly embarrassed to have people see where he lived. It was one thing to hint at a shitty existence so girls would think they could save you. It was another to confront them with direct evidence of that existence by pulling up in front of a house that actually looked too unhygienic even to cook meth in. The roof was patchy and bald, with graying shingles. The once-red front door hung like a bruised, lopsided mouth between the two battered eyes formed by windows with peeling wood frames. Even the remaining snow had survived in brown clumps, like tumor-like growths on the flattened dead lawn. All that was missing were a scrawny dog on a chain and a beater car up on blocks.

"Home sweet home," Leo said. "Hope you brought your manners. Dad probably prepared some hors d'oeuvres." He hopped out of the car casually but still looked sideways down the street for signs of alien life. It was a gesture more for everyone else's benefit. He didn't really think they were in danger. His dad would probably be sitting in the dark on the couch in his underwear.

Leo pulled his keys off his belt as the rest of the group clustered behind him on the front stoop. Maybe it would be better if his dad wasn't inside. Introducing Sarabeth to Mr. Starnick was probably the surest way to guarantee a big romantic fail.

It was a cold thought, but Leo had gone through most of his life not one hundred percent certain he loved his dad. There was nothing lovable about Ed Starnick, as Leo's mom had proven when she and her saggy tits and floppy ass took off for Reno ten years ago to marry a plastic surgeon she'd met in an AOL chat room.

The Starnick men heard from her once a year at Christmas, when she'd send photo cards of her new self. Now surgically enhanced and a deeper shade of orange each year, Denise Mancusi and her personal Dr. Frankenstein always posed in their desert paradise of a backyard. In the pictures, they'd each hold one of their pet tropical birds, which always seemed to be in mid-squawk, probably saying *Fuck you!* The cards accompanied wine-and-cheese gift baskets and said, HAPPY HOLIDAYS TO LEO AND ED STARNICK. GRATEFULLY YOURS, DENISE. Like Leo and his dad were some people she'd done lucrative business with. Which, in a way, Leo guessed she had. Her hate-worthy life in Tinley Hills led to her prosperous new arrangement.

But his mom's leaving hadn't drummed up any emotive loyalty in Leo toward his sad-sack father. Often unemployed, unshaven, and wearing the same baggy-assed Levi's until they started to turn yellow, Leo's dad *was* the hangdog dad from *Pretty in Pink*, that eighties movie. And that made Leo Molly fucking Ringwald.

Leo's house felt darker inside than out. He didn't try the lights, since most nights he came in late anyway and knew his eyes would adjust quickly. The TV skulked, powerless, in a corner, and the overstuffed plaid couch across from it was empty in a way that gave it presence. Leo pushed through the saloon-style doors into the kitchen, seeing it was empty before his boots even had time to squeak against the puke-green linoleum. He gestured for everyone to wait while he felt his way through the mudroom and down the hallway. His father's room was the usual mess: rumpled covers knotted in a ball on the concave queen mattress, old newspapers and issues of *Car and Driver* piled near the bed, small trash can overflowing with empty Old Style cans. For the heck of it, he poked his head into his own room, knowing that his father had no reason to be there but wanting to look anyway.

Everything was as he'd left it. The room would have surprised probably anyone who'd ever met Leo. He kept it neat and sparsely decorated, like someone who didn't spend a lot of time at home or who wanted to be able to escape at a moment's notice. The only objects to give anything away were a stack of library books on the windowsill next to his neatly made bed, an old photo, on the dresser, of his mom holding him at the hospital, and a little wooden box he'd made in woodshop where he kept his emergency weed. He opened this now and pulled out a baggie of his everyday weed, Amsterdam Indica, and the quarter-ounce of Waikiki Queen he'd been saving for a special occasion. The end of the world seemed special enough.

It occurred to him that all he'd brought to the table so far was weed. Maybe he should just hop out his window, get baked in the forest preserves, and see what happened when the aliens' hostile takeover was further under way. He touched his window lock but let his hand drop. Taking a deep breath, he realized he wanted to figure this thing out.

As he revisited the kitchen, everyone stared at him expectantly. He looked back at them without really looking and said brightly, "Not here. But, you know, Dad enjoys an extended happy hour on Saturdays." He opened the fridge and tossed a six-pack of Old Style to Evan. Then he pulled another can of beer out and cracked it open, taking a long swig.

"What's wrong with you, Leo?" Teena said impatiently, with obvious discomfort at her surroundings. In all the time she'd been slumming it with him, she'd probably never realized how apt the term was. "We seriously don't have time to sit around playing *Breaking Bad*." Girl could fire an Uzi, but put her in a house where a maid didn't clean up twice a week and she was as nervous as a Christian fundamentalist at a gay wedding.

"Really, Teena? Because it's not like we're on a schedule. If you hadn't noticed, there's no one here. It doesn't look like there's anyone anywhere, unless you count dead people." Leo set his can down on the kitchen counter. "I really didn't think it would be like this."

Sarabeth caught his eye, and he could see sympathy there— exactly what he *didn't* want.

"What did you think would happen?" She was serious, and he felt grateful to her.

"I don't know," he said, looking from Sarabeth's concerned face to Evan's nervous one to Teena's annoyed one. "I guess I figured they'd colonize, take over the golf course, and start picking people to take back to their home planet. And everyone in town would choose sides and start a special town council subcommittee about what to do, blah, blah, blah. The usual

Tinley Hills bullshit."

Evan laughed. "That sort of makes sense."

Leo shrugged. "Yeah, either that or they'd blow us all up at once. But it's like they just vanished people or something. It's freaky."

"We don't know that," Teena said, but Leo could tell she wasn't that sure of her statement. "Like you said, your dad could be out."

"You're right. So, where to next?" Leo asked, clapping his hands like they'd just finished mini golfing. "Brighton, should we drop in on your folks?"

Evan shook his head. "My mom and my stepdad are at a church fund-raiser just over the county line, so maybe we can wait until we see what's going on in Tinley Hills. What about you, Sarabeth?"

Sarabeth's eyes flicked over to Leo once more, their concern landing on Evan. "I'm not far from here," she said. "My brother left just before me to pick up his girlfriend in Lawn Grove. But maybe my mom is still there."

Sarabeth lived a few miles from Leo in an old part of town, Tinley Town Center. It didn't take long to get there. Traffic along Route 33, usually packed with cars, was a non-issue. The six-lane highway was wide open, without any signs of destruction. No bodies. No destroyed or abandoned cars. No debris. Like they were the first people ever to drive this route. *Or the last*, Leo amended.

"I keep hoping everyone left without us," Sarabeth said. "But you would think there'd be a few people who were just late or something. Did our town become the Bermuda Triangle of suburbs?"

No one answered her, but no one had ignored her, either. They each looked out their windows—Evan's was now covered with plastic bags and cardboard from Leo's garage. Leo knew they were all thinking what he was: Were they the lucky ones or not?

On either side of the road, the lights were out in places where the lights were never out. On the east side of the road, Best Buy, Target, Sports Authority, Chili's, and even the twenty-four-hour Super Foodland stood dark and hulking. A seemingly endless gulf of empty parking spots surrounded each store. It was like someone had just swept all the cars and people away, leaving a neat, tidy, nondescript town behind.

But then Sarabeth came to a stop at the corner of 33 and Harlem. She gasped like the wind went out of her. *Tidy* and *nondescript* didn't apply here. Normally, the intersection was home to a Walmart Supercenter and a Kmart Super Center that had inexplicably been built right alongside each other. They were both open twenty-four hours, and you'd always see at least a couple dozen cars in the parking lot and people walking in and out of the automatic doors.

Both of the giant stores were now missing their tops and stood like brick bowls with their contents strewn around them. Whole aisles had been torn from the stores, and merchandise lay scattered—kids' tricycles and kitschy lawn ornaments and cleaning products and frozen food. And even from here, they could see human arms and legs, a shopping cart with hands still attached to the handle. Where the asphalt wasn't split like

83

a massive gash, there were still cars in the parking lot.

"What happened?" Evan croaked, peering out the portion of his window where they'd used a clear plastic bag.

"I think I prefer the Bermuda Triangle," Teena said.

"How many people do you think . . . died?" Sarabeth asked, her hands tight on the wheel. "Should we check?"

"It's not safe to do a body count," Leo said.

"I just wish I knew why the aliens chose here," Sarabeth said. "What do we have that they want? And why have we only seen one of them, when it's clear more than one did this?"

"We can't get answers until we figure out where they are, and where everyone else is," Leo said. "Let's keep going to check on your mom. Maybe she's home." He felt bad lying to Sarabeth, but he would have gladly been wrong.

Sarabeth lifted her foot off the brake and passed the end of the strip-mallage and maulage. The destruction had been limited to the two big stores.

Now Route 33 shrank down to a two-lane road, along which Old Tinley Hills sprouted up. Town Center comprised five or six straight blocks of Veterans Park, Village Hall, the Tinley Hills Public Library, Wilbur Ross Elementary School (Tinley's first school building, dating back to 1919), and the fire department building, all disturbingly as dark as the rest of the town. Just beyond all this civic pride lay homes, including Sarabeth's.

As they pulled up in front of a two-story, yellow-brick Georgian with actual character, Leo felt a little thrill. This was where Sarabeth *lived. If it wasn't so dark, I might be able to figure out which set of windows is hers*, he thought, chiding himself for being a sappy asshole.

84

Sarabeth put the van into park and gave a heavy sigh as she swung the driver's door open. Leo noticed her hand shaking as it felt for the small gun still tucked in her waistband. She looked into the rearview mirror at Leo and Evan, and then at Teena in the passenger seat. "You guys are coming, right?" Her voice was a tiny delicate object Leo wanted to protect against the night.

In a weird twist of naming irony, there were more trees in Town Center than in the Oaks, so darkness blanketed them. Sarabeth reached behind her, grabbing Leo's hand. Her cool skin against his was a pleasant surprise, but Sarabeth was no-nonsense. "Make a chain so we don't lose each other."

He reached behind him to take Teena's small, warm hand, and with an almost audible eye roll, Teena reached back for Evan's.

"I won't be able to shoot anything if my hands are tied up," Teena said.

"That's not what I heard," Leo joked. Teena pinched his hand, hard. "Ow!" he yelped, feeling like a wuss.

Sarabeth maneuvered up the path, lined with rosebushes in all their winter nakedness, and gasped a little when her front door clicked open before she could put the key in the lock. She reached into the hall closet and grabbed a flashlight, turning it on. She shone it up the staircase, gesturing for the group to follow. At the landing, she ducked her head first into the master bedroom. "Mom?" Her voice sounded small and scared. The beam of light flicked over a floral bedspread, a massive dresser, and a closet left open and filled with row after row of shoes. Seeing nothing, she ducked out and did the same cursory check of her brother's room—the kind of messy guy's room Leo's wasn't—and what Leo presumed was her own room. The only detail he could make out was that Sarabeth's room was pink, since she opened her door just a crack so they couldn't see very far into the space. Her secretiveness just made Leo more curious.

Sarabeth led them back downstairs and through a living room and dining room both cluttered with glass figurines in cases. Most of them were creepy little girls with too much makeup on. So many fragile things usually gave Leo the urge to break something, but tonight he just hoped all the baby beauty-queen statues didn't belong to Sarabeth.

"Is someone brewing coffee?" Evan asked, smelling the air as they stepped into the kitchen. But the room was empty, and more pink than Sarabeth's room. Where did someone even *get* a pink refrigerator and stove? It was like Barbie's grandmother's house. Even the knives had pink handles. As the flashlight scanned over the kitchen island, Leo instantly caught a detail that didn't belong.

"What's that purple stuff?" he asked, already knowing. Dreading. Sarabeth focused the beam of light onto the island. There, sure enough, lay a film of purple slime coating the surface. The coffee smell in the kitchen grew stronger.

"That's the stuff . . . from them," Evan said, a layer of disaster in his voice.

"So they were here, then," Teena said, deftly pulling her Uzi from her jeans and pointing it around.

"Why are you pulling out a gun?" Sarabeth asked her. "They don't work."

"They still work better than nothing," Teena said. "And they . . . the aliens . . . might have a weak spot."

Evan and Leo stepped back and out of the line of fire. Sarabeth didn't move. She slouched against one of the cabinets and slid to the floor, putting her head in her hands.

"Don't be a chicken," Teena said sharply. "The safety is on."

"I don't think that's the problem," Evan said.

"I didn't even say good-bye," Sarabeth said, more to herself than anyone in the room. She pulled her knees up to her chest and hugged them. "I just left. And I even thought, *Someday, I won't have to live with you anymore*."

No one knew how to react to this. As Sarabeth rubbed a tear from her eye, retort-happy Teena looked at Leo and Evan with a face that said, "What do we do?"

"I want to get out of here," Sarabeth said, looking up at them. Right at Leo. He wanted to stroke her hair and tell her it was okay. "I don't want to see any more. I don't want to see. Not her body."

"I don't think there *is* a body," Leo heard himself saying. The theory had started to form in his head when they had seen no people anywhere except where there was clearly destruction. These aliens weren't neat killers. So in order for the town to be so empty of everything, they had to be doing more than killing. "They took her. I think the aliens are abducting people," he explained, not sure if this would make her feel better, much as he wanted it to.

Three pairs of eyes regarded him with something bigger than skepticism but not as big as utter disbelief. Sarabeth fumbled to her feet and stared at the gelatinous substance on the counter. She looked from him to the purple liquid and back at him again. As her juniper eyes rested on him, he couldn't take the look anymore. His dream girl thought he was crazy.

He broke the eye contact and went to the fridge. "Do you have anything to eat? I'm starving." It was a good distraction technique. Plus, he really was hungry.

Sarabeth waved at the shelves, laden with Tupperware containers filled with different, labeled entrees. "Go for it. No one else eats anything I make," she said, pulling an empty plastic container out of a cabinet and scraping some of the purple goo into it without touching it. Once again, Leo was impressed with her brain, and just wished she'd say what she thought of the abduction theory. "The coq au vin is really good, even cold."

Leo and Evan dug into the chicken, still hungry despite the nastiness of the evening. Teena just scowled at them. Like they weren't even there, Sarabeth set her goo-container on the counter, then stepped back into the creepy doll room.

"This is going to seem weird, but there's something I've always wanted to do. And if we're definitely sure aliens attacked, it doesn't matter . . ." Then, she swept her arm across a shelf of the dolls, sending dozens to the floor, where they shattered. The little broken glass limbs were chilling after what he'd seen tonight. "Okay, we're done here."

Leo looked on admiringly. Sarabeth, breaking things. She was even cooler than he'd thought. Or at least weirder. He'd always thought she was a challenge because she was too perfect. Now, he was realizing she was something better than perfect. Clearly, this girl was *complex*.

Hopefully, she was just as crazy as he was.

10

GOING GREEN

Teena McAuley, 2:17 A.M. Sunday,
Sarabeth's Kitchen

"Aren't we going to talk about Leo's theory? I think he's right about the abductions," Teena said as the Gussy Me Up doll shattered to pieces under their feet. Maybe it was the pot they'd smoked. Maybe it was seeing half her hometown empty and half of it destroyed. Maybe it was standing in Cameron and Sarabeth's kitchen with a sense of messed-up déjà vu. It looked almost the same as the last time she'd been here, in fifth grade, when Teena and Sarabeth had tried giving each other makeovers and Cameron had walked in to find them sitting at the pink counter with gross avocado masks on their faces. Or maybe it was because Teena saw the way Leo was looking at Sarabeth, and she wasn't about to be any guy's second choice out of the last two girls on Earth.

Deep down, she knew Leo was probably right. Even when he'd first said aliens were responsible for the destruction at her house and she'd rolled her eyes, she'd had a hunch. Burnout or not, Leo wasn't dumb. Stupid guys, no matter how cute, typically didn't know much about working a female's erogenous zones. And Leo definitely did.

"So, you think the aliens are taking people somewhere to experiment on them?" Sarabeth said, picking up a creepy Gussy Me Up doll head from the floor and examining it. Teena hoped Sarabeth hadn't had some kind of mental breakdown that would work her into a murderous frenzy. It was bad enough to be on the run from aliens. Teena didn't need to be on the run from a homicidal nerd, too. "But what do they want that Tinley Hills has?"

"I haven't gotten that far yet," Leo said. "But everyone needs something. I'm sure we'd invade a planet if it had a ton of untapped oil or, like, endless milk shakes. Maybe their planet needs white people. Tinley Hills has tons of those."

"So they're killing people, like at Teena's and Walmart, and taking people. Why both? And where would they even be taking them to?"

"I have another theory. Those deaths weren't intentional. They landed on us. The giant sphere thing at Teena's fell off their ship." Leo had found a bowl of cold pumpkin gnocchi in the fridge and was plopping the little dumplings into his mouth. "Where did this come from? Enrico's? It's really fucking good."

He swallowed his food and grinned at Sarabeth. Teena wanted to puke. Here she was, backing Leo up, and Sarabeth still got all the love. That bullshit about the way to a man's heart being through his stomach must have been true.

"I made it," Sarabeth said shyly. *Speak up, already, Betty Crocker,* Teena thought, annoyed by the sweet, doe-eyed-ness she herself would never have. Deep down, she knew Sarabeth wasn't doing anything to deserve her wrath. Deeper down, she knew that what was really bothering her were the feelings she was still having for Leo. When he'd shown up with the pizzas tonight, she'd realized she wanted more than revenge; she wanted him.

"This? And the chicken?" Leo tossed a piece in the air and caught it in his mouth. "Marry me."

Teena wanted to dump the bowl over Leo's head. "Leo, can you stop eating? Sarabeth, can you stop playing Dexter with that doll head? And Evan can you stop . . . just stop. They have to have a ship. We just haven't found it yet. You can't expect them to set up District Nine in a few hours." She took a few steps toward Leo, to show she was one hundred percent behind him.

Evan looked at Teena hopefully. "Maybe Teena's right, and we just need to find where they're taking people." Teena should have been grateful for the support but was disappointed instead. Sarabeth got sexy Leo and she got virginal Evan Brighton? *Whoopee!*

Teena rapped her Uzi on the countertop. Everyone jumped. "That's the first right thing you've said, Evan." Then, in her most damsel-y voice, which was tougher than she'd wanted it to be, she added, "We don't want to wait for the aliens to sniff us out, or whatever it is they do." She fixed her eyes on Leo and stared until she got him to look back. Then she smirked like she was thinking something dirty. Which she was, a little. Bingo. Leo put down Sarabeth's puke-worthy gnocchi and grinned back.

"But the one thing is, if they've already been here, maybe we're safe," Evan said, looking at Teena like he wanted her support for staying at Sarabeth's. As if she'd waste her remaining time on Earth at Sarabeth's house, especially if Cameron wasn't home.

"Dude, no one is going to be safe until the aliens are gone," Leo said, looking cute as he strode to the center of the kitchen. "Here's the thing: They'll find us and take us. You have to believe me on this: Teena's house and all those dead people on Route 33 are collateral damage from landing. But if they were here for an intergalactic killing spree, there'd be dead people everywhere. They're taking people somewhere. That's why things are so empty. And if we're the only people they haven't found yet, then we need to hightail it the hell out of this house before they do."

Teena's eyes flicked from Leo to a photo of Cameron on a shelf over the breakfast table. He was wearing his football uniform and gazing into the distance, like a model for men's cologne. What if he'd been abducted en route to picking up that slut-fest girlfriend of his? She imagined Cameron, tied up and alone, sitting next to Nina's devoured remains. Teena would burst in and gun down the alien. (Once she found that weak spot she knew they had.) Grateful, Cameron would confess he'd wanted to be with her all along, and she'd finally have him where she wanted him. Grateful and vulnerable. When he finally kissed her, maybe she could put Leo out of her head once and for all.

"I agree," she said, and without thinking, she grabbed Leo's upper arm, and a little fizz swelled beneath her skin. She hated that his touch still had so much power over her. She hated how it was dawning on her that the reason she'd been so determined to hook up with Cameron tonight was because she wanted Leo out of her head. "We're not safe here. Plus, all the pink is giving me a headache. No offense, Sarabeth."

"None taken," Sarabeth said, and Teena could swear she saw Sarabeth looking possessively at Leo's arm. "Though I remember you felt differently in fifth grade. I quote, 'I wish I could live in your kitchen. I love pink.'"

Teena rolled her eyes and looked at Evan, knowing she'd have his buy-in, no problem. He was such a puppy dog, she almost felt bad. Almost. But he'd live. Maybe.

As she fluttered her eyelashes at Evan, his Adam's apple rose and fell with his nervous gulp. Too easy.

"So, here's my idea," Teena said with authority. "Let's find these motherfuckers' ship."

Leo flashed Teena one of the grins he'd been giving Sarabeth all night. That would show her. Leo put the lid on the gnocchi and then grinned at Sarabeth. The same grin he'd just given Teena. "As long as I can take this gnocchi for the road."

Whatever. Teena was cheerleading for him, and all he cared about was Sarabeth's stupid food. Teena collected her stuff, plus an extra Diet Coke, and led them all to the door. Sarabeth took one last sad look around her empty house, and Teena almost felt bad for her, before she remembered what her own house looked like.

93

Teena marched like a general out to the van, glad to have everyone following her plan, even if they didn't all agree with it. Leo did, and that was what mattered. And Evan might have been tentative, but she knew he'd choose her over Sarabeth any day.

Sarabeth was still driving, but riding shotgun actually made Teena feel more in control. She leaned back in her seat, scanning the horizon for signs of life

At the end of her block, Sarabeth put on the brakes.

"Why are you stopping?" Teena asked.

"Stop sign," Sarabeth said. "Habit. And, I don't know which way to turn."

"Well, where are we going, exactly?" Evan asked.

"Maybe just drive around till we get some answers," Leo suggested. "I'd take a left."

Sarabeth started to roll forward when Teena saw something that made her scream, "Stop!"

Sarabeth jolted the van back to a halt.

"People! Survivors." Teena pointed to a house on the corner with a huge front yard. Across the expanse of lawn, Teena caught the eye of a little girl clutching her teddy bear. Teena wasn't the type to cry at Hallmark commercials, but a tear almost came to her eye at the sight.

"They must know about the attack and be trying to leave," Evan said from the backseat.

Teena ignored him and started to wave at the little girl, when out of the house loped an alien, its jelly-coated skin glinting in the moonlight, and grabbed her by the arm. Behind it came two more, each clutching one of the little girl's parents.

"Do those look bigger than the first one we saw?" Leo asked.

Before she even had time to think, Teena found herself jumping from the passenger seat and pulling her gun from her waistband in one smooth motion. Sarabeth swung the van over to the family's front yard, and the aliens—who'd paused mid-stride but didn't let go of the family—stumbled a little as the headlights landed on them. The father tried to pull away, but the alien yanked his arm behind his back, while the mother and daughter trembled as their captors gripped them tighter.

Teena caught the little girl's eye again, and a wide smile came across the child's face. She lifted her tiny foot and stepped, hard, on the alien's massive knobby one. A guttural noise emerged from its mouthless body, and its co-captors bristled just enough to loosen their grips on the family. The father grabbed his wife and child, and they started to run toward the Gussy Me Up van, behind Teena. Teena silently cheered herself. That made three more people who wouldn't get captured tonight.

She pointed her gun at the trio of the now empty-handed aliens, still a good thirty feet away. She was about to fire, when suddenly out of the darkness came a half-dozen more aliens. As moonlight spilled down on them, they grabbed the family and two of the advancing aliens. Before Teena could blink, the aliens and their captives zipped away into the air. On their backs were clear glass ovals with green flames crackling inside.

Oh, God, Teena thought. The aliens had jet packs. They could fly. How could four high school students possibly win this thing?

As fear climbed in her throat, she realized the boys had jumped out of the van and taken position next to her as she faced down the remaining alien, who'd apparently been left behind to kill her.

"I've got this," Teena said, even though she secretly felt better with the guys out here, too.

"Don't shoot. Let's go before they take us, too," Leo said, staring at the spot where the family had disappeared just seconds ago. "Guns don't work."

"I have to kill these things," Teena said, anger filling her heart. "I have to try." She moved in with the gun, clicking a fresh clip into place and littering bullets into her alien adversary's head, chest, and stomach as it moved toward her. Once she'd locked on a weak spot and killed the first immediate threat, she'd kill every last one. It was the only way to save anyone.

Bullet-ridden, the alien wobbled toward them, and Teena backed up a few steps, bumping into Evan, who was standing beside her like a bodyguard, gripping his bat and ready to swing. Leo held up a pink-handled cleaver he'd taken from Sarabeth's kitchen.

Sarabeth was still in the van, the motor running. "Please, let's go!" she yelled.

Teena rattled off another succession of shots into the alien's throat. Now it was only about fifteen feet away. As the bullets pierced the silvery membrane with satisfying splats, the thing doubled over and started to retch green ooze onto the sidewalk. Evan reached out and pulled her backward by the shoulder so that the ooze wouldn't hit her feet.

"Ha! See? I found its weak spot! The throat!" Teena sneered at Sarabeth, whose green eyes grew so wide they threatened to swallow her face.

She felt better than when she'd won prom queen as a junior. Knowing these things could be killed meant the four of them could win. And Teena believed that if a battle could be won, she would be the one to win it. She pointed proudly at the dying, puking alien. Now they could save everyone.

"Holy shit!" Leo yelled, but not necessarily in a ding-dong-the-alien's-dead way. Teena swung back around to where the creature had fallen onto the sidewalk. The green ooze was mutating into a dozen little green masses that looked like tiny, four-legged goblins with big egg-shaped eyes on the tops of their heads. They were almost cute, like demented lizards from the Littlest Pet Shop. But in seconds, a dozen little beasties were charging at Teena, fast, leaping from the ground and flying toward her face. *Flying. Fucking flying.* As if the sharp silver claws emerging from their tiny green feet weren't enough. She screamed as one came right at her, its claws out. She stumbled backward, dropping her Uzi in the process.

Lying on the ground, Teena clutched her neck, bleeding where one had scratched her. The things came at her in a buzzing swarm, and she held one arm across her face, fearing what was next. She scooted toward her Uzi and plucked it off the ground, but was so heavily surrounded she couldn't even raise the gun to fire. But then the ground crunched as Evan's feet landed in front of her. He planted himself in batter's stance and started to swing—big, sweet, graceful swings that connected with goblin after goblin in a satisfying symphony of splatter. Some hits brought the goblins instantly to the ground, while others sent the goblins soaring on a home-run trajectory, until they exploded mid-air with a tiny squeal. She pulled her

97

hands from her face to watch, disbelieving. Evan didn't miss.

"Get. In. The. Van," Evan commanded her and Leo, who sliced through the air with his cleaver but was making much less progress against his fast-moving targets. Teena and Leo scrambled into the van just as Evan pelted the last little beastie far into the distance. No sooner had that goblin burst into bits than the alien on the ground belched again, this time more green liquid than before, and that green liquid quickly bubbled into at least a hundred more goblins.

They flew at the van like a flood of bats, and Teena could tell that even Evan was no match. He backed in through the open door, swatting the beasties he could and landing on the floor of the backseat with a thud. Leo slammed the door closed just as one of the goblins tried to get in, and cut the thing in half. Its top half, its oval eyes wide, fell onto the center console, sliding onto the floor of the front seat between Teena and Sarabeth. Teena lifted her foot and crushed the thing like a bug, satisfied as it gave a final breath.

Sarabeth sped down the block as a stream of the goblins followed, beating against the windows as they flew at the van with abandon. The window Evan had knocked out—the plastic bags rippling as the van picked up speed—was weakening as the things hit it with their claws. Evan and Leo kept whacking the goblins away.

"It's fucking impossible!" Leo shouted over the din of the goblins' persistent buzzing. "One goes down and another one attacks."

Fortunately, Leo was wrong. Eventually, some of the goblins grew bored and flew away, until just one persistent beastie remained. This one was not as wily as its cohorts, and even looked large and slow, like a goblin version of Dave Brandt, the now-dead lineman. It bobbled against the front windshield, its sharp teeth set in a grin.

Sarabeth turned on the windshield wipers, but they just hit goblin Dave with slurping thwacks. Teena had another idea. She rolled down her window, leaned out, and killed the thing with a quick burst of gunfire. It squealed as it skidded off the hood and onto the street. The tires rolled over it, rendering it a pile of flat green slime.

The threat gone for now, Teena turned in her seat to look at Evan, who was still at attention with the bat but looking exhausted and spent.

"Thank you," Teena said. She meant it, and hoped she sounded sincere. Evan's sweater was tattered from where the little things had tried to bite him. His blood streaked his forearm, and splatters of green alien ooze covered his shoulders and hair. Teena reached out and pulled a loose thread from his upper arm, where the sweater was shredded. She surprised herself by letting her hand linger there. Evan was wearing soft cashmere, like the snuggly sweaters they sold at King Clothing, the kind Teena loved to nuzzle her face in. Since when did Evan have nice clothes? "Are you okay?"

Evan nodded, rubbing a trail of slime away from his eye. The fact that he didn't say anything or seem to care if he got credit made his saving her even more heroic, Teena thought.

"Dude, your foot," Leo alerted him, cutting into the moment. Attached to Evan's shoe was one of the goblins, half flattened but still moving. Evan took his bat and crushed it. He fell back into his seat and leaned his head back, putting a strong jaw on display.

Teena tore her eyes away, reminding herself he was a goody-goody church boy. Home-run hitter or not, it would take more than the end of the world before Evan Brighton scored with her.

11

CATCH MY DRIFTER?

Evan Brighton, 3:51 A.M. Sunday,
Sarabeth's Van

Evan's hand didn't loosen on the bat until they'd gotten back onto Route 33. They had to be going at least eighty miles an hour, and Sarabeth's eyes were glued to the road. Suddenly, she swung a wide left into the IHOP parking lot and pulled up alongside the restaurant, next to the machines holding the *Chicago Tribune* and the *Tinley Herald*.

Through his shredded plastic window, Evan could see the papers were from Saturday. Saturday morning, when he'd barely been sure he'd have the guts to go to Teena's party, much less imagined becoming one of its only survivors. It was now early on Sunday, the time when Evan figured the papers were normally printed. Would someone come to fill these boxes? Would there even be papers? It didn't seem like anyone was left to write the headlines. Besides the family they'd failed to save, they hadn't seen a single other person. Were the aliens taking over everywhere? And how was it possible that *he* was one of the last people on Earth? Or at least in Tinley Hills. With Teena McAuley, of all people. Which only made the fact that he'd probably still strike out with her all the more pathetic.

Under the restaurant's trademark blue roof, the lit windows looked like empty, lonely eyes. If Evan had been with his stepdad, Godly Jim Gibson, this would have been a sign. And those green goblin bastards would be some swarm from hell, and the big purple aliens minions of Satan. "If God didn't make it, then someone's trying to fake it" was one of his Soul Purpose catchphrases.

The IHOP might have been creepier for not being dark, like everywhere else. Under the fluorescent lights, plates of food sat half-eaten and abandoned. Either people had collectively just given up on their Rooty Tooty Fresh 'N Fruitys and decamped for Denny's, or something more sinister had occurred. Leo must have been right. The aliens had taken everyone. And their cars, judging by the parking lot. The only car was an old silver Airstream motor home, the one people at Ermer called haunted because it had been in the parking lot for as long as anyone could remember. Rumor had it, a crazy old man lived there, but no one had ever seen him.

"Don't you guys feel like we're in some kind of weird IHOP commercial? Like, 'Intergalactic attacks keeping you up at night? IHOP is open twenty-four hours,'" Leo said. Both girls shot Leo dirty looks from the front seat, but Evan didn't mind Leo's attempts to lighten the mood.

"Why did you stop here, Sarabeth?" Teena asked. The greenie's scratch on her neck wasn't as bad as Evan had initially worried it was, but she'd been quiet ever since they'd gotten back on the road. Evan wished he could comfort her, but he was having a hard enough time comforting himself.

"The lights were on." Sarabeth shrugged. "It seemed like the only place to go, as usual."

Evan laughed to himself. The guys on the baseball team always came here after practice or after they went out for the night. Waffles were the best way to soak up a six-pack of Bud as it sloshed in your stomach. Evan had never really been invited. And now here he was, at four o'clock in the morning, with Teena McAuley. And she didn't even seem to hate him. It was sort of like he'd made lemonade from the lemons of the evening, even though he probably should have used them to wash out his eyeballs to forget what he'd seen tonight.

"I'm sorry we couldn't save that family," he said softly. The dead bodies at Teena's were gruesome, but seeing that little girl's fearful expression would haunt him forever.

For ten seconds too long, no one answered.

"It's not your fault, Evan," Sarabeth said. "It's not any of our faults. Who saw jet packs coming? I just hope we can find out where they're taking people before they capture us."

He appreciated the honesty. And then he wondered how much easier his life would be if he could just crush on a girl like Sarabeth and not like Teena. Of course, if he liked a girl like Sarabeth, then Sarabeth would probably be the girl who thought he was a pathetic loser. Plus, she didn't know it yet, but Evan predicted she'd be into Leo before the night was through. Or before *they* were through, whichever came first.

"There's no way in hell we can stop them." The others stared at him like he'd just lit his hair on fire. "What? I'm allowed to say *hell*."

Silence. Evan could tell he'd freaked them all out a little, just like he had with the window. "All that crap my stepfather spouts about locusts and fire and brimstone doesn't scare me. Most days, I think it's all BS. But this isn't the end of days. It's real."

"What are you saying, Evan?" Teena asked, her big brown eyes designed to make you wish you were alone with her, or in Evan's case, made him wish he were the kind of guy who had a clue what to do if he got her alone.

"I'm scared. Call me a wuss or whatever," he said, looking into IHOP at an empty high chair facing a plate of chicken fingers, like some macabre museum exhibit. "But I'm scared."

"I'm scared, too," Sarabeth said.

Teena looked from Sarabeth to Evan, and he steeled himself for an admonishment. "Fine. If it will help you guys get over yourselves, I'm scared, too," Teena said reluctantly.

They all looked to Leo, who was staring out the van's window at the Airstream camper. Evan hoped Leo wouldn't play the cool-guy role and blow this all off like alien invasions happened every day for guys as chill as him. Not for the threat Leo's attitude might pose to Evan's manhood, but for what kind of liar you'd have to be to not admit this was terrifying.

Leo scratched his head with his knuckles, shook his hair out, and turned away from his window to look at them all. "Shitless," he said. "I'm scared shitless. So call me a pussy, too. Or did you say *wuss*? I prefer *pussy*." He grinned at Evan, like they were two guys getting psyched up for the big game. Despite playing in many big games, Evan had never had anyone to get psyched up with. He liked having Leo around.

The van was silent for a while as it sank in that their terror was something they all had in common. It was almost relaxing, sitting there, sharing a collective fear.

A pounding came at Leo's window. Leo jumped, grabbing the pink cleaver. Evan cocked back his bat wildly. Sarabeth grabbed a can of Mace from the center console. Teena whipped out her Uzi again, then put it down with a shaking hand.

It took a second to realize the face was human. And old. And not entirely clean. Under the awning lights of the IHOP, Evan could make out a formerly white beard, now yellowing, that hung from a craggy, weathered face to the man's chest, over a shirt that read I'M A FANITOBA OF MANITOBA, which was layered beneath a hairy brown blanket that looked like it had been made from Ewok skins. The man rapped on the window again, smiling. Surprisingly, he had a full set of teeth that were very white, very even, and obviously fake.

"What the fuck?" Leo exclaimed, opening the van door a crack.

"Don't open the door, Leo!" Teena yelped.

Leo shook his head. "Seriously, Teena, all the shit we encountered tonight and you're freaked out by this dude," he said. "Anyway, he's a living legend. It's Winnebago Guy."

"Who're all of you? And why's there no one in the IHOP?" the man asked, bringing his face close to Leo's. Even from his seat on the other side of the van, Evan smelled the bacon grease, vinegar, and cigarettes. "And who's got a light?" He waved a messy hand-rolled cigarette in Leo's face but looked past him, toward Evan. "What about you, son?"

Evan shook his head and pointed at Leo. "If he doesn't have one, then no one does."

Leo fumbled in his pocket for his Bic lighter, which he handed to the man. The man poked him once on the shoulder. "Well, come on, you can't expect me to smoke out here in the cold. Let me sit down. That's not a Winnebago, by the way."

"Well, that's just what we call you," Leo said. "It has a nice ring to it."

The old man shoved past Leo into the van and sat on the floor between Leo's and Evan's seats. "No smoking in the van," said Sarabeth, who'd been staring incredulously. Then she rolled her eyes. "What do I care? Go ahead."

Teena looked at her, exasperated. "What is wrong with you guys? You can't use an alien invasion as a reason to let a crazy drifter into the car."

The man puffed on his cigarette for a long time and then looked at Teena with twinkly, mischievous eyes. "Alien invasions? You got wacky tobacky? Wanna share?" He sniffed the air twice, his smile disturbingly new on the old face. "And I'm no drifter. I took up permanent residence over there." He pointed at the Airstream. "Problem is, can't find my lighter. Checked everywhere but my ass cheeks. Would use the stove, but last time, I almost took my beard off. You all still didn't answer my question about why the IHOP's closed."

"We're under attack," Evan said. "Everyone else is missing. We haven't been caught yet. We think the aliens are taking people, but we don't know where."

"Damn commies," the man said, offering his cigarette to them.

"Did you hear anything? Or see anything?" Leo asked, turning down the cigarette as he packed some weed into his bowl and lit it.

"Seriously, Leo, you're smoking up *now*?" Sarabeth said. "I mean, I got it before, but don't we need our wits about us or whatever?"

"Look, this dude has lived in that RV by the IHOP for fucking ever. I've *never* gotten to see him. The IHOP is void of any people, another first in its twenty-four-hours, seven-days-a-week history. Plus, we just realized that we're probably all gonna die. So yeah, I'm smoking up, SB," he said, inhaling deeply and holding the smoke in. "Why not enjoy what's left?"

"That's my motto, and I've been enjoyin' what was left since 1976," the man said, folding his long legs up like a spry yogi. He was wearing bike shorts and big fuzzy brown slippers under the Ewok blanket. "That little spot, where my silver beauty sits, that spot is a piece of unincorporated land. And I occupy it. I even got a full bar in there. I'll serve ya, too. Shots are a nickel. Bring your friends. I don't card or nothing. Just ask for me, Abe."

Abe poked Evan lightly on the shoulder, and he couldn't help but feel a little better. He'd always appreciated a harmless weirdo, since he was a little kid. In weekly White Sox games with his dad, sitting in the cheap seats, they'd met a homeless guy who believed he was part dragon and part Viking, an elderly lady with flame-red hair who claimed she could summon pigeons (it seemed to work), and an amateur magician who

107

dabbled in portable pyrotechnics (he'd been thrown out of the game for shooting two fireballs out of his sleeve after a home run).

"So the only bar in Tinley Hills is in the IHOP parking lot?" Evan asked. Tinley was a dry town, which was one of the reasons Godly Jim liked it so much.

The man's eyes twinkled happily. "Yup. Now, what are you kids talking about, aliens?"

"Aliens. Big, slimy, purple, indestructible aliens," Teena chimed in. "Aliens that puke puddles of green shit that turns into little, nasty, flying goblins . . ."

"Greenies," Leo piped up. "I'm calling them greenies, and if we survive, I'm going to breed a strain of pot and name it Mean Greenies."

"Anyway," Teena jumped back in, clearly annoyed with Leo's interruption, "they killed about a hundred people at my house, and they're kidnapping everyone else."

"Yup, does sound like we're all gonna die. I should be getting back to my beauty," Abe said. He flicked Leo's lighter and waved it around, the flame shimmying. "Can I have this?"

"Why don't you come with us?" Evan asked. Teena and Sarabeth reeled around like they wanted to capture Evan's brain as it ran away from his body. Leo looked at him with quizzical admiration, he thought.

"I like that idea even better," Abe said, scrambling up from the floor to sit between Leo and Evan.

"And you can have this book of matches. I'm hoping this lighter is lucky," Leo said. He pulled some Phat Phil's matches from his jacket pocket.

Still grinning, the man took the matches and raised them over his head like a trophy. He lit another cigarette and leaned back in the seat between Evan and Leo. Leo hit his pipe hard and tried to pass it to Evan.

"Not right now, man," Evan said. "But thanks." He didn't function as well as Leo did when he was high. Maybe because he'd done it only once.

"Okay, so now that we've all admitted we're terrified and we picked up a drifter, we need a plan," Sarabeth said. She was right, Evan knew, and he wanted to be the one to send them on the right path, not a deathly one. But he didn't know what that was. If only he could be on the mound. On the pitcher's mound, everything always became so much clearer. On the mound, he felt like he could see in front of him and behind him and into the past and into the future. There was a stillness on the mound. Wisdom. Perspective.

It came to him then, how they could get some perspective.

"What's the highest point in Tinley Hills?" Evan asked, getting excited to finally have an answer to something. "That's where we need to go. We could figure out where the aliens are taking people."

"Yahoo! An adventure!" the old man yelled. He pointed out the window at the mobile home. "But if we're really under attack, I'm not leaving Janie here. She comes with."

Leo nodded as he hit his pipe, again, for a long time. "Evan, I like your thinking. And, believe it or not, I know just the place." He exhaled slowly and dramatically, keeping everyone in suspense like he was the hookah-smoking caterpillar from *Alice in Wonderland*. "We go to High Point. And we bring Janie."

"You hear that, girl?" Abe hollered out the window to his vehicle. "We got a plan!"

Evan grinned for what felt like the first time in forever. Leo might have been very, very, very high, and Abe might have been very, very crazy, but they were just the votes of confidence Evan needed.

12

LET'S GET HIGH

Sarabeth Lewis, 6:15 A.M. Sunday, Lagrange Road

"It's too funny," Teena said, half chidingly and half knowingly. "Leo, you predictably horny asshole. Of course you think instantly of High Point."

Sarabeth sighed. Teena and Leo had probably been there together. Of course, they were more experienced. And of course, Sarabeth and Evan sat there uncomfortably, like when you watched an R-rated movie with your mom and the characters started getting naked and you tried to pretend like you didn't care and like you didn't ever think about sex, but you squirmed in your seat uncomfortably so your mom knew you *did* think about sex and were in fact thinking about it at that very moment. It was like that, but possibly worse.

"It is the right spot," Evan said, a little shakily, the tone of someone who hadn't been there.

"It's always the right spot," giggled Abe gleefully.

There were, however, bigger fish to broil, or sauté, or grill (frying wasn't Sarabeth's thing) than her own awkwardness. Sarabeth was driving up LaGrange to Archer Avenue, headed for the first time in her life to High Point, the best known and most uncreatively named make-out spot in all of Tinley Hills. These were not the circumstances she'd expected for her inaugural High Point visit. *No, scratch that*, she thought, *it* would *take an alien invasion before any guy invited me to High Point*. Even more laughably, she now had to lug around the silver motor home that Abe claimed he couldn't drive himself because of an expired driver's license. She thought he, like the rest of them, just didn't want to be alone.

She hated that as soon as the words *High Point* were out, her mind went to an image of her and Leo alone, in a much different situation. It was probably a contact high or something, since Leo kept flicking his purple Bic for another hit, but her lips tingled, and she wondered what it would feel like to be up at High Point, just her and Leo. Sitting shoulder to shoulder. He'd offer her his pipe, and she'd take it, and the smoke would crackle its way down into her lungs, and she'd hold her breath and then melt down into her seat. As she exhaled, all her Sarabeth-ness would peel away to something new underneath. Something new, but there all along.

A two-lane highway shrouded by thick evergreen trees, Archer Avenue was dark and empty, dark and empty being the cliché theme for this whole night, post-alien landing. Everything was starting to feel pointless. Even if they got up to High Point and saw something, what were they going to do about it? They were four random classmates with mediocre—and, it turned out, probably detrimental—gun abilities, a pink van with a missing window, no strategy whatsoever, and now a weird old man who was romantically entwined with his silver camper.

Her mom was either dead or captured. Somehow, she felt confident her brother, Cameron, was still alive, thanks to her twin-dar. Knowing Cameron, he'd befriended the aliens and was now negotiating an intergalactic peace treaty.

"SB, think much?" Leo's voice from the backseat jolted her from the alternate reality Sarabeth was crafting in her head. She turned around to look at Leo, whose eyebrows were raised cockily, his lips up in a half grin, and she couldn't decide if she thought he was cute in spite of being totally irritating or totally irritating because she found him cute.

"Yeah, you've been sitting at this stop sign for, like, thirty seconds," Teena said, looking at her nails like someone who couldn't be more bored. Sarabeth had to hand it to her: Teena was admirably cool for someone who'd only recently nearly been de-skinned by flying green goblins.

"Don't be scared, Legs," Abe said, pulling out a little black gun. "I'm packing heat." She turned, feeling her eyes go wide in her head as he stuck the gun in his mouth.

Sarabeth shrieked, hurling herself toward him in an effort to pull the gun away from him. Leo, Evan, and Teena all did the same. Their heads collided with a painful *thunk!* in the open space between the front and back seats.

"Hold on, I'll share." Abe pressed the trigger, and the gun shot a stream of clear liquid. Sarabeth looked closer and saw it was one of those water guns that Tinley Hills had banned years ago because they looked too realistic. "Gin. Made it myself." He pulled another squirt gun, this one a more obvious pastel blue, from his other pocket. "Orange juice in here. Wanna drink?" Abe aimed both barrels into his mouth and squirted out his oddball cocktail.

As Abe tilted his head back and swallowed, rubbing his belly beneath the Ewok blanket, they all burst out laughing.

"You all sure you don't want a drink?" Abe asked, pulling out a flask to refill the gin gun. "I don't trust no one who can't hold their alcohol."

"Dude, you're, like, my spirit animal." Leo laughed.

The sun was still hidden, but pink was seeping into the dark blue sky. Feeling embarrassed, like Teena and Leo had read her High Point thoughts—and grateful that Evan was silent and probably thinking weird High Point thoughts himself—Sarabeth drove along the winding road that led gradually to the precipice of High Point. To call it a precipice was akin to calling the brown brick slab known as Tinley Hills Village Hall a notable landmark. High Point was only a precipice at all because it rose a couple of stories above the rest of pancake-flat Tinley Hills. (It should have been called Tinley Hill, since High Point was the only thing close to an elevation it had.) Making High Point seem like a bigger deal than it was were the signs that appeared along the road, alerting drivers to TAKE CAUTION ON INCLINE, even though they really should have read SERIOUSLY, JUST DRIVE LIKE YOU NORMALLY WOULD.

Near the top of the peak, the road widened, and Sarabeth pulled to the side and put the van in park. She'd walk the couple hundred feet uphill, to get a good view of everything.

Sarabeth jumped from the van before the rest of them, not out of eagerness to see the aliens again, but more because she needed a break from everyone. As someone used to spending her Saturday nights alone in her room, she wasn't quite ready to be part of this messed-up Breakfast Club. But even as she traipsed a bit ahead, her long strides didn't put everyone else very far behind her. Their ragtag group was filled to the brim with bravery, apparently. Either that, or the idea of remaining in the van with Abe, who was still drinking out of his squirt gun, scared them.

Evan had been right. Gaining some elevation did provide the best vantage point. Sarabeth could see the spaceship before she even reached the rim of High Point. Everyone else saw it, too, judging by the chorus of low gasps behind her.

The ship was huge and had landed just beyond Orland Ridge Mall, on an empty parcel of land that was going to be the future Shoppoplex. A purple glow emanated faintly around the ship's behemoth hulking darkness. It was shaped like a giant Frisbee with a massive diamond pushed through its middle. Purple and green lights pulsed within it.

Around it was the town of Tinley Hills, neat and tidy, like a diorama of suburbia. Little square houses lined straight rectangular blocks, separated by even black strips of road. Nothing moved. It was like the whole town had stopped breathing. Or was bleeding, in the case of the sections of Tinley where the ship had laid waste to everything.

"There it is," Leo said, right behind Sarabeth. "Puts the fucking Death Star to shame."

"It makes the Death Star look like a koala bear," Evan said, absentmindedly drawing circles in the dirt with his bat, his jaw hanging open and, Sarabeth noticed, quivering slightly. "How do they even get it off the ground?"

"I think it's getting it back on the ground that's the hard part," Leo said. "Look at what got destroyed. See? They didn't mean to demolish Teena's or Walmart or anything. It was a shitty landing."

He was right. The chaotic areas of Tinley Hills fell in a straight, diagonal line, and the ship's trajectory was readily apparent from up here. Teena's house was the first bump, then the ship must have lifted back up, crashed down again over Walmart and Kmart, and then bounced one last time over the Orland Hills Mall and onto the vacant Shoppoplex property.

"Don't get me wrong, but my house being collateral damage doesn't make me feel that much better. I still don't get why the space station from hell had to land here," Teena said, no longer as calm and collected as she'd been in the van. She paced back and forth, her steps sinking into soggy piles of dead leaves—the winter thaw took away fall's satisfying crunch. "Or why we want to stand up here, looking at it and wetting our pants."

"It helps because we found it, you know? We found it," Leo said, getting excited, the way he sometimes did when he played something on the cello that he'd just made up. "We know where these douchebags are taking people. Friends and family are probably down there, at the worst welcome wagon ever. We at least know what our mission is, should we choose to accept it."

As they stood in a circle, Sarabeth looked around, at Leo, and

Evan, and Teena. They'd made it this far. That was big, wasn't it? "Good work, everyone," she said, feeling like maybe there was a reason she was here and part of this group.

Leo held up his hand for a high-five. Evan took him up on it first, then Teena, and then Sarabeth. Then Evan high-fived Sarabeth and Teena, too. Teena turned to Sarabeth, high-fiving Sarabeth in one of the most awkward uses of the gesture ever witnessed, and not just because of their height difference. As Sarabeth's and Teena's hands touched, Leo enveloped them in a hug and guided them toward Evan, who joined the hug, too. It felt nice. Calming. Warm. Safe. *My first group hug*, Sarabeth thought.

Proving to herself that she could ruin any moment, Sarabeth couldn't resist looking over Leo's shoulder to the ship beyond, and the quiet landscape around it. Why was everything so still? She understood the Tinley Hills abductions—she'd witnessed one, with that family. But up here, it felt like the whole world had gone silent and still. What if no one was *anywhere*? Something like this would normally merit some military helicopters, tanks, the Army evacuating people, or at least it did in the movies.

It was with that thought that her eyes landed on something just beyond the ship. Hundreds of cars, stacked one on top of the other on tall metal spears, like olives for a cocktail.

Sarabeth drew back from the group hug, suddenly cold. She pointed at the sickening sculpture. "Guys, look," she said as everyone took a few steps away from each other and stared at the scene.

"Do you think people were in their cars when they were

117

. . . skewered?" Evan asked.

Leo grimaced. "For their sake, I hope they were captured," he said. "Unless being captured by them is worse than being killed by them."

Sarabeth shuddered as another chill zigzagged down her body.

"Guys, do you think anyone is left?" she asked softly. "Like, anywhere?"

"Well, Abe is in the van," Leo said, but even he didn't have the energy to give the line the usual joking edge.

"I thought we'd see someone from up here," Sarabeth said. "But we're it."

She could almost hear Leo, Evan, and Teena's spirits deflating, and felt bad for being the cause. *No wonder you don't have any friends, Sarabeth*, she told herself. What was the point of being hopeless in a hopeless situation? She wanted the high-fives back, silly as they seemed.

"Wait, I have an idea. Aren't there stand-up binoculars up here?" she asked, directing the question toward the High Point experts, Teena and Leo.

"Binoculars? Why would anyone need binoculars when they're getting busy?" Teena said, rolling her eyes. The bitchiness was reassuring.

"Charming, Teena. There are," Leo said, a little sheepishly. "Just past that tree stand there. They're fifty cents, though." He fished some change from his pocket and dropped a few warm quarters into Sarabeth's cool hand.

Her fingers closing around the change, Sarabeth made her way up the hill a bit more, where two sets of standing binoculars faced the ship and town. She dropped in Leo's money and peered through the viewfinder, hoping to see something that she could get excited about.

As she focused the lenses and trained them on the ship, she saw something that made her feel like they stood a chance. A long shot of a chance, but a chance nonetheless.

"We shouldn't give up hope!" Sarabeth yelled back toward the group, still looking down at the ship. "The ship may be big, but it's not all space-age technology." She felt a grin spread across her face behind the cold metal of the binoculars. It wasn't what she saw, so much as what she *felt* that made her feel a little optimistic.

She peered back at the group, who'd gathered around her. "For as intimidating as the ship is"—she peeked back, wondering how many people were imprisoned in the ship—"it has a front door. And it's open. There are guards, maybe twelve aliens, and who knows what on the other side. But here's the thing. We have an opportunity to save the world."

Leo stepped closer, gesturing to have a look through the lenses. "I'll take it," he said.

"Yeah, we did make it this far," Evan added.

"Great, I'm so glad you're all pumped up," Teena said, turning away to glance at the ship. She gnawed on the inside of her lip. "But take it from a real cheerleader that a team without a playbook isn't going to win."

Sarabeth bristled at Teena's cynicism but let it roll off her. "Well, there's one other thing that might help, but I don't know. I mean, I could be way off base—I probably *am* way off base. But the ship is like a wheel, with spokes coming out of a central hub, that diamond in the center. I think that's the power source. The only power source. It's a dumb design. If we could get inside, we might be able to shut it all down."

"Like a self-destruct button?" Evan said.

"More like a self-delusion button," Teena sighed.

"What's your problem, Teena? It's just a guess, but it's something. Better than guns that don't work," Sarabeth sniped back, pulling herself up to her full five-eleven and feeling like a different person from the slightly slouched girl who'd tried to shrink into her new sweater on Teena's doorstep earlier that night.

"Yeah, let up, Teena. We probably could have saved that family if you hadn't insisted on fighting the aliens," Leo said, stepping between the girls.

"Whatever, Leo," Teena fired back, starting toward the van. "You're only here because you're in need of new vagina."

Sarabeth blushed beet-red, realizing that she was the new vagina. Did that make Teena the old vagina? "You're only good for firing off your gun and your mouth," Sarabeth said, but too quietly.

"You'd be dead if it weren't for me," Teena growled. When she reached the van, she grabbed her guns from the front seat, then started down the hill. "Whatever. I don't need you people. You *losers*. I hope you all have a good time blowing up a spaceship with a baseball bat!"

Teena stalked toward the trees. A distressed Evan looked from Leo and Sarabeth to Teena's small retreating figure. "She can't be out there alone," he said, before taking off behind her. Sarabeth and Leo were alone on High Point. And it sucked, because Sarabeth knew Evan was right. They couldn't split up, not now, no matter what.

"Well, this is the weirdest set of circumstances that's brought me up here with a girl," Leo said lightly, kicking his foot anxiously against the ground. "Though there was this one time I was seeing this chick obsessed with leprechauns, and it was St. Patrick's Day. . . ."

Sarabeth ignored this. She knew Leo went out with a lot of girls; sometimes in string ensemble, she'd hear him on his phone in the corner, making plans in a low, sexy voice. "Evan's right," she said, cutting him off. "We need her. She may be a bitch, but she's the only bitch we've got."

Leo peered once more at the ship below. "Check it out, it's glowing," he said. Sarabeth cast a sidelong glance at the ship, which was illuminated by a deeper purple light than before. Suddenly, a pulsing bright purple lit the sky, and a surge of energy practically burned the horizon. A laser beam shot out from the ship and headed straight for them. Sarabeth and Leo ran, jumping in the van and starting it just as the surge singed the earth below.

In the backseat, Abe shook out of a deep sleep. "Is it the commies?"

Sarabeth slammed on the gas pedal, and the van rumbled down the hill. Teena and Evan were straight ahead. Teena was having trouble negotiating the hill in her boots, and Evan was just steps behind her.

Evan turned and must have instantly recognized the terror in Sarabeth's eyes. Leo pushed open the door, even as the van skidded along the tree line. "Get in, get in, get in now!" he

121

yelled, reaching out for Evan, who grabbed Leo's arm with one hand and scooped up Teena with his other arm. Pushing off the ground with one foot, Evan launched himself and Teena into the van. They toppled in, sending Abe sprawling on the floor of the backseat with them. Sarabeth swung a hard right, and the van careened into a ditch along the road. The trees they'd just sped by burst into flames.

She didn't let up on the gas the whole way down the hill, until the smell of burnt earth grew faint in her nostrils. Then she slammed on the brakes dramatically at the intersection of 183rd and Edgar Road, stopping at the center of what had been the Tinley Hills's busiest intersection.

"Nice driving, Legs," Abe said, looking up at her from where he lay on the floor.

No one laughed, or spoke. Almost dying kind of took the words right out of your mouth.

"This isn't working for me," Sarabeth finally said in a strong, sure voice. "Look, I don't know if I'm right. I don't know if we stand a chance against these things. But we have to try to find out who they've got on that ship, and the only way we'll survive for more than a second is if we stick together. This is do or die. Or do and then run and hide. But either way, we're all we've got. So let's make a pact right now that we try to calm our hormones, forget our cliques, and stop with the petty personal grievances. Because I don't know about you all, but I don't want to die." She wondered where her oratory capabilities had come from. Probably Cameron.

She didn't say it, but she thought, *Because I think I just got a life*.

Teena was the first to speak, even though she was still taking shallow, nervous breaths. "She's right," she said. And she extended a hand that Sarabeth shook.

Sarabeth might have been making a deal with the devil, but going to hell still seemed safer than staying on Earth.

13

STRANGE BREW

Leo Starnick, 7:11 A.M. Sunday,
IHOP

"Story of my life," Leo said from behind the counter of the IHOP, where he was brewing some industrial-strength coffee. "The more fucked-up my night, the more likely it is that I wind up here at some ungodly hour. Only usually, I don't have to make my own coffee."

They'd come here to eat, finally, and to strategize. Teena, Evan, and Sarabeth sat at a booth just outside the kitchen, not speaking but not angry anymore, either. Everyone was quiet but okay. *Humbled* was probably the right word for it. Leo had to hand it to Teena. It took her outburst—and okay, that thing where they were all almost fried to death—to get them to acknowledge the necessity of functioning as a team. Sarabeth's speech helped, too. He grinned. He knew she had it in her. It was always the quiet ones.

"Janie's got some whiskey that'll go good with that brew," called Abe, emerging from the men's room at the back of the restaurant. Leo chuckled as he jogged past. He was comically fast for an old guy. With a merry wave, like some kind of demented Santa Claus, he disappeared outside.

Sarabeth looked up from the table and smiled at Leo. Something had happened between them on top of High Point. It was like, after years of occupying adjacent cello chairs and sharing the same sheet music, they were finally in tune.

"Want help?" Evan asked, getting up from the table and coming around the counter. "I could use some toast. Maybe some eggs. I'll make them for everyone."

"Good idea, Brighton," Leo said, trying to help him along. "I saw a shitload of eggs in that giant fridge." He pointed to the walk-in next to the prep counter.

At the table, Sarabeth, with a serious expression, was inspecting the purple alien jizz she'd gathered at her house, while Teena flipped idly through a Gussy Me Up catalog, still holding her gun. They'd told her to put the gun away, but she claimed it was like a security blanket and promised not to shoot any more aliens in the throat. *Chicks are weird*, Leo thought. Teena was Miss Killer Instinct unless she broke a nail, and Sarabeth could probably run the world but didn't want to speak up.

But then again, maybe dudes were weird, too. Here, Evan had pummeled, like, a hundred of those greenies but lost all testicle strength when it came to talking to Teena, while he, Leo, had bagged Teena easily (emphasis on *easy*) but had barely bruised one of the aliens.

Evan got to work cracking eggs onto the griddle just as the big, commercial-grade coffee brewer sputtered to life. The smells of breakfast filled the air, and Leo stood back and admired their little group. They were going to be okay. Well, okay with each other, anyway.

"Do you think Abe should be back by now?" Evan asked Leo as he flipped an egg off the griddle and onto a blue-and-white plate.

"I wouldn't worry about him. That guy will still be around when these fuckers kill us all. He's got the ultimate plan. Stay in the Winnebago."

"It's not a Winnebago, remember? And anyway, I think he likes riding with us better." Teena smiled, thumbed down the corner of a page featuring glittery red nail polish, and inhaled. "The coffee smells so good."

She was right. It did. IHOP coffee was lucky to smell like hot, dirty water. And this coffee smelled really good. Great, in fact. Like a Kona blend or a French roast or something.

"Brighton, let's go!" Leo shouted, and jumped over the counter, grabbing both Teena and Sarabeth by the wrists. "They're here. They're here."

"I don't see anything!" Sarabeth screamed, reaching for the container of alien goo as Leo yanked her out of the booth. Evan had traded his spatula for a bat and was right behind him.

"Dead giveaway. The coffee smells too good," he said in a panic. They all ran past the hostess counter, knocking it to the ground. Pastel after-dinner mints rolled in a rainbow across the floor, stopping at the slimy purple feet of two aliens pushing through the narrow door, trailing slime on the glass.

"The back, go out the back," Teena directed, barely paying attention as she unloaded a firestorm into the aliens before anyone could stop her. Bullets hit the aliens' throats with a squishy "splurt."

"You said you wouldn't shoot!" Evan shouted, pulling Teena's gun arm back as the purple aliens vomited onto the floor and the green liquid instantly sprang to vicious greenie life. A gaggle of snapping, buzzing, teeth-baring greenies was on them, swarming the restaurant and forcing them into the back of the building.

"I forgot!"

"Put the gun away," Leo said.

"It works on greenies!" Teena said, proving it by bringing down a half dozen with just a few shots. She tossed Sarabeth the semi-automatic from the waistband of her jeans.

So it goes, Leo thought as he charged back into the kitchen, egging the little monsters on. "Come on, you want a piece of me?" he yelled. The little beasts took the bait and surged toward him. He yanked a mop out of the corner, swirled it in cooking grease, and lit it on fire with his purple Bic. Insta-torch. He shouted to the group, "Get down!" and they dove beneath booths just as he swung his flaming mop at the greenies, igniting at least twenty of them at once. Some screeched and fell to the floor. Others continued the charge.

Evan stepped in behind Leo, swatting greenies away with his bat, smashing them to putrefying bits. Teena and Sarabeth fired when they had clear shots, bringing some more down. Some of the burning greenies flew about clumsily, setting fire to the walls and the tables. The fatter, slower ones swarmed beneath the lamps over the tables like giant, evil moths.

Leo ran ahead and kicked open the back door to the alley. "Go, go, go," he said. Teena and Evan skittered out, ducking their heads to avoid the onslaught. Sarabeth stopped right in front of him, her eyes as wide as IHOP's oversize breakfast-platter plates. She held up her lady gun and pointed it right at Leo. *What the fuck?* She'd been smiling at him, and now she was going to kill him? Did these things have mind-control powers, too? She fired. The bullet whizzed so close to his head he could hear it. With a horrible high-pitched squeal, one of the greenies fell to Leo's feet like some kind of amphibious bird. Sarabeth took his shaking hands in hers and pressed the van keys into it.

"You drive," she said, looking deep into his eyes. He'd never felt more like a man; she was putting her life into his unsteady hands.

They raced to the van, where Evan and Teena were still fending off a seemingly never-ending supply of greenies, which clung to the van like barnacles on an ancient ship. Leo dove in and started the engine as the girls leaped into the backseat and Evan took the front passenger seat.

"What about Abe?" Sarabeth yelled in the commotion.

"He said he would be in the trailer," Evan said.

Out of the corner of his eye, Leo saw a buzzing cluster of greenies at the edge of the IHOP parking lot. Leo's intestines unfurled in his stomach as he realized that beneath the greenies was Abe's reedy shape. The greenies had their teeth and claws in him, and through the mess, Leo could just make out blood dripping onto his yellowish beard. It was too late to help him. "So much for our end-of-the-world party, old man," Leo said sadly.

"Should we leave the trailer? Lose the weight?" Teena asked. Leo could swear he saw tears in her eyes.

"No," Leo said. "Janie stays. I'm not going to let the aliens get her."

"You're right," Teena agreed, without an ounce of sarcasm.

"We're sorry, Abe," Evan added, sounding as dejected as Leo felt. "But we have to go." He pointed to the greenies, which were detaching from Abe's carcass and starting to speed toward the van.

Leo floored the gas pedal. "We need a base. We'll use the mall until we figure out how to take them out. These fuckers are going down."

The van didn't handle like Leo's usual piece of shit. It was like driving a much larger, more cumbersome piece of shit, only this time he was driving it while towing a silver motor home while under attack by vicious outer-space birds. The greenies kept launching themselves at the van, only, unlike smaller pests, most of them didn't smash and die when they made impact with the windshield.

"I can't see!" he yelled. Evan was already doing his best. He'd rolled down his window and was half out of the van, swatting every greenie he could. In the back, Teena and Sarabeth fastened their seat belts, swung open the doors and began firing, annihilating greenie after greenie, even though the little jerks just kept on coming. At least guns worked on greenies, though their existence could have been prevented if guns had never entered the picture.

A greenie flew up behind the driver's-side mirror, and,

keeping just his right hand on the steering wheel, Leo grabbed a handful of Gussy Me Up flyers that were stored in the door pocket. Flicking his lighter with the hand on the wheel, he held the papers to the flame, then rolled down his window and held out his newest torch. Two goblins flew right into the trap, exploding slime all over Leo's hand. A third came at him, teeth bared, and nicked his arm before it caught fire and flew away, burning, into a billboard for the new Martin Scorsese movie. In the mirror, a barrage of greenies kept laying siege. Sarabeth, Teena, and Evan were doing their best, but the troops needed a break.

Leo struggled to keep the van on LaGrange, heading toward the mall. There were tons of places to hide there, to find supplies, and to get some food and rest. He just wished they knew how to kill the purple guys without starting a greenie explosion.

His torch died out at the same time he heard a hissing pop. Looking like it was wearing a shit-eating grin, a greenie flew away from the van's now-busted front tire. Sparks flew from the dull rim as it ground against the asphalt. They were still two miles from the mall, and Leo strained to see through the windshield. It was a Jackson Pollock painting of greenie guts. He turned on the wipers. They almost bent backward against the layer of gunk. After what felt like a million tries, they finally pushed through, trailing green slime.

When his view was somewhat clear, he discovered he couldn't go any farther. What he saw was:

AlienAlienAlienAlienAlienAlienAlienAlienAlienAlien

AlienAlienAlienAlienAlienAlienAlienAlienAlienAlien
AlienAlienAlienAlienAlienAlienAlienAlienAlienAlien
AlienAlienAlienAlienAlienAlienAlienAlienAlienAlien
AlienAlienAlienAlienAlienAlienAlienAlienAlienAlien
AlienAlienAlienAlienAlienAlienAlienAlienAlienAlien
AlienAlienAlienAlienAlienAlienAlienAlienAlienAlien
AlienAlienAlienAlienAlienAlienAlienAlienAlienAlien
AlienAlienAlienAlienAlienAlienAlien

A row of aliens stood in a line like toy soldiers from another awful dimension. Together, they formed a nearly airtight perimeter along Fordham Avenue and as far as the eye could see. They must have been protecting their spaceship, which Leo had figured was a possibility. He hadn't thought they'd also be blocking his way to the mall. But now the four of them were stuck. If he drove through the perimeter, the aliens would be on them in seconds. If they stopped, the remaining greenies would overtake them.

The only good thing was that it didn't appear the aliens had spotted them yet. "Roll up your windows and get down, everyone," he ordered.

"But there are still greenies out there," Evan protested.

"We killed enough," Leo said. "Look up ahead."

Evan, Sarabeth, and Teena drew inside, pulling their doors shut instantly when they saw what Leo had seen.

"Oh, crap," Evan said.

Leo slammed on the brakes, skidded out into a U-turn and rumbled the van up onto the wide sidewalk in front of Pearl Promenade, an upscale medical building where old ladies got

131

their Botox. He swung down the valet-parking ramp and, seeing that they were free from any greenie tails, stopped the van with a screech.

"No offense, anyone, but we're all gonna die," Leo said. His teeth were chattering in his head, but the rest of his body had gone all loose and drippy, like a bad batch of pizza dough at Phil's. A look at Evan sitting next to him and at the girls in the rearview revealed instantly that they were as shell-shocked as he was. This wasn't do or die. It was do and still die.

He leaned back in the seat and let his eyes drift to a display next to the car-park booth. A female mannequin in a short black trench coat dangled a silver key ring from one finger, like someone excited for a jaunt out of town. He closed his eyes for a solid minute and could see them driving. Well, really, he could see himself driving with Sarabeth in the passenger seat. Teena and Evan were there, but just blurry faces in the backseat. They were headed west, toward the ocean. It reminded him of his mom's breathless message on the answering machine just after she moved out. "Leo, I'm driving west. I'm going to meet the ocean." How she decided Reno was close enough was beyond his comprehension.

"We could just leave town," he said hopefully, more to Sarabeth than the others. She didn't notice, her head already bent over the slime sample again. "We can't go up against the Purple Perimeter, can we?"

Next to him, Evan looked out the window, his face as taut as a guard's at Buckingham Palace. Teena's steely eyes scanned the empty parking garage.

"Why would we leave, when there's still a chance we could

stop them?" Sarabeth asked, still intensely examining the goo, which slid around the Tupperware like a mutant slug. "If I could just figure out their membrane, maybe it would give us a clue how we could destroy them."

Leo was scum. A turd sandwich. A soy-and-bean, vegan turd sandwich. He wanted to run, while Sarabeth, Teena, and Evan wanted to fight. He'd survived an alien attack with the most battle-ready teens in Tinley Hills. So why did his own fight-or-flight response meter waver somewhere halfway between "kick ass" and "get the fuck out"? It was one thing blowing up greenies. That was almost fun. But a wall of those indestructible aliens? Come on. Anyone with half a brain knew the four of them didn't stand a chance. And yet, he knew that his vanmates had better-than-half-brains among them, and they kept gearing up for challenge after challenge. Yup, he was a turd sandwich.

14

GREASING THE WHEELS

Teena McAuley, 8:19 A.M. Sunday, Pearl Promenade Parking Garage

Sarabeth Lewis was smart. Teena knew this. Sometimes her parents liked to ask, "Whatever happened to that smart Sarabeth you used to hang out with?" The idea that Teena herself might have been smart was uninteresting to them. To them, Teena didn't need to be. They always figured she'd go into real estate like Mike McAuley, not because he couldn't wait to work alongside his daughter, but more because he wanted to put their faces on bus benches with the slogan he'd come up with when she was in eighth grade, FATHER + DAUGHTER = OUR FAMILY VALUES ARE YOUR FAMILY'S VALUE. If ever she'd been sure she wasn't a daddy's girl, it was in that moment.

So, yes, Sarabeth was smart, and Teena was expected to lend

her face to her father's business. But she knew she was cut out for something else. Something great. The problem was, she wasn't sure exactly what that thing was.

That was partly why she was upset when her fling with Leo had suddenly ended. Except for some drunken complaints about her father, she'd never had a chance to show him that she was more than just the popular girl he'd successfully bagged. Meanwhile, she'd come to see him as so much more than just some perpetually high pizza boy, and the more she learned about how smart and interesting he was, the more she wanted him to see her the same way.

And now Sarabeth, a shoo-in for Ermer valedictorian, had just appropriated the container of alien goo like she was the only person in this van who could possibly save the world. And that Leo and Evan seemed to think the same way.

"Can I check it out?" Teena asked Sarabeth, prompting the guys to turn around.

Teena raised an eyebrow. It was hard to raise it, given that her face was tight with goo from the greenies. Their blood probably had skin-firming potential. Too bad Greenie Guts would make a particularly gross late-night infomercial.

Sarabeth heaved a sigh. "I've examined it from every angle," she said. "It doesn't look like anything I've ever seen. And it just smells like coffee."

Clearly, she, too, was skeptical of what Teena had to offer. Like a person couldn't wear the best clothes, have the nicest hair, know how to do a good smoky eye, and still be smart and substantive. If they made it out of this alive, maybe Teena would start a non-profit organization to help rich, attractive, popular

135

girls prove they had more to offer than money and looks.

Still, Sarabeth put the container down on the seat between them, nudging it toward Teena. The purple goo was slick and shiny, even in the dim parking structure. Teena picked up the container and pulled the lid off. She dipped one finger into the purple gelatin, which was cool to the touch.

"What are you doing?" Evan's voice went up a few octaves. "We don't know what that might do to you."

It was cute, the way he worried about her. But that was Earth-under-attack hormones talking, she knew. In response, she simply smirked at Evan and pulled her fingertips apart. As she thought, the goo dripped into her palm. It wasn't as sticky as the greenie blood—more like an outer-space vinaigrette.

"So, you guys remember Nathalie Oliverio, right? May she rest in peace." An image of Nathalie's burnt but pretty corpse flashed through Teena's mind, and she shivered. "Well, she always had this wicked oily skin. Like, it was almost impossible to even put makeup on her. It would literally slide right off. So she got Oil Rig, a Gussy Me Up product. Do you know it, Sarabeth?"

Sarabeth nodded, ducking into the back of the van. "Yeah, it's a best seller," she said, starting to dig around in the cardboard Gussy Me Up boxes stored on the floor of the van. "But we don't have any."

Teena waved a hand dismissively, like this was no big deal. She didn't think it was, really. "It's okay. All Oil Rig does is dry up greasy skin. There are other products that might dry out skin in the same way. Sarabeth, can you see if there're any bottles of Otherworldly cologne back there?"

Sarabeth heaved a large box onto the seat next to Teena. As the box sank down, Teena rose. "There's tons of that stuff back here," Sarabeth said, counting boxes. "It was a huge Gussy Me Up failure. My mom can't give it away."

"Probably because one spritz and you feel like a lizard," Teena offered. She looked at the boys, who were both wearing looks of bemused puzzlement. This pleased Teena to no end. Carefully, she tore the tape off the cardboard box Sarabeth had put next to her. Inside, the silver-and-blue boxes of Otherworldly cologne were packed tightly, never before touched. She tore away the plastic and pulled out the bottle, a dark blue orb topped with a silver star. Spritzing the air first, she breathed in. "That is the most awful perfume I've ever smelled," she declared. And it was. It smelled like the water in a vase holding a bouquet of flowers that had gone moldy. "However, watch and learn." Like a game-show bimbo, she spritzed two pumps of cologne onto the alien slime.

Almost instantly, the slick, shiny substance turned to gray dust.

"Oh my god," Sarabeth said, amazed and with a hint of jealousy in her voice, Teena thought. "I can't believe it. Their membrane is a protective coating, and I bet if it dies, they die."

"Pretty sweet work, Teena," Leo said from the front seat, and for once she didn't feel like a piece of meat in front of him. He turned around and looked her right in the eye. Her whole body got a little floaty, realizing he'd honestly meant the compliment.

"That will really help, Teena," Evan said. He leaned in to look at the dust in the jar, making hopeful eye contact with her.

137

"Yeah, again, who knew your extensive beauty regimen would come in handy?" Sarabeth said. The backhanded compliment didn't bother Teena in the least. She was glad to have gotten to Sarabeth. Yes, she knew they were supposed to be getting along right now, but she only had to be nice to Sarabeth's face. And besides, how benevolent was Sarabeth when she wanted to monopolize all opportunities to be Little Miss Brainiac?

"Spoken like someone who's never had a makeover," Teena said, firing back in her sweetest voice. "If we make it through this, we're definitely doing something about those eyebrows."

15

LENNY BRUCE IS NOT AFRAID

Sarabeth Lewis, 8:27 A.M. Sunday,
Pearl Promenade Parking Garage

My eyebrows aren't that bad, are they? Sarabeth thought, touching above her eye to feel how caterpillarlike her brows actually were. "So, what do we do with this new information?" she asked, wondering how many notches Teena had gone up in Leo's esteem, now that Teena was the resident alien expert.

"Yeah, it's not like we can walk up to the aliens and say, 'Want to try some Otherworldly cologne?' like they do at the mall," Evan said.

Leo laughed, and then drummed against the steering wheel, starting slow and building to a quick rhythm. Sarabeth watched his hands on the leather, somewhat mesmerized. "I think I have an idea," he said. "Let's go."

He started the van and revved the engine, a look of childlike glee on his face. He bounced up and down in his seat, seemingly dancing to a song they couldn't hear.

"Where are you taking us?" Sarabeth asked, her body tensing.

"Just chill," Leo said. "It's a surprise. So you guys be upstanding citizens with your eyes on the road, and let me do the kind of shit I do best."

He charged up the valet ramp and into daylight. At the top of the ramp, he turned the opposite way from Orland Ridge Mall and sped down the street, singing to himself. It was an R.E.M. song from the eighties that Sarabeth recognized, and Leo had the lyrics down, impressively shouting them out fast and furious.

His voice was soft but strong, and he carried the tune perfectly. Sarabeth grinned, and started to sing along, humming the melody to fill in the gaps she didn't know, even while realizing she knew more of the lyrics than she'd thought.

Next to her, Teena joined in. They stumbled over the lyrics together, giggling when they slurred a bunch of made-up nonsense over one of the parts where the song became gun fast. Up front, Evan had finally lent his voice to the mix, and his baritone gave the song its bass line. He leaned his head back and smiled.

Looking straight ahead and knowing all the words was Leo, and just watching him sing so assuredly was enough to make Sarabeth feel better about their situation. Actually, together, they were all making her feel better about their situation. Stubborn Teena, solid Evan, and Leo, who felt like the glue to her, even though he'd never agree. She wasn't someone who believed in fate—there wasn't a page in her journal devoted to guessing at her "soul mate." But something about the four of them together right now made her think they weren't just the last people around—they were *meant* to be the last four people around.

This early, it was possible to imagine that Tinley Hills was just a town that wasn't open yet. The sun was out in an indecisive sort of way, and its rays wove themselves between the still mostly bare tree branches. Little strands of cool air from the broken window next to Sarabeth tickled her under the chin, and she grinned as Leo caught her eye in the rearview.

It's the end of the world as we know it, and I feel fine.

In front of her, Evan hung his arm out the window, appearing to catch the breeze with his fingertips.

"I feel better than fine," Evan said to them all. "Is that weird?"

"No," Teena said, bringing a grin to Evan's face.

The van slowed as Leo slid into a parking spot.

"And we're here," he said.

The overly jovial rainbow-hued letters of Toys"R"Us looked monolithic above them, the backward R like some kind of cruel joke from God.

The song in her head stopped abruptly. What the fuck was Leo thinking?

16

A THOUGHT

Teena McAuley, 8:44 A.M. Sunday,
Toys"R"Us

What the fuck was Leo thinking?

17

A THOUGHT

Evan Brighton, 8:44 A.M. Sunday,
Toys"R"Us

What the fuck was Leo thinking?

18

RETAIL THERAPY

Leo Starnick, 8:44 A.M. Sunday, Toys"R"Us

"Seriously?"

Leo knew why everyone was staring at him like he'd sprouted a goat's head. Clearly, they all thought he was nuts, or too high for his own good. But he'd been there for all their plans. Evan wanted to go to High Point. Leo was in. Sarabeth thought the ship had a central, self-destructive chewy center. Leo bought in, more or less. Teena wanted to fuck up bad guys with perfume. Leo thought, *Why the fuck not?*

So now, they could go along with him. His idea was their best shot at getting past that perimeter without being taken prisoner. He knew it.

He strode ahead, feeling kind of excited. Make that really excited.

He was *trying*. He was putting in effort. He might put his turd sandwich days behind him.

That is, if everyone else kept up with him.

He turned and looked at them, jogging back to pluck the baseball bat from Evan's hands. "Hey, remember we said we weren't going to fight with each other? Last people on Earth and all that? I think I'm going to be at least a little pissed at you guys if you can't trust me for a minute."

Casually, like he was flipping some pizza dough, he twirled the bat once, twice, and then he gave one quick swing, hitting the center of one of the automatic doors, sending a shower of glass skidding across the tiled floor. Using the bat, he cleared the doorframe of extra shards of glass and stepped through into the darkened store, the smell of new plastic toys more apparent than usual thanks to the lack of customers.

He looked at his friends—he'd decided he could call them that, unless they all fucked him over right now—and tapped on the sign above his head that showed Geoffrey the Giraffe surrounded by smiling toys. "Come on, guys, think young."

Even though it was only March, the main toy displays were stocked with toys befitting CWWT—Chicago Winter Wishful Thinking. Frisbees. Kites. And water toys by the dozen. Squirt guns, from little pistols to massive Super Soakers. Kiddie pools. Water balloons.

Turning to face the gang, Leo could see the lightbulbs go off in everyone's heads like he'd flicked a switch. One by one, his friends grinned. Leo grinned back. "So, I can tell I needn't explain Operation: Beauty Bomb."

He strode over to a G.I. Joe truck, the kind big enough for

145

two kids to sit in, with battery-powered pedals you pushed to make the car go. He climbed in. The thing was plenty roomy, probably because they had to make toys big enough for fat kids these days. "Evan, come on."

Evan looked intrigued. He loped over and took the seat next to Leo. Leo steered over to a pink Barbie Corvette parked near a display of princess crowns. He nudged the front end of the Corvette and looked at the girls.

"Get in," he said in a voice much different from the who-gives-a-crap tone he usually used. Urgency, an emotion foreign to someone who spent his time actively not caring about anything, had crept in. "Remember those shopping sprees Toys"R"Us used to give away when we were kids? Anything you could grab in ten minutes? No one ever won. Or if someone did, it sure wasn't me. So today, we win. And we spree. Grab anything you want. If it's battle-worthy, great. If it's just something you always wanted, even fucking better."

Teena and Sarabeth faced each other over the top of the pink car, as much as two girls could face each other with an eight-inch height difference between them.

"You should drive," Sarabeth said to Teena, seeing how desperate she was to helm the chunk of pink plastic. Teena plopped into the seat, satisfied. Sarabeth lowered herself into the passenger side and with a grin said, "My legs are too long anyway."

Leo bristled, and he could see Evan gnash his teeth. Things were going so well, they didn't want a fresh girl fight. A weird thought, since Leo had once left work to watch a girl fight at the mall. Forever 21 had that effect on women.

But Teena just swatted Sarabeth playfully, with maybe a hint of bitch, and said, "I'm a better driver anyway."

Evan pointed to his watch. "Okay, so should we give ourselves ten minutes?" He turned to Leo. "Guys versus girls, right?"

"Yup," Leo said, pressing down on the gas pedal so the car leaped forward and knocked over a display of Nerf guns. "But we're all winners."

"Whatever," Teena said, looking around the store to pick what direction to go in. "Ready, set, *go!*" And before Leo could even turn around, Teena had gunned it and the girls zipped past them, giggling maniacally. *Good*, Leo thought. *This might calm down some of the cattiness.*

Leo watched Teena and Sarabeth grab an assortment of water balloons, Super Soakers, and a water-balloon slingshot, and before leaving the front of the store, each took several oversize shopping bags from hooks near the entrance. Dumping their water toys in the bags, they took off in the direction of the girls' toys.

Evan raised his eyebrows at Leo. "That's smart," he said, reaching out of the G.I. Joe truck and pulling an entire shopping cart that had been left in the middle of the aisle. He held it with one hand next to the truck. "This is smarter."

"Nice work, Evan," Leo said, meaning it. Ribbons of giddiness shimmied in his stomach, and if that made him seem like a little girl, so be it. If death awaited, at least his bucket list was one item lighter.

Leo pushed the pedal to the plastic and—despite their collected weight—the truck shot off speedily down an aisle loaded with superhero toys. They plucked Captain America

147

shields and Spider-Man web shooters and Hulk fists from the shelves, rounding the corner and spinning down an aisle filled with kids' sports equipment. Evan pulled Wiffle bats and catcher's mitts from the shelves. On his side, Leo scrambled to toss padded mixed martial arts training gear and joust sticks into the cart. They raided an aisle of remote-control vehicles, grabbing cars and helicopters and even a shark that you inflated and flew with a remote control. They added plenty more utterly useless stuff to their makeshift side-cart—a billion-piece LEGO set to build Hogwarts, creepy zombie-skull balls with eyeballs that popped out, and not one but two replicas of the *Millennium Falcon*. They'd covered half the store and hadn't even seen the girls yet. They were probably doing quite a job on Barbie's Headquarters. He smiled as he imagined Sarabeth selecting an Easy-Bake Oven.

Spinning out into the birthday-party section, Leo saw an item on a high shelf and got an idea. It was perfect.

"It's 9:01. Time's up."

19

EVERYONE'S A WINNER

Sarabeth Lewis, 8:56 A.M. Sunday, Barbie's Headquarters

They were five minutes into their shopping spree, and Sarabeth could safely say she'd never had more fun in her life. Teena's competitive spirit meant they were reaching never-before-felt speeds on the Barbie Corvette. Teena and Sarabeth each wore several princess crowns, and pink flowing capes streamed out behind them. They had one of every Barbie Doll, a Hello Kitty karaoke set, Rapunzel hair extensions, and—just to indulge herself—Sarabeth had picked up an Easy-Bake Oven, even though electricity wasn't exactly available. Her mom had never approved of the Easy-Bake Oven when she was little. "Wouldn't that be like giving you a weight problem on top of everything else?" What "everything else" was had never been explained.

The soundtrack for their spree came from a battery-operated

Kidz Dance radio that played the same three tinny tween songs on a loop. As a twelve-year-old sang about being awesome, it occurred to Sarabeth that they needed to be practical. She hated her inner killjoy, but hadn't getting supplies been part of Leo's plan? "Shouldn't we be looking for stuff that's useful?"

Teena shook her head and smiled, her perfect white teeth glimmering under the fluorescent lights. "This is useful," she said. "In its own way." She reached out and adjusted one of the crowns decorating Sarabeth's head.

Just like that, Sarabeth got it. They were *bonding*. She and Teena, who'd barely thought of each other in the last five years, suddenly needed each other. And Leo had helped her realize it.

Leo. What was it about him? It was like he knew just what she needed, and made it happen. All those times in string ensemble, telling her to loosen up and just play—now here she was, just playing, not caring that she might be reduced to alien garnish, and she was really, truly herself. If she made it out alive, maybe her new life rule would be "Be Sarabeth."

Teena grabbed and uncapped some tacky blue body glitter for little girls. "Oh, smells good, though." She rubbed some on her collarbone and did the same for Sarabeth. It did smell good, in a cheap, lavender-vanilla sort of way.

"Wow, Mommy, don't let your baby grow up to be a pole dancer," Sarabeth said cattily, putting a little more in her hair.

Teena laughed in happy bells. Sarabeth blushed, pleasantly surprised by the effectiveness of her mean comment. Teena swabbed some more on, rendering herself more glittery than was probably fashionable, so Sarabeth did the same, not even concerned they would probably lose to the boys. She and Teena were cracking up laughing, like two old friends, instead of two old friends who were no longer friends.

"Is it just me, or is this stuff making your skin feel really dry?" Teena said.

Sarabeth did notice; the glitter was sucking the life out of her pores. "It's just like the Otherworldly," she said to Teena.

"You're right! And look at this!" She held up another item from the ShimmerGirlz product line, scarily called Gleaminizer Body Glitter Sleepover Spray Shooter, a sparkly gun so friends could presumably have glitter-party wars. "It comes with its own gun!"

Between the ShimmerGirlz glitter and the Otherworldly cologne, their chances against the Purple Perimeter were improving. Sarabeth couldn't wait to tell Leo. If he hadn't led them here, they'd have never found this stuff.

She could tell Teena was excited, too. "How much time do we have left?" she asked.

Sarabeth checked her watch. "One minute."

"I could use one more tiara. You?" Teena was already driving toward the princess gear.

"Yes, please!" Sarabeth was in total agreement with her new best friend.

A minute later, laughing, breathless, and beyond crazy-looking in their royal wigs, multiple crowns, and fairy wings, Teena and Sarabeth spun out into the birthday-party section at the front of the store, where Leo and Evan were waiting, their cart loaded with toy guns and shields and sports equipment.

Sarabeth dropped her bags on the ground, grinning un-self-consciously. She felt shiny, and not because of ShimmerGirlz.

"You won't believe what we found."

Leo grinned back, looking joyful, and her heart flashed inside her. Even though Evan and Teena were in her peripheral vision, she felt like they were alone as Leo took a step closer to her, his hands behind his back. Every part of her, from her throat to the pit of her stomach, felt like nagging spaces she wanted to fill by pulling Leo to her and kissing him for all she was worth. *Be Sarabeth*, she thought. But there was being Sarabeth and there was giving in to her more cavewoman-esque urges, which wasn't the best option at a time like this.

"No matter what it is, I have something even better. For you," Leo said softly, like they were indeed the last two people on Earth. Sarabeth half expected some heavily synthesized, dreamy-vocaled music to kick in, like in one of the eighties movies her mom forced her to watch in hopes of unleashing Sarabeth's inner swoony teenager.

Now her inner teenager was all outer, and she had to fight the oncoming swoon that made her want to sigh loudly. "What is it?" she asked Leo, realizing as she said it that her tone was all bedroom eyes, and not because she was tired.

From behind his back, he pulled a very cheesy, very big-eyed, very pink teddy bear holding a heart that read HAPPY BIRTHDAY. He held it out to her, and she stepped closer, taking the plush bear from him.

"But it's not my birthday," she said, rubbing her thumb over the bear's soft fur. "My birthday's not for a month."

"Well, I thought we should celebrate while we still can." Leo smiled. A loop of hair fell over his left eye, and Sarabeth reached out to push it away without even thinking. Her fingertips brushed the warm skin of his cheek, and her heart shot up another roller-coaster crest.

Yup, he knew just what she needed. The only sad part was having her first romantic feelings for a guy arrive at the same time the world was probably ending.

Sarabeth's fingers were still near Leo's ear. Her eyes were locked on his as she clutched the bear, which she'd already named Pinkie. She realized Teena and Evan were standing there. Evan was blushing, leaning awkwardly against the guys' cart full of toys, pretending to be interested in a set of Pokémon cards. Teena was untangling cheap plastic tiaras from her Rapunzel wig, looking tense and . . . mad? She wasn't meeting Sarabeth's eyes. *Maybe I'm imagining things*, Sarabeth thought. She suddenly felt weird standing there wearing her Belle wig, the brunette swirls cascading down her back. Sarabeth pulled the wig off her own non-swirling, non-cascading hair and hung it neatly on an empty hook.

Teena tossed her wig to the floor and kicked it away like a piece of toilet paper that had stuck to her shoe. Definitely mad. She turned to Evan. "Evan, did you pull that cart around with your pitching arm?" She grinned like a cat who'd found a mouse with a broken leg. Teena sauntered up to him, and with a glance toward Leo and Sarabeth, said, "Let me massage it. We so need your arm."

She dug into Evan's arm, kneading like a professional. Teena kept looking at Leo like she wanted him to take notice. "You're so much more cut than Leo," Teena said. So there it was. There must have been a time when Teena massaged Leo's arm. Sarabeth no longer felt like she was in a meet-cute-romantic-teen movie.

Instead, she felt about as interesting and attractive as Skipper probably felt next to Barbie.

Sarabeth clutched her new pink bear by the arm a little more tightly and gave Leo a halfhearted smile. What was it about girls? Why did they always fight when it came to guys? She turned as far as she could away from Teena, literally—if insincerely—sinking her clutches into Evan. Was it wrong that Leo's return smile made her feel a little bit better? She'd lost Teena as a friend before, so she could manage again. Right?

20

A MAN OF ACTION

Evan Brighton, 9:14 A.M. Sunday,
Toys"R"Us

Teena was all over him. Well, all over his arm. And since his sweater was covered in alien guts, dirt, and his own blood, he was thinking that maybe she really was starting to like him.

The cool thing was, he really *liked* her. And not just in a physical way. There was more to her than her petite, curvy frame, and the little freckle that fell right between her tan shoulder and the top of her collarbone. He actually liked her as a person. She was strong and smart and absolutely fearless, and when she laughed, like she had when she and Sarabeth had spun around the corner minutes ago, he wanted to grab the sound out of the air and carry it around with him like a good-luck charm. Being in lust with Teena the fantasy had been easy, even if he'd been scared shitless of that Teena. The real

Teena was a challenge he actually looked forward to.

But now wasn't the time for that. Leo had brought them here, an idea that proved brilliant, Evan thought. They'd gotten gear and blown off some steam. And the whole trip had reminded Evan that there was a lot worth fighting for. Teena most of all.

Evan knew he needed to be more take-charge if he was going to really land a girl like Teena, last four people on Earth or not. As hard as it was to do, the next time Teena's kneading slowed down, Evan gave her what he hoped was a meaningful look that said "thank you" and stepped into the center of the group. He was still holding a bat in his right hand, and focusing on his hand around the white ash handle made him feel strong and grounded. "Look, I think we should try to take down the Purple Perimeter soon, while we're all feeling good and before it gets dark."

Teena was scowling, and a tiny part of Evan wondered if it was because he'd pulled away before she'd expected him to. He inched a little closer to her again, but she continued to frown. *Ugh, girls.* He wished he could look her in the eye and say, "Frankly, my dear, I don't give a damn." But he did give a damn. He gave a lot of damns.

Leo came up beside him, clasped him on the shoulder, and nodded. "This has been fun, but Brighton's right," he said. "We need to strike while the iron's hot, or whatever. Evan, what do you think we should do?"

"Well, we have all this stuff," he said, gesturing to the rainbow assortment of toys and games in the center of their circle. The girls had stuffed about a dozen shopping bags, and his and Leo's cart was almost overflowing. "Maybe first we need to sort it into piles of useful versus not-so-useful. And take the useful stuff out of the packages."

"That's a good idea," Teena said. She smiled at him, and all felt right with the world again. "I'll start. One pile is fun, one pile is weapons."

She set to work, putting things like LEGOs and Barbie dolls into the "fun" pile, while adding squirt guns and the sparring gear to a "weapons" pile. She was cute as she zipped between the carts, really in her element. It was like watching one of the HGTV shows his mom loved, but with a much hotter host.

Sarabeth tentatively stepped in to help Teena. Evan held his breath and shared a glance with Leo, who seemed to be doing the same. He didn't get the way girls went from friendly to weird in seconds. It kept happening, like an invisible rubber band snapped and tension mounted between them again. But Teena stepped to the side and let Sarabeth help sort through the merchandise. A sigh of relief floating between them, he and Leo began going through stuff, too. They all worked for a while, a busy vibration in the air. It felt good to have a purpose.

After a few minutes, they were at the bottom of the guys' cart and down to the last of the girls' bags. Sarabeth pulled a Captain America shield from the guys' cart. She examined it for a few seconds, turning it over in her hands.

"Fun pile," Teena directed Sarabeth. "It's too flimsy."

"No way," Evan said. "It's badass."

Sarabeth paused with the shield over the fun pile.

"Badass?" Teena asked, with a raised eyebrow. "I never thought I'd hear you swear. I mean, besides *hell*."

"Come on, like you've ever thought about me at all," Evan

blurted, trying to memorize Teena's face as she grinned at him.

"Fine, weapons pile," Teena said, avoiding his comment. But was she blushing a little? Sarabeth smirked, put the shield in the pile, and went back to work.

"Thank you," Evan said to Teena.

"You're welcome," she said, and it was like he had her all to himself, even more than when she'd been massaging his arm. Leo was going through an assortment of action figures, and Sarabeth had begun unwrapping squirt guns from their plastic-and-cardboard packages just feet from them. But Teena was flirting with him, wasn't she? And was he successfully flirting back?

They were standing shoulder to shoulder as Evan opened the girls' last bag, stuffed with some body glitter meant for girls probably too young for body glitter. He started to dump it into the fun pile.

"Nuh-uh." Teena grabbed the bag from him. "That's weaponized glitter."

"Come on, what could that be for?" Evan teased her, trying to yank it away.

"Wouldn't you like to know?" Teena said with a sly smile.

"It dries out your skin," Sarabeth said as she tested the trigger on a junky pink water gun before tossing it into the trash. "Teena found it. It will be great for fighting the aliens."

"Nice," Leo said, looking up from a particularly aggressive set of twist ties holding a Super Soaker to its cardboard backing. "Death by sparkles."

Evan surveyed the weapons pile, satisfied. Leo let out a low whistle. "We're in good shape." He clapped his hands together.

"Okay, what next, Brighton?"

Buoyed by the support, Evan continued and picked up a package of water balloons. "Well, we probably need to make some weapons. It might be good to test the weight of these, for maximum explosion potential."

As soon as he said it, everyone got the same idea. They ran to the family restroom at the front of the store and turned on four of the six taps. There was still water. They filled several dozen of the water balloons, making some extra-big, some small, and some right in the middle. When the bag of balloons was empty, the sinks were stuffed with candy-colored balloons.

Teena picked up the first balloon, a small one, and tossed it at Evan from about five feet away. It bounced off him and even stayed intact when it hit the floor.

"Underfilled," he said. He grabbed a larger balloon that he knew would burst easily, but before he had a chance to toss it, Teena took it and tossed it into the center of the circle. It burst with a huge splash before it even hit the ground. She ducked into a stall, her laughter echoing through the bathroom.

"Holy crap!" Leo shouted, his hair dripping. "That's the ticket." He grabbed a balloon and hurled it at Sarabeth at the same time she threw one at him.

Evan launched a medium-sized balloon over the stall wall at Teena, careful not to throw too hard. It went over the wall, and she shrieked as it exploded. Dripping wet, she ran out, took a balloon from the sink, and hurled it at him. For four glorious minutes, they lobbed the water bombs at one another. And then the balloons that had taken almost twenty minutes to fill were gone, their rubbery guts lying in the puddles on

159

the floor. Everyone was soaked and cold, but grinning happily. It was too bad they couldn't stay at the Toys"R"Us forever, Evan thought.

"Okay," Leo said. "So I think we learned that the best size is a handful, something I've always stated as fact." He went to light a cigarette, but the pack was dripping.

"Perv," Teena chided Leo. Evan felt a twinge of jealousy but reminded himself that was just how Leo talked. And he was right about the handful thing, Evan thought, looking at Teena's not-too-big and not-too-small breasts, the outline of each one super apparent beneath the soaking-wet fabric of her hoodie.

"Is that the best size for you, Evan?" Leo asked. "You're the one that's going to be handling them."

"Uh, yeah," Evan said, half startled and realizing he was staring at Teena's chest.

Sarabeth must have noticed, but instead of saying anything, she actually helped him. "Okay, let's get the cologne from the van and get to work. This might take a while."

21

RHAPSODY IN PURPLE

Teena McAuley, 3:40 P.M. Sunday, Fordham Avenue and 159th Street

It didn't happen often, if ever, that Teena had to question why she was riding in the backseat. If she rode there, it was usually—no, *always*—because she wanted to.

Not, as just now, because Leo and Sarabeth had climbed into the front seats like an established couple who were just dragging around the friends they'd set up on a date. "You sure your arm feels good?" Teena leaned closer to Evan, making sure to bump the back of Leo's driver's seat as she did so, but careful to not disturb the shopping baskets of cologne-filled water balloons they'd worked the past five hours to prepare. "We really need you for this."

Evan gulped and nodded. "Yeah, I'm ready."

She actually felt bad, doing this to Evan. She knew he liked her. Yes, he'd momentarily stunned her in the toy store when she'd been massaging his arm and he'd actually pulled away to become Mr. Take Charge. But she knew he was like a puppy dog that would follow her anywhere, and she'd always been more of a cat person. Still, he didn't deserve to be used the way she was using him. She had no other options, though. Making the guy you liked jealous by paying attention to another guy was one of Teena's specialties, and poor Evan happened to be the only guy she had to work with.

In the rearview, Leo grinned at Evan. "Yeah, man? You sure you're good? Not to put pressure on, but we're counting on you."

Seriously, how could Leo not care about her at all? How was it possible that just last night he was dying to sleep with her again, and one alien invasion later, he suddenly was all a-dither over Sarabeth? Teena ran her tongue over her teeth to check for errant food.

"We're counting on you, too, Teena," Sarabeth piped up from the front seat. "You're our best shot." Her voice was a little feeble. She must have been picking up on Teena's mood. But Teena was hurt. Leo had rejected her. And then, right when they had been bonding, it felt like Sarabeth had dropped her for a guy as soon as Leo had materialized with meaningful eye contact and a teddy bear he hadn't even paid for. She wanted to be happy for Sarabeth. She was obviously stunned by the attention from Leo and had done nothing to actually steal him from Teena. But this was life, not the CW, and Teena wasn't ready to neatly air her teenage emotions.

"Yeah, I know," Teena replied, pulling the pump on her Super

Soaker and pretending to be very interested in the scenery, which was either wasted or void. She was so used to being a queen in Tinley Hills that she'd never noticed how blah it was. The horizon was all parking lots and shopping centers, just like anywhere else. It was weird how different the world looked when you were no longer on top of it.

In the front seat, Leo looked over at Sarabeth. "You okay?" He asked it with the kind of casual concern a guy reserves for a girl he truly cared about. If this were a romantic comedy, Teena would have been wanting the Leo and Sarabeth characters to quit with the cute chitchat and get together, already. As it was, it made Teena want to barf and cry at the same time.

Seven weeks. Seven weeks of summer she'd wasted with him, and not once had he expressed that kind of like for her. Never even "Are you cold?" when they were half naked down in her clammy basement. Yes, their affair had been clandestine, but it wasn't as if Leo even *tried* to make it more than that. If he was feeling generous, she got some free burnt pizza, a hit of his pot, and maybe a compliment on her cute underwear.

She'd set out to host her party and told herself she would finally land Cameron Lewis. But now it was so clear: She was definitely not over Leo. The lame-o therapist her mom sent her to would say that she had daddy issues and that was why she coveted the love and affection of men whose attention was directed elsewhere. But Leo's wandering eye and man-slutness had never bugged her more than it did now. They were all going to die, and she couldn't get a date.

Teena just needed to do a much more convincing job of "liking" Evan, prompting Leo to snap him out of his Sarabeth

163

stupor. Teena wanted Leo to choose her now, not just settle for her once he figured out that Sarabeth would not put out.

Across the backseat, Teena could feel Evan's eyes on her back as she looked out the window at the gray buildings and drab, empty landscape. "Is it freaking you out?" The way he said it oozed thoughtfulness. She cocked her head in his direction to see him eagerly questioning her with his bright baby-blue eyes, half sweet and half bewildered to be talking to her. He looked kind of cute geared up as they all were in foam chest plates with Super Soakers, paintball guns, and jousting sticks strapped to their chests and sides.

She'd be lying to say that, looks-wise, Evan didn't do anything for her. But he was Evan Brighton and so pure he made even Sarabeth look like the class slut. She didn't know if she could handle pure. A week ago, she might have gone out with him on a dare, just to mess with his head or prove she could make a lame guy seem desirable on her arm.

"I'm fine," she said, wondering what this whole experience would have been like if she'd survived with different people, with her so-called friends. Ermer's finest would probably have wanted to use an alien invasion as an excuse to get extra drunk. The guys would have gone through the rubble at Teena's looking for lost bottles of Boone's Farm. Nathalie Oliverio and the rest of her girlfriends would probably still be hyperventilating and hugging one another while they talked about their emotions and tried to start an exclusive Facebook group for survivors.

As per the plan they'd concocted, Leo came down a side street and pulled into the parking lot of a Jewel grocery store. He kept the Gussy Me Up van and Abe's trailer hidden behind a tall hedge that faced Fordham Avenue. Just across the four-lane street from them was one stretch of the alien perimeter, covering the sidewalk and streets between 159th and 161st. Past that was the start of Prichard Estates, a gated townhome community that, even from here, Teena could tell contained no signs of life.

"Ready?" Evan asked her. Teena looked from the aliens to him and gave a single nod. Screw Salvador Dalí and the melting clocks she'd studied in art history class. Aliens lining the sidewalk in front of Red Lobster while Teena shared the backseat with Supervirgin Evan? *This* was surreal.

"Step one, divert," Sarabeth said. With the van still running, she and Leo set down remote-control cars on the pavement, steering them across the empty road toward two of the biggest aliens. Leo's red Lightning McQueen whizzed right over an alien's slimy feet. The row turned to look, closing in on the red car just as Sarabeth's yellow monster truck steered its way into the circle. The aliens were like apes at the zoo, poking the cars with their long, clawed fingers. They looked around for the source of the cars while Leo launched a remote-control helicopter and Sarabeth operated a remote-control inflatable shark.

"It's working," Evan said, watching. "They're taking the bait."

"You ready, offensive line?" Leo asked Evan and Teena, dropping his remote and sending the chopper down into the alien circle. He floored the van toward the distracted group.

Teena and Evan leaned out the large window Evan had broken. Teena pressed hard on the trigger of her Super Soaker, shooting a huge stream of Otherworldly at the aliens. Evan picked up a water balloon filled with the cologne from a shopping basket at his feet. They had a hundred of them, painstakingly filled with cologne. His eyes narrowed and, almost like he was possessed, he hurled the balloon at the cluster of aliens that had gathered away from the perimeter.

Evan's first balloon hit with a massive splash, dousing three aliens clustered around the car. Almost instantly on contact with the liquid, their purple membrane went gray. Beneath the slime, their insectlike faces shriveled like old grapes. Their chests sank inward, and even amid the din, Teena could hear their skin crisping out. Simultaneously, the three turned to dust and burst, clouding the clear, cold air.

"It worked, it worked!" Sarabeth shrieked in the front seat. "You're a genius." She was looking at Teena. Sarabeth shrieked again in victory, and Teena did, too, forgetting that she was mad as Sarabeth high-fived her.

The victory celebration was short-lived. The dead-alien vapor floated overhead, dusting the other guard aliens. One of the creatures looked down the line, seemingly confirming its missing compatriots. All at once, dozens of aliens moved in on the van. Their offensive worked, but they were surrounded.

Teena blasted another stream of cologne out her window, killing an alien instantly. But several more came in its place, reaching in the window, their long claws ripping through the upholstery as Teena backed away from the window and into Evan's lap. He gripped her arm protectively, his hands stronger than Teena had imagined. He hurled a water balloon at the group, killing three aliens. Teena's heart hopped the slightest bit when his warm breath hit her bare neck.

166

She wondered if they'd find them dead like that, Evan holding her. If there was a "they" left to find them.

"We'll be okay," Evan told her. He walloped another alien with a water balloon. As Teena watched the thing go up in a cloud of dust, she actually believed him. Her body relaxed a little, and she took aim again. As she did, one of the aliens lashed out with its claws across the top of Evan's chest. Teena took aim and shot the alien square in the face.

Evan was bleeding. Teena pressed her hands to his chest. "Oh my god," she said, looking into Evan's eyes, wondering if he was going to die.

"It's just a scratch," he said, looking down and wiping away the blood. It was a big scratch, but he'd live. "Thanks for looking out for me."

He turned away from her and lobbed another water balloon at the angry mass of aliens. *Puppy dog*, she reminded herself, somewhat unconvincingly.

Up in the front, Sarabeth and Leo sprayed away at the aliens pressing into the front windows, killing some but unable to fully squelch the onslaught. They were soon overwhelmed as a fresh set of aliens abandoned the perimeter, pushing in on them.

"There are too many," Sarabeth said, pale and ghostly with fear.

"We just need to break through," Teena told her. "If we can get to the mall without a tail, we might be okay."

Sarabeth rolled up both front windows, trapping one alien's arm. Leo squirted the alien's flailing limb with cologne. The arm dusted instantly, raining onto the van's upholstery. Outside, the alien backed away, poking at its damaged limb. The other aliens weren't frightened, though, and continued to come at the van.

Behind Teena, Evan lobbed Otherworldly-filled water balloons with all his might. His angle wasn't great, now that he had to stay back from the window. He was missing as many as he was hitting, and the supply was running low.

His eyes shot to the sunroof above Sarabeth's seat.

"I can throw better if I get out of the van," he said, his eyes fixed on the sunroof, unblinking as he pushed the button for it to open.

"Yeah, but if you get out of the van, they can kill you better, too," Leo said, noticing Evan's wound with concern in his eye. At the front of the van, an alien's claws screeched against the glass. Teena's spine curled at the sound. The van rocked like it had been rammed.

"Well, we're all gonna die if we stay in here," Evan said. Teena was still partially leaning against him, and she felt his body tense, like he was holding in energy he had to let out. "Get me on top."

"If you go, we all go," Teena said, surprising herself. And she wanted to kill these things, which wasn't going to happen when they were trapped like rats in here.

"Fine, but me first," Evan said, getting up. Teena instantly felt the absence of his arm. She watched nervously as he pushed off Leo's shoulder and heaved himself onto the roof.

Teena watched him go, thinking that even puppy dogs could surprise you sometimes.

22

ANGER MANAGEMENT

Evan Brighton, 3:51 P.M. Sunday,
Fordham Avenue and 159th Street

Evan's first thought as he climbed onto the roof of the van was that he'd never been so angry before in his life.

On all sides, the aliens were a sea of purple ooze at least three deep. They rocked the van as they pressed in on the vehicle.

He was angry that the aliens were there, trying to kill his friends.

He was angry that he'd had to see dead, gutted bodies.

He was angry at being forced to do church stuff all the time, instead of going to high school parties.

He was angry at himself for never getting angry until now.

"I need the water balloons," he said, dancing away from the onslaught of alien claws that stabbed at his feet.

So much for intelligent forms of life, he thought to himself.

These things might have a big-ass, scary ship, but they seemed like dumb bullies to him. But you didn't have to be smart to be dangerous. The aliens were rocking the van like drunk guys after a World Series win, pushing so hard that Abe's trailer wobbled behind it. If the aliens didn't kill them directly, then it wouldn't be long before they had the van turned over or on fire.

Leo hefted the basket of cologne-filled water balloons onto the roof of the van and climbed up. The girls with their water guns followed. Evan gave them a hand and then started plucking balloons from the basket like they were baseballs and he was at pitching practice.

He wound up and threw, and a balloon crashed against the alien trying to rip off his foot. Instantly, its skin went gray and the alien exploded. He wound up again and killed two aliens standing shoulder-to-shoulder. Again and again, he fired off pitches that hit their marks perfectly.

He fired a fastball-speed balloon into a cluster of aliens that had abandoned the perimeter and were making their way to the van. The splash hit each of them about chest-high, exactly where Evan had determined the aliens were most weak.

Every pitch came off his hand like it was on fire. The Evan who played in games—a picture of precision and form and thoughtful-but-deadly control—was there, but gone was the usual mental deliberation he subjected himself to on the mound. His body was a weapon against these things, and there was nothing else quite like it to get the job done.

To Evan's left, Leo swung his jousting stick against each oncoming beast's head, disorienting them and leaving them for Teena and Sarabeth to douse with their water guns. The Super

Soakers were starting to fade, though, as the girls reached the last of their fragrant ammo.

As the guns' spray weakened, some aliens would suffer just a wound that created a dead, open patch on their membranes. And the more hideous and scarred they were, the angrier they became. The incensed, disfigured aliens pushed the van harder, rocking it back and forth more haphazardly. Behind it, Abe's motor home scraped crazily against the ground.

Evan struggled to keep his footing on the roof as he kept an eye on Teena. She looked like she might fall into the gap between the van and the trailer. But somehow, she balanced like a tightrope walker on the van's edge, her silhouette delicate against the gray March sky. He didn't know what to make of the way she was all over him one second and ignoring him the next.

But it didn't matter. All that mattered now was protecting her no matter what.

The aliens spotted Teena's vulnerable position and closed in on her. As an alien reached for her foot, she kicked it square in its face. "Die, asshole," she screamed, firing her nearly empty cologne gun. With another swipe, one of the aliens managed to pull Teena halfway off the van's roof, her legs dangling.

"They're going to kill her!" Sarabeth shouted, lying stomach-down on the van roof and reaching an arm out for Teena. Teena grabbed hold of Sarabeth's hand, but the other aliens were rocking the van too hard, and she and Sarabeth slid back and forth across the roof.

Leo and Evan struggled to keep their balance. They couldn't get enough traction to reach down and pull the girls to their feet. The aliens gave another huge push, and the laundry basket of water balloons slid off the roof, the balloons bursting uselessly on the pavement.

"The glitter," Teena gasped, her grip on the roof of the van looking tenuous. If she slid an inch more, the aliens could easily grab her. "Get the glitter stuff."

It took Evan a second, but he remembered flirting with Teena over the glitter at Toys"R"Us. He spied a glitter canister in Sarabeth's cupholder and pointed at it. "That's it."

Leo swung down into the van and tossed the glitter up to Evan. He spotted Teena's glitter in the backseat cup holder and grabbed it for himself before going back up onto the roof. It only took him about twenty seconds, but it felt like hours to Evan as he swayed from side to side, helplessly watching the girls struggle.

"Hey, fuckers," Leo said, shaking his glitter canister. The alien let go of the van to look.

"Yeah . . . assholes!" Evan shouted, now shaking his own canister.

"Prepare to die," Leo said.

"Just douse them, already," Sarabeth said. "We're going to slide right off into the pit."

At that moment, one of the aliens slashed the air with its vicious claws, connecting with Teena's thigh. She screamed as blood started to flow.

"Do something!" she yelped. Seeing Teena hurt was all Evan needed to get even angrier.

Leo and Evan jumped off the van like a synchronized stunt team, pressing the spray tops of their cans when they were just inches from the aliens' lumpy, slimy faces.

The air filled with puffs of glitter, like a bad special effect in a little kids' movie. Evan's heart thudded wildly. If this didn't work, they'd just jumped into a pile of deadly aliens.

Then one alien disintegrated, and then the next and the next. Then the group was gone.

The cloud of glitter that floated down around them felt like New Year's confetti. Evan turned his face upward, letting the shiny specks coat his face.

"Holy crap!" Evan said, feeling fifty feet tall. "That was fucking awesome!"

23

WINNERS

Leo Starnick, 4:47 P.M. Sunday, Fordham Avenue

It was almost sad that the aliens were all reduced to dust. Well, dust and some glitter streaking the cracks in the concrete. After a hard-fought battle, you wanted some kind of aftermath scene. Just to prove you hadn't dreamt the whole thing.

"Nice work, man," Leo said to Evan. He scanned the empty horizon and felt almost as satisfied as if he'd just cleaned his plate at a fancy steakhouse. *Actually, food would be good right now*, he thought.

Next to him, Evan's sweater was crusty with his own dried blood. His face was dirty, and he looked spent, like someone who'd been running for days. But as Evan rubbed his arm, his face was one of a man satisfied with a job well done.

They were leaning against the van, next to the open back

window. Thanks to the aliens, the Gussy Me Up van was dented in places and tilting, due to the greenie that had taken out the front tire earlier. But the van was still driveable, and attached to it, Abe's trailer was still in good shape. Part of Leo wanted to look inside, but another part of him wanted to keep it sacred. The old man's death had hit him harder than he'd ever say.

Behind them, in the van, Sarabeth was trying to bandage Teena's cut using some torn-up Gussy Me Up polo shirts. If he ignored her wound, with her windblown hair and her melted-off makeup, Teena looked just a weensy bit like someone who'd just gotten lucky.

In contrast, Sarabeth still looked calm and composed, even though she'd fought as hard as anyone. Leo smiled to himself as Sarabeth bit her lip in concentration. He knew she'd left the battle behind her already, and her mind was working in overdrive thinking about what came next. They'd made it past the perimeter, but that just meant they were one step closer to the ship.

"I'll be fine," Teena was saying insistently. She looked out the broken passenger window at the guys. "Maybe we should hit the ship now, while we have momentum. The mall will just slow us down."

"We won that battle because we prepared for it," Leo said. "We're out of supplies. We're tired. Let's stick to the plan and get to the mall."

The sky was growing dark, and the air was colder. Across Fordham Avenue was an old strip mall that hadn't been updated since the seventies. Instead of the faux Tuscan oranges and yellows that many of Tinley Hills's new shopping plazas had, this one was just gray and flat, and in the parking lot was a Stop 'n' Smoke, a tiny shed that sold cigarettes at a drive-through window.

"You know what would be good about now?" Leo said to Evan. "A cigarette."

"I don't smoke," Evan said.

"And I've been thinking about quitting," Leo replied. "But something about fighting off aliens makes the health risks seem like less of a big deal."

Evan seemed to consider this. He looked at Teena in the backseat until she finally looked back up at him. She smiled.

"What?" Teena asked. "I'm okay, really."

"Okay," Evan said, blushing beneath his dirty face. "Let's go."

Sarabeth looked up momentarily from her work and caught Leo's eye with a half-smile he couldn't quite decipher. He knew he liked it, though. He smiled back at her. "Be right back."

He and Evan jogged across the empty street and pushed on the door of the Stop 'n' Smoke. It was locked. He still had a pistol tucked into his jeans, so he fired a shot at the lock, like they did in movies.

He was hoping the door would blow open. Instead, the bullet lodged itself next to the knob, the sound of the shot echoing through the empty town. He tapped the door with his foot. It creaked open.

"At least guns work for something around here," he told Evan as he walked in and scanned the various cartons of cigarettes. Evan minded the door, keeping watch on the van across the street, probably worried about leaving the girls.

Leo quickly scanned the tiny space, wrinkling his nose

at menthols and Marlboros. "So, I've always been more of a Camel guy, but maybe this occasion calls for something fancy. A Nat Sherman, perhaps." He crouched down to see under the register, where the premium tobacco was kept. He grabbed a box of Nats, a box of Camels, and a second Bic—a green one, for backup.

"How many more of those aliens do you think there are?" Evan asked.

"Man, I don't know. We at least need more supplies. We can't take chances."

"Um, chance taken," Evan said, pointing down Fordham. "They must have heard the shot."

Dozens of aliens were coming toward them. They were about a quarter mile away, marching in unison, and not slowly.

Without talking, Leo and Evan dashed across the street. Leo jumped into the van, and before Evan even had his door half closed, Leo pressed the gas and zoomed down the nearest side street, hoping the aliens wouldn't see them.

The girls looked at the road behind them. "It was the gunshot, wasn't it?" Sarabeth said.

"I fucked up. I'm sorry," Leo replied, careening down Sayre Avenue, a quiet residential street that abutted the mall. He kept an eye peeled for other aliens or—he hoped—other non-captives, but the street was as empty as the rest of the town.

"You didn't know, man," Evan said next to him. "I thought we might be in the clear, too."

Leo parked at a far corner of the mall parking lot, just near the Shoppoplex construction site where the ship had landed. There was still a cluster of trees that hadn't been taken down, and a set of Dumpsters. Even when things were normal, this particular part of the parking lot had been dark and scary, and female mall employees were urged not to park there.

The four of them were all breathless and cagey. Their victory high was gone.

"I don't think they saw us," Teena said, looking tense. "We're safe for now, but we need to move quickly."

"She's right," Sarabeth said, an edge creeping into her voice.

Leo had imagined this moment differently. He hadn't even had his victory smoke yet.

No, he thought. *The aliens aren't going to take this from us.* "Slow down, people," he said. "Let's let the mall tell us what to do next."

24

MALL FOR ONE, AND ONE FOR MALL

Sarabeth Lewis, 7:12 P.M. Sunday, Orland Ridge Mall

Sarabeth had never been much of a mall person.

Maybe it was because she never had anyone to go with, but any time she actually needed to go to the mall for something, she ran the errand like she was a contestant in the Hunger Games—moving fast and praying for her survival.

She'd once made the mistake of believing the mall was a place where a person could just shop. Last year, on a kick for new kitchen supplies, she'd been eager to peruse Sur La Table and Williams-Sonoma one Saturday afternoon. After picking up a few things, she'd gone for a snack in the food court. She picked a table where she could sip her cappuccino, nibble on her croissant, and read the newest issue of Bon Appétit. But Orland Ridge Mall was no Parisian café, where a woman dining alone was almost a cliché. She'd barely gotten through the Letters to the Editor when she felt eyes on her. Every table around her contained a cluster of girls her age who apparently thought she was some new, highly undesirable species. Teena and her friends made up one of the clusters. The other tables weren't even girls she knew from Ermer, but apparently her solo shopping excursion had egregiously broken some girl code. They'd looked at her and looked away, as if afraid that eye contact would freeze them into stone social pariahs.

After that day, she got it. Orland Ridge Mall wasn't a place where people—at least people her age, who were supposed to be living the best years of their lives—just shopped. They *hung*. And to hang, you needed a group, which Sarabeth had never had.

But now, walking through the parking lot of Orland Ridge— empty save for errant plastic bags and crushed Big Gulp cups that blew across the asphalt—it occurred to her that she did have a group.

A group that had just maneuvered its way past an actual perimeter of outer-space thugs using some of the worst beauty products ever invented.

Her life was officially too weird for its own good.

Teena yanked on the handle of the glass doors like she owned Orland Ridge Mall. Which, in a way, she did.

"It's locked, dammit," she said. Then, despite her bad leg and the fact that she couldn't have weighed more than a hundred and ten pounds, Teena hefted up one of the three-foot cylindrical stone ashtrays outside the entry doors. With a determined look in her eye, she positioned herself with the ashtray like a battering ram, ready to drive it though the locked glass doors.

Leo stepped between the ashtray and the glass. "Wait, don't do that," he said, pulling a key ring from his pocket. "I have the key."

Teena scowled at him, the kind of cute scowl that guys liked and Sarabeth would never manage, no matter how many alien attacks she survived. "You could have said something," she said, putting down the ashtray with a thud. "I have to pee."

"Keep your pants on," Leo said. He pulled the keys off his belt loop and casually opened the door to the mall, as if every teenager had mall keys. Sarabeth's insides puffed up like a blowfish. A tingly blowfish. Leo, Mr. Rulebreaker, was trusted with keys to the mall.

Very adorable, Sarabeth decided. She just wished that "being Sarabeth" also meant knowing what to do when you liked a guy for the first time. The locks clicked open.

Leo breathed in deeply. "Ah," he said. "Mall sweet mall."

He held the door open for them, pointing down various corridors like a tour guide. "Bathrooms, down there. Movie theaters, that way. Bubbling water sculpture, straight ahead."

As Sarabeth stepped inside, she was startled by how still and quiet everything was. The kiosks where salespeople chased you with flat irons and greasy hand lotions slept like hulking, motionless buffalo. The stores, with their grated gates locked tight, looked like deserted, heavily merchandised jail cells.

In the dusk, the small potted birch trees that ran down the center of each wing became skeletal sculptures from a Tim Burton movie. Rays of moonlight flowed in from the overhead skylights, bathing everything in a dark blue wash. It wasn't too dark to see, but it wasn't light enough to make their haven feel a hundred percent safe.

"I think we should stay together," Sarabeth said, catching Leo's eyes. His tangle of hair was more of a mess than ever, and she could tell he was as tired as she was, but the smile he flashed gave her a burst of energy that started at her heart and worked its way out.

"I think so, too," Leo said, just to her. A little connection fizzed between them. She knew that the little glances and touches, and the flirtation, and the teddy bear might have been part of some Leo scheme to have a little fun with her. But she really felt something real was happening here. And if she was wrong, and this wasn't the real thing for him, it was real for her, and she wanted to act on it.

Sarabeth pictured the world being normal again and bringing Leo home as her date. Cameron probably would give her the thumbs-up, but Cameron liked everyone. Her mom, not so much. But if Leo was a hero and not just a pizza-delivery boy, maybe even Olivia Lewis could forgive his unkempt, shaggy hair and marijuana habit.

"So, we're going to sleep here?" Evan asked, making his way to the water feature and splashing his face.

"Yeah, for a little while. We need to fortify our operation," Leo said, rubbing a palm of cool water along the back of his neck. "I thought we'd make our way to Bed Bath & Beyond, to enjoy the beds and beyond. Sorry, ladies, but the showers are fakes."

"Honestly, Leo, if they're still out there, we should be moving as fast as we can. Otherwise, it's like we took out the perimeter for nothing," Teena said, splashing her own face with the fountain's water. She wrinkled her nose. "Chlorine, how refreshing."

"Look, we need weapons, and we need food, and we need a plan. A little rest wouldn't hurt, either. The mall has everything, including places to hide," Leo countered. "And it's like home turf for us. We need this."

"I agree we need some supplies. But how can we get what we need when all the gates are locked?" Evan said, scanning the storefronts, his eyes tired.

Leo shook his head and jangled his keys proudly. "There are back entrances to all the stores," he said. "And I have a master key. Phil may be a scumbag, but he's got connections. Actually, he probably has connections because he's a scumbag."

Evan got to his feet and slapped Leo on the back appreciatively. "A nap in a real bed will feel good after today." He grabbed his baseball bat and started to head down the corridor toward Bed Bath & Beyond.

"Okay, fine. And maybe we can crack open one of those giant popcorn buckets by the registers," Teena said, stretching her back. "I'm fucking starving." She hoisted her Uzi on one shoulder and started to follow Evan and Leo. Sarabeth didn't move.

It wasn't even eight o'clock. Sarabeth was tired, but she didn't want to sleep, not yet. How often would they have the mall to themselves for a whole night, with no worries that anyone would catch or stop them? If it was their last night on Earth, why not make it count?

"We're not going to make camp already, are we?" Sarabeth asked. "I mean, we have the full run of the mall with someone who has the keys. When does that happen in real life?" She gestured expansively, as if they were about to spend the night at Versailles, or the Metropolitan Museum of Art, like in *From the Mixed-up Files of Mrs. Basil E. Frankweiler.*

The grayed-out signs for the As Seen On TV store, the Vitamin Shoppe, and Baby Gap weren't necessarily deserving of Sarabeth's prize-showcase hand gestures. But so what if it was no hall of mirrors? They all might be decorating some alien's mantel come Monday. They needed to take what they could get.

"Sarabeth's right," Leo said. "We might be dead tomorrow."

Sarabeth bit back the goofy grin that threatened to appear on her face. Who wanted to think about tomorrow when she had Leo Starnick tonight?

As her heart beat rapidly in her chest, she realized something. Crushes were *fun.*

You might think making the night matter means that someone—ahem, Sarabeth—is about to lose her virginity. But this isn't prom. And while it's certainly a good way to spend a possible last night on Earth, giving up your V-card isn't something you want to do in the bedding department of J.C. Penney. Or maybe you do. No judgment. But having the run of a whole mall is much more of a one-of-a-kind experience than some clumsy fumbling in the dark.

You don't need nitty-gritty details. Just think, what would you do if someone gave you and a couple semi-strangers keys to the mall for one evening? Mind you, the power's out, so you'd have to make do with what's available.

Would you go to Macy's and try on the most outlandish formalwear, while blasting a gimmicky CD of early nineties dance music on a battery-operated boom box? Sure.

Would you hit up the bulk candy store and not use the sanitized silver scoops, but instead hand-sample every gummy confection available?

Would you hold races from one end of the mall to the other on roller skates, scooters, skateboards, and mountain bikes you pilfered from the sporting goods store?

Would you raid the fridge at Subway and make the biggest sandwich you've ever made and eat the whole thing? Only to follow it shortly with a raw cookie-dough chaser from Mrs. Fields?

It might sound like a movie montage, but when you have to pack a lot of life into a little time, the montage is your only option. And you best enjoy it while it lasts, because what comes next is never easy.

25

I'LL DRINK TO THAT

Teena McAuley, 12:23 A.M. Monday (aka Casimir Pulaski Day), Orland Ridge Mall

Teena's stomach ached. She'd overdone it on the Swedish Fish—they were her weakness. Normally, because she was not Fatass McEveryGirl, she'd eat only one Swedish Fish at the end of each day. She had to rein herself in like that. If she had even two, all hell broke loose, and she'd commit fish-icide, downing the little red swimmers faster than you could say *Ja*.

She'd done that today. All this end-of-the-world, last-night-on-Earth talk was getting to her. So was the fact that Leo was still in la-la land over Sarabeth.

They were making Teena sicker than the gummy ball lodged beneath her ribcage. They'd giggled over conversation hearts at the candy store as if Teena and Evan weren't even there. In

Macy's, Sarabeth had tried on a green strapless prom dress, and Leo donned a tux with a matching cummerbund. In the food court, Sarabeth and Leo had eaten halves of a sandwich like they were in the middle of Central Park with doves tweeting melodiously overhead.

She wanted to let Sarabeth have him. She really did. But every time they shared a glance or laughed at one of each other's jokes, Teena just plain hurt.

Now the four of them were preparing to camp out at Bed Bath & Beyond. Since several hours had passed with no sign of the aliens, they decided they had some time to relax and strategize at a less frantic pace.

They were gathered in the outdoor furniture section, each wearing a Snuggie. Teena had held out for as long as she could, but now even she was draped in pink fleece. Among several deck chairs were a cluster of Crock-Pots they'd filled with scented candles, like a campfire. A schizophrenic odor cloud of vanilla, pine, Tahitian Dream, coconut, Sea Breeze, and jasmine hung in the stale store air. Propped up between two inflatable palm trees was a whiteboard where Sarabeth had started to scribble drawings of the ship, and lists of necessities, like perfume, flashlights, and first-aid gear. But Leo, with his irritating concern for Sarabeth's well-being, had convinced her to finish it later, after she got some rest.

Now Leo and Evan were playing bartender at one of the thatch-roofed tiki bars that everyone in Tinley Hills seemed to purchase after returning from a Sandals vacation. In a town with no bars or liquor stores, people made sure they could drink heavily at home. Leo had lifted several bottles of booze from a cabinet next to his boss's desk. He hadn't had the key for it, but picking the lock had proved easy.

"What do you guys want?" Leo asked, trying to catch a bottle of tequila behind his back. Evan reached out and grabbed it before it hit the floor. "Sarabeth, you seem like you have a refined palate. No girly, fruity stuff for you. Something with a little burn maybe, like a whiskey and Coke?"

Teena's jaw clenched at what felt like an inadvertent dig at her own taste for drinks with paper umbrellas.

"Whatever you think," Sarabeth said, practically melting in a puddle at Leo's feet.

"Whiskey it is," he said, and with a smirk toward Evan, added, "Dude, think you can mix up something pretty and pink for Teena?"

Teena did an isometric abdominal crunch, holding the muscles taut as she counted to ten in her head. She'd made a New Year's resolution to calm herself this way every time something bothered her. It didn't help with the bother, but after several months of being irritated, she did feel a nice firmness in her obliques.

Ugh. So Leo had picked someone else. What was in the McAuley DNA that couldn't take coming in second? She was teasing poor Evan with suggestive arm brushes. Next, she'd be giving Church Boy lap dances just to piss off Leo. Wasn't a life-or-death situation enough to correct her mean-girl ways?

Leo finished mixing two whiskey drinks for him and Sarabeth, leaving Evan shaking a pink fruity concoction that Teena found enticing in spite of herself. And in spite of her stomach's sea of Swedish Fish.

He poured the drink into two tumblers with flamingo necks for handles and handed one to her, looking a little proud of himself. "I think it's a strawberry daiquiri. But it's pretty strong," he said, taking a sip and grimacing as he double-checked the recipe in *The Bartender's Handbook*. His puzzled pursed lips were cuter than Teena wanted to admit. "I don't have a ton of bartending experience. But I figured, why not?"

Teena sipped. *Why not?* was right. The cocktail was good. Evan must have been heavy-handed in both the daiquiri mix and the rum because the little chill running over Teena's skin ceased, leaving her instead with the milky warmth of being rum-soaked.

Across from her, Sarabeth was nursing her cocktail. She probably didn't like whiskey any better than Teena did. And yet, her flushed cheeks and easy sips indicated she was having a good time. Sarabeth looked up and caught Teena staring at her. She smiled the kind of smile one girlfriend smiles at another one when she's talking to a guy she really likes and she wants her friend to squeal with happy-for-you glee. Teena took another gulp of her drink and tried to scoot closer to Evan to see if Leo would notice, even as a little voice inside said, "Give it up, already."

Coupled with their exhaustion and the adrenaline-fueled nature of the last two days, the booze worked fast. Teena felt like she was thirteen again and had just taken her first shot of Rumple Minze in Becka Gierstakas's basement. Now that things had slowed down, the totality of their situation dawned on Teena. They weren't just pre-gaming; this very well could be her last drink ever.

"Don't you guys think it's weird that there's no military evacuating the town or anything?" She looked at her co-combatants expectantly. "Seriously, where is everyone?"

"I thought we established that the aliens were taking everyone." Leo drank. "Just absconding with them."

"Yeah, to their ship." Evan drank.

"Teena's right, though. How is it possible we've seen only, like, three other people? This is a big town." Sarabeth drank. "And what about people from other towns?"

"Why are you guys debating? Aliens are fucked-up shit. Maybe they put everyone to sleep in their houses." Leo drank. "If you've ever read any alien theory, you'd know that experts believe they're more efficient than humans and might even be able to bend space and time, or execute mass mind-control."

Teena raised an eyebrow. "Are you for real? Alien experts? Who believes that shit?" She smirked at Leo. He could say what he wanted about her being bitchy, but she knew he was turned on by girls who didn't fall for his bullshit. "And why are you reading alien theory?"

Leo smirked back at her, and for a second, she could feel that familiar crackle of his. He might have acted like it was just sex between them, but he'd always found her a little interesting, too. "Let's just say I read it because I—unlike some people—never believed aliens were outside the realm of possibility." He sounded peeved, but he was grinning at her. *Bingo*. She drank, this time with satisfaction.

"Maybe the military is scared. Or unprepared." Evan drank. Their roundtable discussion had become a remedial drinking game. You spoke, you drank.

190

"Whatever, I still think it's fucked-up. You don't just let your whole town get wiped off the map by aliens." Teena drank.

"Maybe *every* town is getting wiped off the map." Sarabeth drank.

"It doesn't matter. For all we know, we're who's left. And I'm pretty sure we're teetering into wastedness," Leo said. They drank. Teena hated that Sarabeth was swigging whiskey while she was downing a daiquiri, but she had to admit, Evan's cocktail was really good. If she could just transplant a little of Leo's swagger into Evan, she could almost picture kissing him. He'd probably play with her hair. She loved that.

"So, what do you guys think you'll do if you survive? Like, do we just finish high school?" Seated cross-legged on the floor, Sarabeth leaned in Leo's direction. She put one hand on the floor for balance, and it wasn't lost on Teena that Leo put a hand down, too, causing their pinkies to just barely touch. Teena suddenly wondered if the aliens could erase relationship memories, like in that *Eternal Sunshine of the Spotless Mind* movie. She needed Leo out of her head.

"Well, there's some question about whether I'd finish high school, ever," Leo said, giving his whole focus to Sarabeth, like his interaction with Teena from moments ago was barely a memory. "Of course, if they take out Ermer High, maybe my permanent record will be vanquished."

"Oh, please," Teena said, "you're practically a genius." Leo looked at her again and smiled appreciatively. *Score another point.*

"What do you think you'll do, Sarabeth?" Leo said, turning right back to the gangly Snuggied succubus.

191

Sarabeth looked up at the ceiling, her oversize anime eyes reminding Teena of an annoying Zooey Deschanel type. "I know I need to finish high school, but the whole accredited-college thing is seeming a little lame to me all of a sudden." She sipped her drink like some bitch out of an F. Scott Fitzgerald book. Leo's attention brought something out of her. It was like watching a butterfly emerge from a cocoon, without the nasty larva stage. Sarabeth was really, truly happy. "I think I want to go to one of those cooking academies in France. Just imagine, buying fresh ingredients at the markets, walking on cobblestone streets that are actually old and not just . . ."

". . . and not just some developer's way of making a new mall seem upscale?" Leo finished for her.

Cobblestones were a marker of upscale retail. Teena fumed. Why did Leo so aggressively scorn her world?

"Yeah, I used to want a baseball scholarship. But it's not like I'll make the majors. Maybe it'd be good to bum around for a while," Evan said, refreshing his flamingo drink with another pour of rum. He gestured at Teena, offering to add some to her drink. She grabbed the bottle from him and poured with abandon. Evan didn't seem to notice her irritation and smiled sweetly.

"Dude, free college?" Leo said. "I have a cousin who's still paying for her art history major ten years later. I'm not usually the voice of reason, but why not just go and use the chance to study something really useless." He gestured with his tumbler of whiskey, like the world was at Evan's feet.

Evan laughed. "Maybe. Whatever will piss my stepdad off the most would be awesome. Something like evolutionary science."

192

Leo raised his glass. "Cheers to that," he said. He and Evan clinked. Leo dismissively clinked with Teena, then lifted his glass to Sarabeth. "Cheers," he said in a whisper.

Fuck. This.

No one had even asked her what *she* wanted to do after this was over. It was like they assumed she would die, or like she was already dead. This was so not a normal day in the life of Teena McAuley.

Again. Fuck. This. If it was so easy for Leo to ignore her, maybe she just needed to do something he couldn't ignore. Subtlety wasn't her style, anyway.

Step one. Lose the Snuggie. She pulled the pink blanket-dress over her head, and even though the cold air hit her instantly, she reached her arms over her head with her chest out and sighed into the stretch. During their mall adventure, she'd traded her hoodie and torn jeans for a snug V-neck and a new pair of Paiges.

Step two. Eye contact with Leo. "Can I try some of that?" She gestured to Leo's tumbler. He shrugged and handed it to her, but she could tell that he was curious. "Thanks," she purred, and tossed back a healthy swig. Handing him the glass back with one hand, she wiped her mouth with the other lustily. "That hit the spot."

Step three. Acquire target. She turned her gaze pointedly to Evan. "Evan, would you come with me?" She asked this in her sweetest voice. As he stood up, in a voice much less sweet, she added in the loudest whisper she could manage, "I want to show you something in the bedding section." The word *bedding* was like a trigger. Evan's blue eyes went wide, even though he

193

tried to nod like girls used the word *bedding* around him all the time. Sarabeth actually blushed. And Leo looked at her for just a few seconds too long, as if to say, "What are you doing?"

She grabbed Evan's hand and began to pull him away.

Leo knew what she was doing, or at least what she was pretending to do. If he didn't like it, he knew exactly where to find her.

26

A CASE OF BED HEAD

Evan Brighton, 1:17 A.M. Monday,
Bed Bath & Beyond (Bedding Section???!!!??)

This was unreal.

No, wait, for it to be unreal, Evan would have to be feeling totally calm and cool. But the rum felt like it was trickling out of his pores stickily, and the hoodie and jeans he'd "borrowed" from Macy's during their mall party suddenly felt like they were made of hot, heavy iron.

Finally, something was happening. He'd done something right.

Well, Leo had helped him do something right. When they'd all been trying on prom gear at Macy's, Evan had helped Leo tie a bow tie while Leo had dispensed girl advice.

"Look, man," Leo had said. "When it comes to chicks, it's like . . . well, it's like fighting those fucking aliens. You know how when you're in the middle of it, all you're thinking about really is you? It's kind of that way with girls. The more you just think about you, the less you're thinking about them, and the more they start to want you because they can't believe you're not just thinking about them."

Evan had questioned the advice. "But you're not doing that with Sarabeth."

"Different. Sarabeth's still new at this. She needs to realize that life outside the cocoon is safe. But Teena never had that shell. She was born a butterfly. And butterflies never land on you when you run around, trying to catch them. But if you stand still . . ."

Evan had raised an eyebrow. "There's a lot of metaphors going on," he'd said.

"Girls *are* metaphors, dude," Leo had said. Evan thought it was the smartest thing anyone had ever said.

Now, as Teena tugged him away toward the bedding— Bedding! They were about to bed!—section, all metaphors were unnecessary.

He walked behind her, his left hand dragging his bat uselessly at his side. When they kissed, what was he supposed to do with his hands? He didn't want to put them anywhere lame that would be a turnoff. But he didn't want to just grab onto her breasts or her butt. It seemed too forward and, honestly, uncreative.

They crossed behind a display bed fitted with a leopard-print comforter and another, more rigid bed done up in a crisp nautical motif. Both seemed a little threatening to Evan, their overly pillowed tops more a warning than a welcome. He knew

196

they weren't going to do "it"—well, didn't know, but didn't want to presume, either. He'd be happy just to touch her face and hold her close to him and have her kiss him back. He could deal with dying a virgin. But if he was going to die, it would at least be nice to know his feelings had been returned.

As she wove between more of the puffed-up display beds, Teena kept looking over her shoulder, but not at him. Evan wondered if the aloofness was her way of playing it cool. He wished he had some music or something. It felt so quiet now that they were alone, and the silence felt too big for him to fill when he had so much else on his mind.

Teena made her way past a red satin display bed that reminded Evan of coffin lining, or those *Twilight* movies. She looked so tiny among the tall shelves stacked with pillows and mattress toppers. Not looking right at Evan, she started running her fingertips over various sheets, assessing the thread counts. Evan wasn't sure if this was an important part of their night together, or if he was losing her.

"So, what were your plans for this weekend if we hadn't been attacked by aliens?" He thought it was a kind of funny question, and he came up beside her as he asked it. She'd traded her heeled boots for a pair of flat boots, and he realized how much shorter she was than he was. He'd have to crouch down kind of weirdly for a kiss to even work.

Teena shrugged, not looking at him but studying the diamond pattern on a set of Egyptian-cotton sheets. "I probably would have wound up here somehow," she said, with a little laugh. "The mall, I mean."

This wasn't going well. He hadn't expected Teena to take the lead necessarily, but he hadn't expected her to do comparison shopping on bed linens. He took a few steps back and sat down on the nearest bed, which bore an ugly floral comforter that reminded him of his grandma's house.

Teena flopped down next to him. "I just can't believe it," she said, grinning up at him even as her eyes still traveled the store. "I wonder why we survived."

Ah. Now her lack of eye contact made sense. She was just on the lookout for other aliens. She *needed* comforting. He needed to make her feel safe.

"I know, but I think the captives are alive. We're going to save them," he said in his best tough-yet-sensitive action-movie-hero voice. He inched a little closer to her on the bed, so that his arm was extended behind her back but not yet touching her. He wasn't sure how to go about this. He'd kissed girls at church functions before, but no one he'd felt an overwhelming need to kiss. And certainly not Teena. "And . . . it's going to be okay."

He sounded cooler than he felt. As his words slid into the air between them, their slick, silvery promise actually pulled Evan's face toward Teena's.

And then he kissed her.

Without even thinking about it, he'd kissed Teena McAuley. His skin fizzed, and his heart leaped into his throat, and if those sensations were too girlie to be having, then so be it. This was amazing. And she was definitely kissing him back. Was time slower or faster? One one thousand, two one-thousand. Three one—

Teena pushed him away.

"Are you kidding me?" She'd sprung up off the bed before

Evan even had time to fully open his eyes again. "Why did you do that?"

Evan blinked and tried not to look at her full lips, which he still felt should be on his. Which *had* been on his. He hadn't imagined it. Right?

"Because," he said, not coming up with anything. Why would he do that? On what Earth did guys like him get anywhere with girls like Teena McAuley? Apparently, not even an Earth that might be on its way out.

Teena stared at him, still expecting an answer, which made him feel like he was disappointing her even more.

He tried to sit up straight on the bed, but the mattress had gone lumpy and saggy thanks to years of strenuous work as a display model. So he stood up instead and crossed from the bedding section to the bath, as if taking a figurative cold shower. The distance gave him perspective.

"Because, you invited me to the *bedding* section. Remember? All day long, you rub my arm, you whisper in my ear, and ten minutes ago, you practically dragged me away from Sarabeth and . . . Oh." *Now* it made sense. Teena was into Leo. And Leo was into Sarabeth. So . . .

"This is about Leo and making him jealous." Evan began grabbing oversized towels as Teena watched, puzzled. He'd seen a couch in the employee break room on their way in. He'd sleep there and not disturb Sarabeth and Leo. The beds here might have been more comfortable, but he wanted to be as far away from Teena as possible.

Teena stared at him, her mouth slightly open like she was simultaneously hanging on his every word and unable to believe someone like Evan would dare speak to her like he was. Empowered, he continued.

"But even if you got Leo, what, you'd be hoping that some other guy would be jealous? That is, if anyone else is still alive. Is it all a game, or do you actually give a shit about anyone besides yourself?"

He turned away from her, the load of towels heavy in his arms. Maybe there was some girl out there who'd go for a guy like him, but it clearly wasn't Teena. Right now, he didn't even *want* it to be Teena. He went in the direction of the break room, plucking his baseball bat from where it was leaning against the shelf of throw pillows.

"Wait, Evan, I'm . . . I didn't mean to hurt you," Teena called after him, her voice weak. He was tempted to look back at her, but he didn't have the strength to handle whatever apologetic tack she'd try on him.

"Forget it," he said, hoping she could hear the finality in his voice. "I don't want to waste whatever time I have left on you."

27

FIRST DATE

Leo Starnick, 1:22 A.M. Monday,
Bed Bath & Beyond

So this was what shy felt like.

Evan and Teena had left about five minutes ago, and Leo and Sarabeth had basically been sipping their drinks and half grinning goofily at each other ever since. He didn't quite know what to do. He was a guy who prided himself on being a natural, on not having any studied and practiced "moves," but right now he could have used some.

Every time he looked over at Sarabeth, seated on the outdoor double chaise longue next to him, he was struck dumb by how much he liked her. Right now, acting natural was making him feel like an idiot.

He wasn't used to it.

He was the guy who read girls like books—and by books,

he meant simple books with no subtext, like the Berenstain Bears, not fucking James Joyce. But Sarabeth was more complex than *Ulysses*. A metaphor, like he'd told Evan. No, a metaphor wrapped in a simile with some intransitive verbs for good measure.

Their legs were touching on the lounger, and they were both looking up at the ceiling, as though there were a starry sky to see above them and not just a banner encouraging couples to start their wedding registry at Bed Bath & Beyond.

"So, what do you think Teena and Evan are up to?" Leo finally asked, cursing himself almost as soon as the question left his lips. It sounded kind of creepy to ask, plus it brought up Teena. Sarabeth didn't yet know about him and Teena, and he really didn't want to make her insecure. And besides, he knew what they were "up to." Teena had led Brighton to bedding. Leo was glad his advice to Evan had worked, and it didn't sting even a little to see Teena saunter away. He was happy for them.

Sarabeth swirled the liquor in her glass. "I don't know," she said. "I mean, I don't think we should bother them. Unless it's an emergency."

Leo reached out and grabbed her arm. "Believe me," he said. "I don't want to be anywhere but here." It was total cheese, but it was true.

Sarabeth's long lashes fluttered against her cheek as she raised her eyes to look at him. "Really?"

Leo shook his head and laughed, almost disbelieving. How could she not see right through him? He felt like the skin above his chest should have gone transparent by now, so she could see his heart single-mindedly beating away while ticker tape that read SARABETH over and over again came spiraling out of it.

He took her hand. "Yeah, really," he said. "I mean, well, how do I put this? Remember that day in string ensemble, when I was trying to pull off that mash-up?"

Sarabeth squinted at him. "You mean the Chopin-meets-Pantera thing?"

Leo grinned. "Yeah, that one. You practically ripped my balls off over that. I mean, you didn't, and I thank you for that, but you totally let me have it. It was unusual."

"What, because usually girls are impressed when you mix classical string compositions with death metal?" Sarabeth raised an eyebrow.

"No, they're probably not, but most wouldn't tell me so," Leo said. "You have conviction."

"Sometimes I wish I knew how to break the rules like you. You get to be Mr. Improvisation, and I'm still looking for sheet music to play along with." Sarabeth looked at her bent knees with a half-smile. "Also, I think I said I would snap your bow in half. Your balls never entered the equation."

She was too much. Leo tried to determine if she'd moved a little closer on the chaise longue in the time they'd been talking. Or had she moved farther away?

"Well, you've been breaking the rules tonight. It was half your idea to take this recess at the mall. If it makes any difference, I've liked you since then." Leo searched her face for some reaction, but he didn't feel like she had one. Oh well, it felt good to just tell her. He'd never been so honest with a girl before.

"Since four hours ago?" Sarabeth smirked.

"No, since that day in string ensemble."

Now would be the time to kiss her. Right? When had he gotten so neurotic? He felt like his life would be incomplete if he died tomorrow not having kissed Sarabeth.

He looked at her, trying to gauge her face for a sign. He couldn't tell. She was staring back at him, but he wasn't sure if her studious look was one of mutual admiration or one of how-do-I-tell-this-creep-to-leave-me-alone? He could lean in and go for it. Or he could keep talking and hope she seemed more receptive.

But then she was kissing him. While he was trying to man up, Sarabeth had taken matters into her own hands and kissed *him*. And the kiss was . . . good. Good verging on life-altering. And was that her tongue flicking ever so faintly against his? Holy shit, she was a good kisser.

Okay, he could die now.

Then her hands ran up his back, her graceful fingers lightly brushing his neck.

All right, he could die now, but he really hoped he got to stick around for more of this.

In response, he touched the sides of her face, his fingertips running along her jawline, tickling the delicate skin of her neck just under her ear. She kissed him harder, and he let his hands wander down her sides, the curves of her body pressing into his palm as he did so.

Hard as it was to do, he pulled back from her and twirled a strand of her hair around his finger. "Is this just an end-of-the-world thing, or do you like me, too?"

Sarabeth just grinned devilishly. "Maybe a little bit of both."

She kissed his jaw, and then his neck, right alongside his throat, and he sucked in a breath at how insanely good it felt. His baser instincts wanted more of her, all of her, but the noble Leo, who had just started showing his face tonight, knew she would be worth waiting for.

He pulled back from her again. "So, can I ask you something really cheesy?" He started playing with Sarabeth's hair again, partly because he liked the way it felt around his finger and partly because he liked the way she looked at him when he did it, like it was a totally novel sensation for someone to be touching her hair like this.

"Of course, I'd expect no less," Sarabeth said.

"If we survive this thing, will you be my date for prom?"

She raised an eyebrow. "Prom's in May. I'd hope you could at least take me mini-golfing before then."

Leo rolled his eyes. "Total given. Haunted Trails." He named the horror-movie-themed putt-putt course a few towns over. "But I need an answer on prom."

"I'll pencil it in." Sarabeth's half smile raised the bar on all half smiles till the end of time.

"Pencil? You don't pencil in prom. That's pen all the way."

"Pencil. You might back out on me if the theme song is some irritatingly forgettable ballad from a very special episode of a CW show."

"Nope, I'm in for all the slow dances. And I'll even get one of those tuxedo belts that match your dress, like we tried on at Macy's."

"Cummerbunds?"

"Cummer what? Sorry, Sarabeth, I'm not that kind of boy."

She laughed then, throwing her head back and giggling wildly. Leo knew that he was a goner.

He kissed her again, so that he wouldn't blurt out *I love you* and freak her the hell out.

They went on like that for a while, kissing until they both needed to try breathing for a little while. Sarabeth laid her head on Leo's chest, and he wrapped his arms around her shoulders. Their bodies fit together nicely, he thought.

"Should we get some sleep?" Leo said.

"We could try," Sarabeth said, and he liked that he could hear in her voice that she was enjoying this as much as he was. "First, I need to find a ladies' room."

Leo sat up, easing Sarabeth up with him. "There's one just inside the mall. I'll go with you."

Sarabeth smiled. "That's okay," she said. "I have to maintain some mystery, don't I? I'll take a flashlight."

She grabbed her flashlight and a Gussy Me Up tote bag where he knew she'd stashed a notebook with some drawings she'd done of the ship. Leo wondered if maybe she'd written something about him in the little journal, too, and that was why she didn't leave him alone with it. She kissed him once more in a way that made him look forward to prom and not for the reason most people looked forward to prom. He wanted to see her come down the stairs in some dress made amazing because she was wearing it. He wanted to slow dance with her for all the world to see. Forget his bull-crap, kiss-her-once-die-happy sentiment of moments before.

She'd given him what he wanted to live for.

28

JUST ANOTHER SAD LOVE SONG

Sarabeth Lewis, 4:21 A.M. Monday, Orland Ridge Mall

Sarabeth almost skipped to the bathroom, her lips feeling fuzzy and a little raw from Leo's two days of stubble grazing them. And grazing them. And grazing them . . .

She passed the Claire's boutique and Gloria Jean's Coffees. She flitted past the site of her earlier party-outfit anxiety, Charlie. She hung a left down the hallway where the mall bathrooms were, shining her flashlight down the long corridor. A little creepy, but nothing she couldn't handle.

Especially after what had just happened. She'd kissed him. Her first kiss, and she'd gone for it. She'd surprised Leo Starnick. She'd kind of surprised herself, too.

She hoped that this side of her wasn't coming out just because it was the end of the world. She didn't want her new self to retreat back into its neatly organized shell when all this was over. *If* all this was ever over . . .

She used the restroom and stopped on her way out to look at her reflection, shining the flashlight into the mirror so she could see. Her mouth was bright red and a little chafed from kissing. The skin around it looked a little bitten. Her hair was matted down on one side, and her chest was a little flushed. She had never looked better. Okay, yeah, so she definitely had the goofy expression of a crazy person, but a wildly happy crazy person.

She was in love. Wasn't she? She didn't have anything to compare it to.

"How messed up am I?" she asked the mirror un-self-consciously. "Who falls in love when they're surrounded by violence and carnage, weirdo?"

She shrugged. Maybe people did fall in love in dire circumstances. Maybe it was part of what kept the world going. Because even without an alien attack, it wasn't like the world was normally all puppies and kittens and rainbows. A lot of it sucked, and people fell in love amid the wreckage all the time. They laughed and kissed and went to prom. Ha, prom. She was going to prom. It was like she'd finally joined the teenage human race.

Sarabeth's whole life felt new. She felt new. And not just for being in love. If she could survive this, everything else really didn't matter.

Even so, she still needed to wash her hands before she returned to Leo. She didn't want to fight aliens while fighting one of those late-winter colds. The tap ran freezing cold, but she closed her eyes and soaped up her hands, singing the song they'd all sung in the car that morning.

"It's the end of the world as we know it, and I feel fine."

And then, she smelled coffee. Really, really good coffee.

It took her a few seconds to remember that the Gloria Jean's down the hall was not brewing today. Nothing was brewing today.

She opened her eyes, saw the purple aliens' reflections in the mirror behind her, and screamed.

Have you ever screamed?

Like, really screamed.

Not one of those fake shrieks you do when you see someone you haven't seen in a long time and feel like you have to make a bigger deal out of it than it is.

Not an "OMG, this roller coaster is so fast and we're all going to diiiiieeeeeeeeeeeee!" scream.

Not a movie scream. In the movies, no one gets a true scream quite right.

Really screaming isn't something you do on purpose. It's something you can't not do. It's like a giant hand is reaching down your throat and ripping out your entire voice all at once. It burns. And it leaves a mark. The kind that no one knows is there but you.

So, you may think you've screamed before. But if you're lucky, you never have and you never will.

THIS IS NOT A DRILL

Teena McAuley, 4:29 A.M. Monday,
Bed Bath & Beyond

Sarabeth's scream ripped through the mall, making a beeline for Teena. Teena shot up off the floral bedspread where she'd been curled up. She ran through the store, doom pressing down on her.

Though it took her just seconds to reach their camp in the outdoor furniture section, Leo was already tearing out of the store. He must have tripped over the Crock-Pot of candles, because a rainbow of wax had congealed on the floor. At least nothing was on fire. Evan was steps behind him, baseball bat in hand, not even looking back for Teena, just racing out into the mall corridor to find Sarabeth.

Normally, this show of emotion for someone other than her would have irritated Teena, but right now, she couldn't have cared less. She had been jealous of Sarabeth, yes. She'd wished she was gone, yes. But in the last couple hours, since Evan had taken her down a notch, she'd realized Sarabeth wasn't the problem. She was.

"What the fuck?" she huffed, her heart still skittering madly in her chest as she caught up to Leo, running alongside him. They clipped past Gloria Jean's, Claire's, and GameStop. Leo looked straight ahead, his face pale and panicked. She looked over her shoulder for more aliens. The mall seemed as empty as when they'd arrived. "Why weren't you with her?"

Leo was a ghost. He stared blankly, like all his words had left him.

"Where was she going?" Evan asked, matching Leo's long strides. He avoided Teena's eyes. She was avoiding his, too, but out of shame, not anger. She'd used him, and he didn't deserve it. At least there was no time to make heartfelt apologies. She didn't know what to say anyway.

"Where did she go, Leo? Did you piss her off?" Her breath came out fast, and her heart vibrated in her chest.

"No," he croaked. "She went to the bathroom." He turned down the corridor that led to the restrooms. The hallway was lined with posters for store sales and new movies. Except for the eerie and dark quiet, it almost looked like life was going on as usual.

Leo slammed open the door for the women's restroom. Empty. Teena's stomach rose and dropped as the door shut behind them. They checked every stall twice and then they checked the stalls of the men's room with the same frantic energy.

"Maybe she's in the mall," Evan said to Leo. "Maybe she ran."

The guys took off back down the corridor, yelling Sarabeth's name. Teena hung back, looking for clues. In the rush to find Sarabeth, they'd forgotten flashlights, but Teena's eyes had adjusted, and some moonlight still filtered in through the mall skylights. There were no overt signs of a struggle. Actually, there were no signs Sarabeth had been here at all. Teena checked the women's restroom for the third time, stall by stall as if she could have missed something. Nothing. She turned to go find the guys. Before she got to the door, she skidded across the floor, landing on her butt in a puddle of something that felt like salad dressing and smelled like coffee.

Dread pulsed through her. Okay, they'd definitely been here. She stayed on the floor, crawling to follow the trail of slime. *I must really like Sarabeth if I'm on hands and knees on the floor of a public restroom*, she thought. The trail led to an employee exit door that took her to the parking lot. But that was all she could see. She could hazard a guess that once outside, the aliens had used their jet packs.

As she got back inside, Leo and Evan were still calling for Sarabeth. She ran in the direction of their voices and found them each standing at opposite ends of the decorative fountain, hollering and craning their necks in search of Sarabeth. They both looked as hopeless as she felt.

"They got her," Teena said. "I found a trail of slime leading out the door."

"Why did they go without the rest of us?" Leo asked, seeming angry that he hadn't been taken.

"Maybe they knew she was our best hope of surviving, and

her boyfriend just let her take off unattended," Teena said, surprised it didn't sting to call Leo Sarabeth's boyfriend. "I knew we should have gone straight to the ship."

"Gee, thanks, Teena. I wouldn't have realized what an asshole I was without your help," Leo said. His hair was a mess, and he looked older without his mouth drawn up in its usual smirk. "I get it. I'm a fuck-up, case closed."

"Leave it alone, Teena," Evan said in a low, cold voice. "It happened. There's no going back now."

He still wouldn't look at her. Teena held in the tears that wanted to emerge. She didn't have anything to say in response. This was worse than being rejected by Leo or taken to task by Evan. It felt like they didn't even want her there.

She wanted to snap necks and bust heads and shoot the shit out of something.

This whole ordeal was just too much to take. But she needed to be more than angry. She wanted to take the higher ground for a change, not just carry out revenge for her own purposes. So she said, in what she hoped was an inspiring voice, "No, but we can go forward."

"I know," Leo said, turning his back on her and heading to the employee exit.

"Where are you going?" Teena asked, feeling bad that she'd blamed him. It wasn't really his fault. They hadn't been prepared, and they had needed the rest.

"Isn't it obvious? To the ship, to save Sarabeth," Evan said as he followed at Leo's heels. His tone was matter-of-fact, and cold.

"You can't just go. You're not ready." Teena ran out in front of them.

Leo rolled his eyes. "You would say that. You hate her, anyway."

"I don't hate her," Teena said, knowing it was true. "I want us to save her. But we can't if we die."

"Fuck, two seconds ago you were blaming me for not going straight to the ship," Leo said. "And now, when it's more important than ever for us to get there, you want me to hang out at the mall a little longer?"

"I'm sorry for what I said. But you weren't totally wrong last night," Teena said, desperation coating her words. She tried to connect with Leo, so he'd see her motives were true. "We can't just storm in unarmed, like you said. We probably should have spent the last night preparing, but all of us were having fun, not just you. I don't regret anything that happened." She gave Evan a meaningful look. It had been a good kiss. If only she hadn't cut it short.

"Fun's over," Leo said. "I'm going. Evan, you with me?"

"Absolutely," Evan said. Teena was still on his list of regrets, clearly. "I don't want to stay here, that's for sure." He practically hurled the remark at her like one of his fastballs.

"No," Teena said definitively. "We split up and gather supplies in the mall. A half hour, tops. You know I'm right. We wouldn't have taken down the perimeter without our Toys"R"Us trip."

Teena crossed her arms over her chest. He didn't like listening to her, but she could tell Leo knew there was some truth to what she was saying.

"Fine, then fifteen. You guys can help or not," she said. "Just so you know, I can do a lot in this mall in fifteen minutes."

30

THE MOST INTERESTING MAN IN THE WORLD

Leo Starnick, 4:41 A.M. Monday,
Bed Bath & Beyond

An air horn sounded, jolting Leo out of his daze. This was why he hadn't wanted to wait. The longer he did nothing, the more of a shit-funk he got in. He hated himself for encouraging them to camp out at the mall in the first place. Last night, half—no, three-quarters—of his reason for wanting to camp here was to see what might happen with Sarabeth. And now he knew what happened, and it fucking sucked.

He was in the kitchen section of Bed Bath & Beyond. Evan was wandering the store with a shopping cart, but Leo kept seeing him put items back. Teena, meanwhile, had disappeared into the mall proper and was probably giving herself a fucking makeover. Like she actually cared about Sarabeth.

He sighed, scanning the shelves and feeling cagey. There was nothing here that would help him take over an alien ship. Melon ballers? Avocado slicers? His head was starting to throb with a whiskey headache.

The air horn sounded again. Closer this time.

What the fuck?

He made his way toward the sound and saw Evan coming at him from the opposite direction, the only thing in his cart a bottle of cleaning solution. This was a waste of time. They needed to move.

Staring at them from the end of a long aisle of multicolored curtains was Teena, looking tiny and elflike in oversize Jackie O sunglasses. She was wearing the foam sparring pads they'd gotten from Toys"R"Us around her mid-section, with the toy Captain America chest plates Evan had worn during their perimeter battle. The armor was placed over a tight, shiny spandex bike shirt and matching bike pants. On her feet were polka-dotted rubber rain boots. She looked ridiculous.

"Look alive, fuckers," she said, blowing the air horn again.

She squeezed it once more, and Leo and Evan both cringed in agony.

"Do I have to use this thing again? Come on, what did you find?" She sounded the horn again, this time aiming it right at them before they even had a chance to move, enjoying their pain.

Leo simply showed his empty hands, feeling edgy. Evan shrugged down at his cart.

"Well, whatever, I covered your asses. Literally. I'm armored, and I've got spandex for you, too," she said, gesturing to a cluster of shopping bags at her feet. "And we're fortified. I raided the perfume counters. Britney Spears's cheapo colognes are super drying." She reached into an oversize Michael Kors purse slung over her arm and pulled out the purple perfume bottles.

Evan pointed to a weird R2-D2 machine with a hose attachment at Teena's side. "What's that for?"

"It's a Super Sprayer," Teena said. "It's basically a knockoff of a power washer. Half the Macy's perfume counter is in there. It won't last long, but we should be able to hose a whole bunch of aliens down with it."

Leo knew he was looking at Teena like she'd just pulled the cure for cancer out of her purse. To his left, Evan was just as incredulous. "Did you go to a hardware store?"

"No. There's a creepy junk store in the mall, down by Shitty Arcade and the store that still sells Looney Tunes ties. You know, the gross section. Don't you pay attention to anything?" She matter-of-factly gave them each a nail gun. "I got these there, too, so you'll have them in case of a greenie attack. Though you'll probably suck at firing those, too."

"Guns don't even work," Evan said.

"Well, we don't know what's on the ship, now, do we? And, as long as I don't go for the throat, we can still slow things down, if we need to," Teena said. "Just let a girl have her guns, would you?"

Leo held up a hand. "Hold on a second," he said. "I need to get my bearings."

He went over to the whiteboard, where Sarabeth's rendering of the ship was drawn. She had started drawing arrows and circling areas of the ship, but between the shock of losing her and his ever-growing hangover, he couldn't remember what she'd said about them all. Plus, she'd never finished, because they'd all been so intent on getting drunk.

"We don't have a chance," he said, pointing at the board and realizing he didn't think he could say Sarabeth's name. "She had all these ideas for where to go and what to do, and now she's gone."

Teena nodded, almost solemnly. "I know. I was being totally self-absorbed and an utter bitch. I wasn't paying attention, either."

"As usual," Evan said, leaning against a shelf full of throw pillows.

"Yeah, like usual," Teena agreed, pulling down her sunglasses and looking at Evan. Leo saw Evan twitch a little before he turned away.

Teena looked ready to go. And in his heart, Leo was ready to go, too. He wanted to save Sarabeth. But trying to rescue her also meant he might fail to rescue her. And if he failed . . .

He rocked from side to side on the balls of his feet, thinking of every eventuality. They could do this, right? He could tell his deliberations were making Evan nervous.

Not Teena. She grabbed two loofahs off a nearby display and lobbed one at his head and one at Evan's.

"Snap the fuck out of it!" Teena yelled like a drill sergeant. "Do you know what today is?"

"It's the day we go save Sarabeth," Leo said, hoping he sounded convincing.

Teena lobbed another loofah at him. She threw pretty hard,

and it scratched him near his eye. "Damn straight, asshole. But today is also Casimir Pulaski Day. Do you know who Casimir Pulaski was?"

"No one knows who he was," Leo and Evan answered simultaneously.

"I do. Casimir Pulaski was exiled from Poland and recruited by none other than Ben fucking Franklin to fight in the American Revolution," she said. "He trained soldiers, he fought, and you know how the revolution turned out. It wasn't the life he expected, but he took it, and he worked it."

Evan looked at Leo. Leo looked at Evan. Both of them wore expressions of pure puzzlement. Teena McAuley knew who Ben Franklin was, let alone who Casimir Pulaski was? The world really was ending.

"What?" She picked up another loofah. Leo and Evan both winced, but Teena didn't throw. "Of course I know who Casimir Pulaski is. My mom is three-quarters Polish. Look, my point is, like Casimir, I didn't expect to wake up on the last day of my three-day weekend at Bed Bath & Beyond, and especially not with Evan Brighton and Leo Starnick. Now all I really want to do is march through the front door of that ship and kick some alien ass. And save my friend Sarabeth."

"Did you just say your friend Sarabeth?" Leo asked, realizing her name came out easily this time. He was starting to feel more confident. Teena knew how to give a speech.

Teena blushed, something Leo had never seen her do. "Yeah, I said my friend." She turned away from Leo and glanced at Evan with semi-sad eyes. "It turns out I didn't realize how much she meant to me until too late."

Evan swung his bat, seeming sprier than he had a minute ago. Looking at Leo but not really at Teena, he said definitively, "Then let's go save Sarabeth."

Leo wondered for a moment what had gone down between Evan and Teena in the bedding section. He knew he didn't have time for petty gossip, but he actually gave a shit and wanted them to be happy. It was a new feeling for him, caring about others' happiness. While he was at it, he thought of his father and hoped he was safe. Maybe Leo and Ed Starnick had some bonding to do when this whole thing was over.

"Okay, one thing," Leo said, looking at Teena's cache. It was a strong start, but like she said, her robot sprayer would only work so long, and he really didn't want to get close enough to spritz the aliens with cologne. No one killed anything by spritzing it. "We need more weapons."

"We can fill our water guns with perfume," Teena suggested. "We could try to find some water balloons."

"Water guns, fine. But we don't have time to be pouring perfume into water balloons again. We need alcohol. The real stuff." He got excited. Why hadn't it dawned on them before? If the alcohol was the drying agent in perfume they needed, wouldn't full-on alcohol be fucking awesome against the aliens? "Shit, why does Tinley Hills have to be a lame dry town?"

"We have a bar," Evan said, spearing the air with his bat victoriously. "We brought it with us, remember?"

Leo felt a smile creep across his face. He knew they'd been saving Abe's trailer for something.

"Janie!" they said in unison. Looking from Teena to Evan, Leo could actually imagine them winning this thing.

The morning was silent. And not the kind of silence you could cut with a knife. It was the kind of hard-edged silence that *was* a knife. The hulking metallic mass of a ship loomed just beyond the mall like a huge blemish on the horizon. It was still dark out, and Leo, Evan, and Teena crept across the mall parking lot toward Janie, Abe's trailer.

"I can feel every leg hair in these pants," Leo said, wriggling uncomfortably in his spandex. His balls felt like someone had put them in a Ziploc bag. He wasn't quite sure the uniforms had been Teena's best choice, but he'd gone along with it as a gesture of good faith.

"Yeah, I wish I had gone up a size," Evan said, squatting a few times in an effort to stretch the pants while straightening out the Iron Man chest plate Teena had affixed to his armor.

"Stop whining," Teena whispered, her footfalls soft on the pavement. "If you really hate them, take them off when we're in the trailer. Just remember, right now, you're aerodynamic, and the spandex won't get caught on anything. Jeans might."

She had a point.

In addition to the spandex, Teena was wheeling the Super Sprayer in a kids' wagon behind her. Evan, of course, had his bat. Teena also had a squirt gun filled with perfume but still insisted on carrying her Uzi and extra clips of ammo, even though neither Leo nor Evan thought this was a good idea. Leo and Evan had oversize water guns filled with perfume, plus the nail guns, which they carried in backpacks. Their bags also held extra bottles of cologne, plus cans of hair spray, which Teena claimed would at least partially dry out the aliens. They were planning to load up further with what they hoped to find in Abe's trailer.

As they traipsed through the dark, Janie shone, practically winking at them.

Leo could feel excitement growing in his belly. Losing Abe had been a blow, but he just might be able to help them, after all.

He climbed up the metal steps to the silver door, tugged on the handle, and opened it softly.

As they stepped inside, Leo could swear he heard angels singing.

"This is not at all what I expected," Evan said, looking around.

"That dirty old man lived *here*?" Teena asked, stunned. "I mean, may he rest in peace. This is nice. Not my taste, but nice."

Leo whistled low and slow. "Yeah, Janie's got some pretty guts."

The inside of the mobile home was like a futuristic, high-class bordello. Or, like the Wizard of Oz's vacation home. The walls were covered in a deep, emerald-green paper with flocked dark green fern leaves—but not in a seventies gigolo kind of way. It looked brand-new, like something from a fancy Vegas hotel. The wall nearest them was lined with a sapphire crushed-velvet couch wide and long enough for two people to sleep comfortably. Two armchairs in a soft, silver-gray leather sat opposite the couch, with everything gathered around a low coffee table made from gemlike, iridescent fiberglass. The table contained the only Abe-like thing in the room, a massive ashtray overflowing with cigarette butts. The centerpiece of the wall opposite the couch was an enormous flat-screen TV. It rose up behind a Lucite bar that sparkled under the blue-gray overhead lights. Shelves on either side of the TV contained amber, blue, and clear glass bottles showcasing every liquor and spirit imaginable. They twinkled and gleamed temptingly under museum-quality track lighting.

"Wow," Evan said, looking up reverently.

"We found the mother lode." Leo smiled. He had to make sure Sarabeth saw this. "Abe, you magnificent bastard."

Leo slid behind the bar and started to pull bottles down from the shelf, lining them up on the clear bar top. "Take whatever you can carry, the higher the proof the better."

They started to fill their backpacks with vodka and whiskey and gin. If a bottle had no label, they'd smell it to see if it was strong. If two bottles were half empty, they combined them.

Their work was almost done. Only a few bottles remained, and to Leo, the atmosphere had gained a pulse. Next to him, Evan and Teena worked contentedly. This was the team that would save Sarabeth, and the world.

Then something clattered in the back room. His heart rocketing up his throat, Leo snatched a bottle of Wild Turkey off the bar and held it aloft. Evan pulled out his bat. Teena whipped out her gun, pointing it toward the sound. Terror growing in his eyes, Evan gently guided her arm down. A greenie attack in these close quarters would be very bad indeed. Teena pulled a squirt gun from her bag instead.

Leo took a deep breath and just listened. Utter silence. He squinted at Teena and Evan, as if to say, "Did we imagine that?"

Teena looked toward the source of the sound and, when no new noise emerged, tucked the plastic gun into her tight spandex sleeve. Evan and Leo lowered their weapons, leaning against the bar. They all started breathing again.

Then, something jumped up onto the bar behind them. In unison, Leo, Evan, and Teena screamed like the terrified teenagers they were. Spinning around and ready to fight, they all aimed their weapons at a . . .

. . . cat?

"Meow," it said, mockingly, Leo thought, before slinking around Teena's outstretched arm, purring loudly.

She checked its tag. "Knickers?" she said. "Isn't that how English people say *panties*?"

Leo laughed. "Our Abe, a perv to the end."

The cat brushed by him and jumped from the Lucite bar to a small shelf that Leo hadn't noticed before. It contained an Albert Einstein action figure and a photo of a younger, cleaner Abe, his arm around a pretty redhead. The woman reminded Leo of Sarabeth. He slid the photo into his backpack. He had to show her. Also on the shelf was a small bottle with a handwritten label that said PURPLE PEOPLE-EATER. Leo uncapped it and sniffed.

The aroma alone was enough to get him drunk. He had a good feeling about the stuff, so he put it in his pants pocket.

"We ready?" Evan asked, working his arm through the strap on his now-laden backpack.

"Let's go save the world," Leo said, even though he still wasn't sure how they were going to do this.

Teena petted the cat one more time. It pressed itself against her palm and purred.

"We'll be back for her," Leo said, hoping he was right.

They stepped outside into the dawn's weird pre-sunrise

light. It was just past five a.m. Leo could see the scene drawn in his mind. Him, Teena, and Evan, standing together with a wide swath of nothing between them and the ship. Showdown.

The ship had landed on a large empty parcel that used to be Walt's Wheat 'n' Stuff, a commercial bread bakery where Leo's dad once worked. It had shut down seven years ago, and the bakery had stood dormant until now. Most of the buildings were cleared away to prepare for the new Shoppoplex retail, dining, and living community. Construction was supposed to start in May on the 356-condo, 12-restaurant, 24-movie-screen, 72-store "experience" advertised on a big banner that hung on a chain-link fence. There were small piles of stone and rubble left from the demolition, but not much else.

Their packs were heavy, but they each had a spring in their step. Despite her small size, Teena effortlessly pulled the wagon containing the Super Sprayer behind her.

After cutting through the few trees that remained between the mall and the new shopping center, they came to the chain-link fence and stood behind a massive Shoppoplex banner that covered most of it. Leo used a paring knife he'd taken from Abe's bar to cut a hole in the banner. He peered through binoculars—another Teena find—at the entry ramp onto the ship.

"There's the front door, as it were," he said, handing the binoculars to Evan. "Complete with alien doormen."

About a dozen of the purple aliens stood on either side of the ramp, their massive forms casting huge shadows against the ground. Leo's confidence started to fade. When they'd taken out the perimeter, they'd had the van and been on their own turf. How were they going to get past those guys?

"There are only about twelve of them," Evan said, his voice wavering a little. "We've handled more than that."

Teena took the binoculars from Evan. "At least they don't have weapons," she said.

"That we know of," Leo corrected her. "Besides being indestructible, able to spew greenies, and having fucking talons that could run right through us like those samurai knifes that cut through shoes."

"Thanks for that," Evan said sarcastically.

The aliens shifted ever so slightly down the ramp. Leo tensed. Evan cocked his bat back, ready to fight.

"Do you think they saw us?" Leo asked.

"I don't know. Their eyes are so unreadable." Teena shuddered. "Not even eyes."

"For our sakes, I hope they're blind," Evan said. "But I don't think you can abduct a whole town without seeing it."

They were freaking themselves out, Leo knew. They needed to make a move.

"So, should we run straight for them? Or do we need a cheer or something?" Leo said.

"We need to get over the fence first," Teena said, gesturing to the twelve-foot-high barrier that separated them from the aliens.

Evan gulped. "With all this stuff? And the Super Sprayer? They'll see us for sure."

Leo shook his head. "There's a piece of fence that's open just down the way from here. My buddy Frank was trying to start a pot farm here."

He led them to a spot where the chain link had been cut and

pushed to the side. They put their packs down on the other side first and then carefully crept through, making themselves as narrow as possible. They pulled in the Super Sprayer last, cringing every time it rattled in the wagon. The aliens, a few hundred feet away, hadn't seen them, it seemed. The scattered piles of construction rubble probably helped shield Leo, Evan, and Teena from view.

They tiptoed over the crunchy dead grass that covered patches of the construction site that hadn't been bulldozed. With each step, the ship looked more alive to Leo, like if it wanted to, one of the spokes could reach out and grab them all, shake them, and render them people-jerky. Leo remembered the power surge from Friday night, and a chill rose in his spine.

A twig snapped beneath Evan's feet, and all three of them jumped.

"It was nothing," Leo said, trying to sound calmer than he felt. "Keep walking." He kept his eye on the ship, waiting. The aliens weren't going to let them just walk right in, were they?

Then, the sky lit up purple and Leo knew instantly what was next. The spoke nearest them emitted a burst of bright violet fire, just like the laser that had almost killed them all when they were looking down at the ship from High Point. Only this time, they were right next to it. Close up, the fiery blast was a thousand times scarier.

Leo threw himself backward as the purple flame whipped forth. He felt heat through his pants and deep into his body, like his bone marrow was melting. This couldn't be good. He looked back at Teena and Evan, wanting to scream out a warning, but the words were ashes in his throat.

Teena's eyes met Leo's as they widened in terror. Then Evan dove past Leo's line of vision and crushed Teena's body with his own. They disappeared from sight, and Leo closed his eyes, trying to protect them from the heat crackling against his pupils. He rolled away from the surge, covering the back of his neck with his hands like they used to do in grade-school tornado drills.

What good would it do? This was it. They were all going to die. For all he knew, Evan and Teena were already crisp corpses, and he was next. The laser snapped angrily right next to him. He opened an eye to see flames spark against the dead ground. Then the spoke powered down, the purple laser retreated, and the flames, apparently finding nothing to ignite besides a few dead leaves, died out. He dared to open his other eye, and ahead of him, saw Evan crouched over Teena, shielding her. A blackened trench remained—if they'd been three inches to the left, they'd all have been dead right now. But now there was no doubt the aliens had been targeting them.

Teena and Evan were starting to rise to their feet, somewhat awkwardly, as if they were trying to help each other up without touching.

"Thanks," Teena offered to Evan, obviously trying to get him to make eye contact as he just nodded and held a hand out for Leo to get up.

Leo dusted off his spandex, looking at their motley crew. They stared back at him, panic etched on their faces. The fear was at odds with their shiny spandex outfits and made him grin in spite of everything.

"Good thing we wore these aerodynamic pants."

31

IN FOR THE KILL

Teena McAuley, 5:22 A.M. Casimir Pulaski Day,
Shoppoplex Construction Site

"They must have seen us," Evan said from behind a big pile of gray bricks they were using to shield themselves while they tried to regain some semblance of composure. Or as much composure as a person can have after yet another near-death experience. Evan still wasn't talking to Teena, but his willingness to serve as her human shield had to show he still cared, right?

"Yeah, we're fucked," Teena agreed, pulling the miraculously intact Super Sprayer wagon back to their hiding spot.

"It's okay," Leo said. "They're not moving in on us."

"They probably figure they'll kill us when we get closer," Teena said.

"If we're lucky, they think we're already dead," Evan said.

Ha, progress, Teena thought.

They were within a hundred feet of the ship. Twelve alien guards stood rigid and ready, daring them to intrude.

"I have an idea," Evan said, taking the wagon from Teena.

He stepped out into the open as if he was done creeping around. The Super Sprayer rattled as he pulled it toward the ship, not really trying for stealth. Teena wanted to call out to him, or better yet, run and stop him. But the look on his face was so determined that she also wanted to see what would happen. Evan Brighton had her full and complete attention.

He stopped about twelve feet from the end of the ramp. Now he had the aliens' attention, too. Despite their expressionless faces, Teena thought they remembered Evan, or maybe remembered all of them. How awesome would it be if the aliens were scared of them?

But then the left row started to advance on Evan, walking single file down the ramp and extending their claws. Just looking at the claws was enough to make the gash on Teena's thigh throb. They could slice right through Evan. She grabbed Leo's hand next to her, pulling him along. "He needs our help," she said to Leo.

They ran toward Evan, who didn't take his eyes off the aliens as he turned on the Super Sprayer and reached for the hose.

"Hey, jerks," he said, pointing the hose. He pressed on the handle. Nothing. Teena's heart sank. The machine wasn't vibrating or rumbling; it was dead. Evan pressed futilely on the handle again, his stupefied face devolving into an expression that said, "Oh, shit."

Time had stopped, and instead of her life flashing before her eyes, Teena saw her would-be killers and what they would do to them. The aliens were huge, and they were close, and their claws alone were enough to leave the three of them lying in ribbons of spandex and skin on the ground. Teena could hear Evan gulp.

"I said, hey, jerks," he tried again, shaking the hose. At the very least, the failed machinery had the aliens' interest for now. Teena quietly pulled out her perfume gun, catching Leo's eye so he'd do the same. He already had his out and aimed.

Before she could fire, she was lifted into the air, as an alien slid a long claw under her backpack strap and shook her, sending her gun to the ground. Next to her, another alien had Leo in the same unfortunate position. The aliens stomped on the toy guns, steam rising from beneath their feet as the perfume splashed their flesh, not enough to kill them because the tender membrane covered the aliens' torsos, not their legs. Teena looked into the creature's netted, buglike eyes and saw her own terrified face a million times.

Then the biggest alien wrapped a claw around Evan's back. The straps of his toy chest plate ripped as the claw ran over them and the Iron Man shield fell to the ground as the alien lifted him. Evan, who had saved her again and again, was going to die, and she couldn't do anything about it.

"Hey, Evan," she croaked, feeling some satisfaction as he turned his head as much as he could to see around his captor. As he watched, Teena kicked the Super Sprayer, hard, with the side of her foot and said a little prayer. Suddenly, the machine hummed and gurgled to life. If they made it past this, he had to forgive her. "Try again."

He pointed the hose at the alien that had him several feet

off the ground. He pressed the button, and Teena held her breath. The cologne cocktail came shooting out, turning his alien to dust. Evan landed on the ground in a pile of its ashes. Still on the ground, he aimed the spray at the aliens holding Teena and Leo. The creatures' deaths were instant, and Teena and Leo hit the ground with thuds. Teena didn't mind the pain in her tailbone. She was alive.

"Hell, yeah!" Leo yelled, getting to his feet and helping Teena to hers.

Evan aimed the hose at the three aliens who'd been blocking the foot of the ramp. They each burst in rapid succession, like exploding dominoes.

"The other ones, get the other ones," Teena said, pointing at the other six aliens that were now coming at them from the side.

Evan aimed the Super Sprayer, but this time, it just shot a dribble of cologne onto the ground. "Shit," he said. "It's empty."

"And our guns are dead," Leo said, pointing at their crushed squirt guns.

The six aliens had them surrounded, three to a side with claws extended and ready to avenge their freshly dead brethren. Teena had one foot on the ramp. Leo was just behind her, and Evan was still on the ground, next to the now-empty Super Sprayer. The second any of them tried to reach into their packs, the aliens would kill them. But the ramp was wide open. She could run right onto the ship. Leo and Evan would follow. She just wished she could ensure Evan could get up from his vulnerable position at the things' feet. She looked back and saw the beasts holding devices that looked like shiny green golf balls.

"What are those things?" Teena asked, just as one of the aliens let go of his. It zipped through the sky, hovering between Teena's and Leo's faces, where it shot out a sudden burst of green fumes that clouded over them.

"What the fuck?" Leo said, trying to move away from the fumes. His legs seemed glued to the ground. "I can't move."

"Me, neither," Teena said, her legs frozen as a hardening sensation took hold of her torso, then her arms. She looked back into Evan's scared face as her own stopped moving.

32

DEEP FREEZE

Evan Brighton, 5:29 A.M. Casimir Pulaski Day,
Shoppoplex Construction Site

Evan had only seen a body so waxy and fake-looking once in his life. His father's, when it had been all made up and laid in his coffin at the wake. Bad as that had been, this felt almost worse. Teena and Leo were completely frozen and lifeless. And there were still six more aliens, five of them holding the devices that had made statues of his friends. If he weren't still down on the ground, he'd be a mannequin, too.

He reached next to him for his bat, yet again. His security blanket. Then he skittered backward in a crab walk, away from the cluster of aliens, and got to his feet, still taking steps back from the aliens as he rose.

He cocked his bat like he was at home plate and felt the pull of a tear at his eyelid. He wiped it away, squinting at the aliens like they were opposing pitchers. They were, in a way. One at a time, the aliens hurled the tiny green balls at him. Evan gritted his teeth and smacked each ball into the horizon. The aliens paused to watch them soar. He hoped they were scared shitless.

Evan breathed deeply as the last alien held up its green ball, seemingly taunting Evan as he rolled it around in his clawlike six-fingered hand.

The alien let go of the orb, and it zipped toward Evan, catching him off guard. He swung, and he missed. Panic froze Evan's heart, and he grabbed for the ball as it hovered for a split second in mid-air. He lobbed it back at the cluster of aliens, and they frantically tried to grab for it, their claws clashing in air. Before they could get it, green fumes burst forth.

The gas froze the aliens, same as it had Teena and Leo. The emptied ball fell to the ground. With light footfalls, the same kind he'd once used to sneak downstairs early on Christmas mornings, Evan crept up to the aliens. Inches from them, he could see every crease in their skin and could sense no feelings or emotions behind their netted, bulging eyes. He looked back at Teena and Leo, frozen in time. Maybe Sarabeth was the same way, or worse. And what about the rest of the town?

His earlier tear finally poked its way out of his eye. He pulled some perfume from his backpack and misted the air at the center of his six frozen attackers. The droplets floated then fell from the March sky onto the aliens' wet-looking skin. The gooey purple coating quickly went gray, like one of those time-lapse nature videos that showed flowers blooming and dying in seconds. Then he was alone in a cloud of dust-colored confetti.

And that was it. He waited for other aliens to rush out of the ship to kill him, waited for another burst of fire, a greenie attack, something. But nothing happened. He sat down on the ground and put his head in his hands. He was on his own. The guy who couldn't get a girl was the last guy on Earth. Awesome.

"Dude, what are you sitting there for?" Evan looked up to see Leo cracking his neck, then his knuckles. Next to him, Teena was stretching her arms over her head like some kind of post-apocalyptic yoga instructor.

"You guys aren't dead?" Evan said. He jumped to his feet and, without thinking about it, hugged them both. Leo slapped his back like they were bros. Teena held on to his arm longer than necessary. He covertly brushed away the tear on his cheek.

"Just stiff," Teena said. "Did you kill the rest of them?"

Evan shrugged. "It was nothing."

It was still hard to talk to her. *Better*, Evan thought, *to just get on the ship, and free the residents of Tinley Hills*. Teena had affirmed that he was not the guy for her, so maybe he would rescue some other girl who recognized his good qualities. Someone who didn't mind that he wasn't as funny and laidback as Leo, or as cool and popular as Cameron Lewis. It could happen.

Leo and Teena were halfway up the ramp. "You coming, dude?" Leo called.

Evan nodded. He'd plan his new life later. He flipped his trusty bat up onto his shoulder. If they survived, he would have it mounted over his fireplace.

It should have been a big deal, stepping onto the alien's ship. But Leo just loped through like he was sliding into class late.

Teena hopped over the oval door's bottom edge, like she was stepping over a puddle. Why did she have to be so completely cute? Behind her, he kept his head down and soldiered forth, onto the ship. He wished that things were different, and that Teena felt for him what he felt for her.

But he could win only so many battles. And there were more to come. He could feel it.

33

ALL ABOARD

Leo Starnick, 5:37 A.M. Casimir Pulaski Day,
Aliens' Ship

As Leo stepped onto the ship and was faced with a second ramp—this one a moving sidewalk—and another door, he wondered if this was how Alice felt in Wonderland, only he had alien murder on the brain, and she'd just smoked up with caterpillars. "No turning back now," he said, half to himself, half to Teena and Evan. They stepped onto the ramp and were headed deeper into the ship, as if it were their unalterable destiny. After a few moments, the ramp deposited them onto the floor like groceries at the end of the cash-register belt. The strong scent of coffee loomed thick in the air, and they all looked around nervously. This part of the ship was empty, which was almost more unsettling.

They were in a long, white hallway that stretched out on

each side of them in a circle. Looking down the corridor in either direction, Leo tried to figure out which way would lead them to the captives. If it weren't for the lives-on-the-line factor—and his overwhelming need to find Sarabeth—it would have been cool to look around a bit. All that time thinking about aliens, and now he was on their ship.

"Should we split up, or stick together?" Evan whispered.

Leo pursed his lips. "If we go the same way, we could all die. If we split up, we could all still die. I don't know."

Teena sighed like she was annoyed with them both. "Look, I know I complained louder than anyone about the four of us getting stuck together, but we should stick together. I don't want to lose you guys."

Leo saw her look right at Evan as she said it, but Evan just looked down the corridor. Leo almost felt bad for Teena. "You're right," Leo said to her. "How about we go that way?" He pointed right, based on nothing more than a hunch. The ship was a circle, but he thought if he was leading prisoners on board, it would be easier to steer them into a right turn than a left one.

"Works for me," Evan said. Teena nodded in agreement.

The corridor was gleaming white, like being inside an iPod. It surprised Leo. He'd been expecting something more . . . gross. Like maybe purple alien goo covering every surface of the ship's interior. Or at least more darkness to set the mood. As it was, tube lights lined the walls, giving off green and purple glows. The ship hummed like the inside of a refrigerator and was almost as cold.

With every almost-too-easy step, Leo felt his nervousness

increase.

"Where are they?" Leo said. "Don't they need to go about their outer-space asshole business?"

"We did kill a lot of them," Teena said. "Maybe there just aren't many left."

"Or maybe there's a lot of them on the other side of these walls." Evan gestured down the corridor. "The ship is big."

"You know, they probably want us to find them," Leo said. "Like, what's behind door number two? Hey, you're dead!"

"I don't even see any doors," Teena said, furrowing her brow.

"Yeah, that is weird," Evan said, slowing down.

Leo hadn't seen a door, either. He stopped walking and studied the wall. Teena and Evan stood behind him, like he had a clue. On closer inspection, he found tiny seams where it looked like the white walls opened in some way. But he couldn't tell if they slid open into the wall or pushed open into a room. Maybe they even lifted up, like garage doors. Evan and Leo exchanged a glance. They positioned themselves on each side of one of the seams. They pushed. Nothing. They pulled. Nothing. They tried lifting up from the ground. Nothing.

During their feeble show of manhood, Teena had wandered away.

"Hey, what's this?" She was pointing at a section of the wall that wasn't smooth. It resembled a pair of white puckered lips, only vertical and tall enough for an alien to fit through.

"Not to be vulgar, but I'm seriously afraid this is some kind of alien vagina situation," Leo said, poking the soft spongy door and watching it pulse in and out. "Ew, squishy."

Before any of them realized what was happening, green

241

tentacles shot out from the door and yanked them inside, dragging them along a cold, damp floor. Leo pressed against the constricting tentacles, but the more he resisted, the tighter they got. Just ahead of him, through the dark, he saw Evan kicking and Teena, caught by the leg, being dragged on her stomach.

Pfft! Pfft! Two bursts of sound punctured the air.

"*Eeeeeeeeeeeeeeeeeee!*" The inhuman squeal pierced Leo's eardrums.

He heard another *Pfft! Pfft!* behind him. Suddenly, the tentacles loosened, drooping down around his mid-section. Teena stood over him with a nail gun and gave him a hand getting up. Then she vanished into the dark. Then he heard the nail gun again, and another squeal of agony.

Teena emerged from the darkness with Evan in tow. Leo coughed into his sleeve, trying to regain his breath. "What was that?"

At their feet was the creature Teena had killed. It had no face, just a beach-ball-sized green center, now punctured with nails, from which the ropy tentacles emerged. The dead tentacles lay like tangled ropes of seaweed at their feet.

Ahead of them was a dimly lit staircase leading down into the bowels of the ship.

"What do you think's down there?" Evan asked.

Leo had been hoping to stumble on the holding bay, but why would the aliens guard their prison with what was basically a plant? A violent plant, but still. "I hope something," Leo said, brushing the end of a tentacle off his shoulder. It fell to the floor with a splat. "I'm starting to feel like this ship is empty."

"Me too," Teena agreed.

Leo walked first down the slippery ramp, stopping to listen for signs of danger. They could barely see ahead of them. On the last step, his body went rigid, like a panicked exclamation point.

They were in a dim, but not entirely dark room that was teeming with aliens. But unlike the ones they'd encountered before, these were slightly smaller, with deeper purple skin and long green tendrils sprouting from their heads like hair. Dead, dented sockets took the place of the other aliens' fly-like eyes. The effect was as chilling as the chamber's cool, damp air.

If they backed up the stairs before these things saw them or, really, sensed them, maybe they'd survive.

Leo took a step backward, knowing his friends would get the hint. But his foot lost traction on the stairs, and he slid off, landing with a loud splat on the gooey floor. The room of aliens collectively lifted their heads, their green snakelike hair swirling in mid-air.

As if on cue, the aliens opened their wide, gaping mouths. All at once, they let loose a barrage of greenies. The little flying aliens emerged from the aliens' mouths in dense clusters, hovering in the air for a split second before releasing a massive, eardrum-breaking squeal. And then they flew right at them.

"They can't puke greenies unless you shoot them!" Leo yelled over the din.

"These are the female aliens!" Teena screamed. "This is a nest!"

"Let's not make it our tomb!" Evan shouted, as he raised his bat yet again.

Teena dialed up the pressure on her nail gun and let loose

243

a storm of nails into chamber. As they met their targets, the nails pierced the baby greenies, which fell to the floor of the nest, writhing uselessly.

Leo pulled out his nail gun and started to shoot as four greenies, stuck together in a slimy ball as they flew, came at him. The first nail fell limply to the floor, as did the second and third. He dialed up the pressure. Still nothing. The nail gun was busted. A greenie dug its teeth into his armor, so he fumbled in his backpack, emerging with the paring knife he'd taken from Abe's trailer. He swiped the air uselessly as the greenies began to surround him. He felt like he was standing in someone's stomach and couldn't get traction on the soft, slippery floor.

Evan was ahead, in the thick of greenies. He swatted away, and Leo could see the little hatchlings explode in mid-air. But even Evan was having trouble. His mid-section was covered in at least a half dozen of the creatures. Leo heard Teena fire her nail gun several times, and he hoped she'd come to Evan's aid.

Leo could barely see as the greenies clung to his armor and buzzed around his head. With a good swipe of his knife, he cut a few down, and through the gap, he saw that another greenie swarm separated him from Evan and Teena.

"Use your nail gun!" Teena yelled to him.

"I can't! It's broken!" Leo yelled back.

"Piece of crap," Teena swore. "I'll use the Uzi."

"You can't see in here, Teena," Evan said behind her. "You might fire right at Leo."

"Yeah, no firing at Leo!" Leo yelled back. A greenie seized his upper inner thigh. Leo froze. It was going to bite his balls.

He fucking needed his balls.

His trusty purple lighter. He had tucked it into the waistband of the spandex. Now he pulled the sweaty Bic out and flicked it into life. He held it to the ball-biting greenie, feeling the heat on his thigh. The little beast caught fire and let go. *Sweet*. He proceeded to ignite the rest of his greenie attachments. They squealed and dropped to the floor, forming tiny fire pits where they fell.

He had an idea. Pulling out his hair spray can, Leo yelled to his friends, "Take cover!"

Teena and Evan hit the floor just as Leo sprayed a stream of hair spray and set fire to it, making a torch. The giant ball of greenies ignited like something straight out of hell. Their mothers must have sensed the greenies' pain because they writhed and screamed as if they were the ones on fire.

The greenies were burning, and through the flames, Leo's eyes landed on another white puckered door, just beyond the mothers' nest. If they could make it past the female aliens, they could get through that door.

Leo gestured to his friends to follow him, and they started to run through the smoky haze of flaming greenies.

"Why aren't the big ones doing anything?" Teena asked, looking at the dormant female aliens. They were still, save for the snakelike movements of their green hair.

"Because they're going to give birth again!" Leo shouted. "There's a door back there."

"You think it's a holding chamber?" Evan asked.

"Whatever it is, it's gotta be better than this," Leo said as the mama aliens started to move and sway. He pulled his Phat

Phil's Pizza polo from his backpack.

Leo used his knife to cut the shirt in two pieces, then pulled Abe's bottles of tequila and Jack Daniel's from his backpack. He uncapped them and shoved each shirt piece down a bottle neck to make a wick. He soaked the cloth with Abe's cheap gin.

He took a swig of the gin for himself and handed the Molotov cocktails to Evan.

"I'll light, you throw," Leo said. He looked at Teena. "Get ready to run."

Leo ignited the first bottle, watching the flame take hold and crackle its way up to the bottle top. Evan hurled it toward the aliens, where they were clumped together most tightly. Even Leo could see it was hardly a perfect throw—the bundle was an odd shape and flew shakily toward its target. It landed at the edge of the ring of aliens. The bottle didn't even break.

"Shit," Evan said. Leo grimaced. The little fiery bundle hardly looked like it would do anything.

"Look . . ." Teena pointed to the nest. The aliens were starting to open their mouths, ready to let loose with more greenies.

"That one was just practice," Leo said encouragingly, giving the second bomb to Evan. He lit the wick. The bottle arced overhead, starting to fall right in the center of the aliens.

All at once, two things happened.

The mama aliens pulled back their mouths, regurgitating another swarm of greenies into the air.

And the second bomb dropped, the bottle bursting with a violent pop at the center of the nest. Shards of glass and balls of fire flew through the air, landing scattershot throughout the nest. A few of the aliens' hair caught fire, and the tendrils whipped through the air, igniting greenies and other mama aliens. Meanwhile, the exploding fireballs were landing all around them, and the first bomb—the one at the edge of the nest—burst, sending glass into the air.

Leo, Teena, and Evan ran toward the door, trying to shield themselves from the whips of flames all around. They fought to get past the mamas, which were now trying to escape in an unorganized cluster. In front of them, the newly born greenies flew haphazardly, colliding with one another. Some were on fire, and the greenies that weren't in flames set in on other greenies, gnawing and biting one another like little cannibals.

Leo cut a path toward the second door, his arms sticky with dead greenies. Evan was behind him but waiting for Teena, who'd stumbled over a dead mama aliens' ropy green hair. "You go," Evan said to Leo as he went back for Teena.

Leo shook his head. "Get her," he said to Evan. "I'll hold the door."

Teena had broken free, and Evan pulled her up, nodding to Leo to go. Behind him, Leo heard Teena say sweetly, "You didn't have to wait for me."

It made Leo want to hear Sarabeth's voice again.

He just hoped Door Number Two would get them closer to her.

Leo pushed on the spongy surface, and he, Evan, and Teena plopped out on the other side.

34

LOOKS LIKE WE MADE IT

Evan Brighton, 5:53 A.M. Casimir Pulaski Day, Aliens' Ship

Evan hit the ground, hard. Solid ground: Already an improvement over where they'd just been.

"Holy shit, we found it," Leo said, under his breath.

"We found *them*," Teena said, awed. Evan had had a feeling that the nest had been guarding something important, and he'd been right. Before them was a sea of people that filled the room as massive as an airplane hangar. It looked like half the town was there.

"Wow, how are we going to get all these people out of here?" Evan couldn't believe they'd made it. There'd been moments when he'd thought they'd only find the captives if they were captives themselves. Now the three of them stood there, looking from the crowd, to one another, and back to the crowd. From

Teena's and Leo's matching expressions of surprised delight, he could tell they felt like he did: Now that they'd found everyone, how did they make sure not to screw it up?

"I wasn't expecting it to be so . . . lively," Leo said, scanning the crowd, probably looking for Sarabeth.

The people were distracted and frantic. They hadn't even noticed Evan and the others arrive.

"Yeah, I thought they'd seem more mind-controlled or something," Evan said, peering over the half wall they'd come out behind.

"It's better they're not," Teena said, starting to move out into the crowd. "We should move in. Look for your families, or anyone you know. See if there's a safer way out than the way we came."

Evan and Leo breathed matching sighs of relief, both glad to have someone taking charge. Teena led the way, and they stepped into the crowd. No one turned to look at them, which was awfully odd, given their spandex uniforms coated in green guts.

Evan didn't see anyone he knew until his eyes landed on the far side of the room, where several hundred people turned inward, all focused on Godly Jim, probably preaching to his new targets in the middle of their circle. At least Evan's mom was among them. He wanted to go to her, but he didn't want Jim to slow the rescue down. There was a lot of saving to do, and Jim couldn't help.

"What is everyone doing?" Teena wove past some women in their nightgowns.

"Arguing and panicking," Leo said. "Listen." As they

cut through the clusters of people, they heard snippets of conversation in the crowd.

From a woman in a short leopard-print robe: "I can't die. I can't! I haven't slept with anyone since my husband left me."

From a young mom, clutching her baby to her chest: "I wish we had moved to Lawn Grove when we'd had the chance."

From one pajama-clad dad to another who looked ready to throw down: "We need to figure out how that thing works, so we can use it against them."

"Look for this thing they want to use." Leo sidestepped a crying toddler.

"I think they mean that," Evan said, pointing across the room. "By the other door out."

A line of shriveled corpses hung like rag dolls above a door similar to the one Evan and Leo hadn't been able to open. Beneath the corpses, a half-dozen aliens pulled yet another body from what looked like a tanning bed, or a human-sized panini press. The aliens started to string up the body alongside the others.

"Oh my god," Teena said, staring from the bodies to the machine. Her skin had gone green. "Did that machine do that? How?"

At that moment, an old man broke away from his group of senior citizens, a crazed look in his eyes. He held a ballpoint pen aloft in one hand and a pocketknife in the other. "I fought in World War Two. I'll kill you all!" he yelled, running wildly at the aliens.

The old man was two feet from the door when one of the aliens reached out a claw and punctured his side, like he was meat for a shish kebab. The alien tossed him onto the panini press and closed the top. The alien pushed a button, and as the room of people fell silent, the machine hummed to life. The man's withered scream echoed through the chamber. Within about thirty seconds, two spouts at the foot of the press shot out blood and water into massive tubes that disappeared into the ceiling of the room.

Teena gagged, covering her mouth with her hand. The crowd reacted the same way, women crying, men wringing their hands, everyone staring at the aliens in fear and then turning away, as if staring too long would make them the aliens' next target. No one spoke or moved. The device obviously didn't just drain humans. It prevented uprisings.

"No wonder no one wants to leave," Leo said. "They can't leave."

"They can't stay, either," Evan said. There weren't really that many aliens guarding the room, probably because their intimidation technique worked so well. "We can take them out the door we came in. Now that we killed the nest, there's no threat left back that way."

Leo was still eyeballing the crowd. "Do you think everyone is in this room?" Evan knew he was talking about Sarabeth.

"She's gotta be down there somewhere," Evan told him.

"I haven't seen my dad, either, but he blends in. Sarabeth's a tall redhead. I feel like I would have seen her." His voice was sad and dejected. "Where else would they have taken her?"

Teena's face registered his question, and a grin spread across her face. "It's not about where they brought her. It's where she went once she got here."

A look of realization dawned on Leo's face. "The center of the ship!" He shook his head, amazed. "It's a little nutty, but how sweet would it be if she's right?"

"But how would she have gotten out without getting killed?" Evan said, looking around. His focus kept landing on Godly Jim's crowd, and anger welled up inside of him. His stepfather could have been trying to get people off the ship, instead of using them as an audience.

"I'm not sure," Leo said jumpily. "I need to find out."

"You're right," Evan said, trusting that Sarabeth would have figured something out. He took off his backpack and pulled out his squirt gun and two pints of whiskey. He tucked the Super Soaker into his body armor and the pint bottles into the tight waistband of his bike shorts. He looked from Leo to Teena. "You guys find Sarabeth. I can handle this."

The chatter in the room was growing again, back into the nervous and panicked crescendo it had reached before the old man tried to attack the aliens.

Leo squinted at him. "Are you sure?"

He nodded. "Sarabeth needs you more." He was already moving toward his stepfather. "I need to handle this alone anyway."

"But how are you going to get people out with the aliens in here? They'll kill you," Leo said.

"Not if I kill them first." Evan patted his Super Soaker. There were only six aliens. He'd killed that many by himself when Teena and Leo had been frozen. "They won't even see me coming."

"Thank you," Leo said, patting Evan's back. Teena looked at

him with concern and squeezed his hand. His heart swelled, unwittingly. He squeezed her hand back and hoped it said what he needed to say.

Evan merged into the thickest part of the crowd as Teena and Leo went back the way they had come. He got a few looks here and there, but people were so consumed by their fear that they didn't seem to care about the guy with the Super Soaker and the baseball bat. He passed behind his stepfather and listened to Godly Jim's irritatingly self-satisfied voice.

"God sent these beings to take us away," he crowed. "We should be proud. We should be honored. We've been chosen."

He had his full preacher drawl going, and Evan prickled at the way his mother stood, nodding dutifully, at Jim's side. The crowd around him was at least a couple hundred people and growing. Godly Jim was having the time of the end of his life.

Evan would handle him later. He knew he needed to kill the aliens first if he was going to save anyone.

The six aliens lined up by the door weren't as big as the ones outside the ship. They didn't even bristle as he approached them, extracting his Super Soaker from his padding. They probably thought he was just another dummy they could put in their human juicer.

He stepped right up to the aliens and, before they could do anything, pulled the trigger on his gun. A jet of perfume streamed at the first alien's chest, and then the second's. They both went up in little clouds. The remaining four aliens moved in on him, and he fired again. The gun jammed. He stumbled backward, suddenly wishing he'd kept Teena and Leo for backup.

He fell to the floor, hoping someone in the crowd would help. But people had turned away, like they had with the old man whose carcass had been added to the aliens' collection. He knew his trusty bat wouldn't do much good against these indestructible creatures, so Evan pulled the two pints of whiskey from his waistband. He uncapped the bottles as the aliens reached for him, their sharp claws only millimeters from his throat.

"Have a drink," he sneered, as he splashed the booze at the aliens, hitting three of the four where he needed. They turned to dust right at his feet. But the last one was still on him, its bony, purple foot stepping on Evan's ankle. It leaned down over Evan, so they were face-to-face.

Each bottle had maybe a shot's worth of alcohol left. He raised the bottles over his head and then swiftly smashed them, right into the alien's mucous chest plate. Broken glass protruded from the alien's skin, and green blood shot onto Evan's hands. Just when he started to fear there hadn't been enough alcohol left, the creature's skin crusted over, its slime drying up instantly. He kicked the dead alien away. It was dust before it hit the floor.

"He just killed the aliens!" someone shouted.

A crowd started to gather around him. "You killed them!" "Are we free?" "How did you do that?" "Thank you!" "What do we do now?"

Evan liked the attention, he had to admit. It felt better than either of his perfect games. Without a beat, he started directing people toward the far door, telling them it was safe and not to be intimidated by the burned-out nest. In groups, people started to leave.

There were thousands of people still left, though, and some hadn't noticed that their captors had been dispatched. Including Godly Jim's new flock.

Evan made a beeline for the makeshift church service.

"The Lord works in mysterious ways." Jim gave his folksy grin, his preacher bellow carrying through the high-ceilinged space. "Look at my wife. Her own son—my stepson, but I think of him like he's my boy—went missing in all this. And she's struggling—by golly, is she ever. But she knows she'll see him again after all this is through. Maybe they're taking us somewhere more special than Earth. Or maybe they're sending us to the heaven we know is up there for us. Either way, we welcome the Lord's plan."

It was too much for Evan to take. He didn't know what bothered him more: Jim's statement that Evan's mom was cool with his possibly being dead or that Jim had called him "my boy."

"Actually, I'm right here, *Dad*," Evan called, giving the word an ugly edge. "In case you hadn't noticed, I killed all the outer-space sorts."

He sidled up next to Jim. With his protruding gut—"God gave me plenty, and I said thank you" was one of his lame jokes—Evan's stepfather was larger than Evan in girth. But Evan was taller and leaner, something he'd never registered when he'd been doing everything Jim said for the last six years or so.

The weekend had shown Evan some things. Things like he might not get the girl, but he didn't have to let her treat him like crap, either. Things like he could forgive and forget, for

255

the right person. Things like he needed to stop drinking after three rum-based cocktails. And most important, he was his own man.

"You're not listening to this crap, are you?" He summoned his voice and pushed his words out over the crowd. "He's a fraud."

Jim stepped in front of him. "Everybody, this is my boy, Evan." Nervous laughter. "He clearly has been watching too many of Hollywood's movies, and he thinks our heaven-sent friends are our enemies."

Evan's mom came up to him and threw her arms around him, despite the dirt and congealed guts that clung to him. "I was so worried about you," she whispered as Jim stared. "I'm so glad you're safe."

Evan hugged her back, beyond grateful she was still alive. But today, he couldn't let his mom get in the way of him finally telling Jim off, once and for all. "We have to get off this ship," Evan said, his voice a croak. His mom looked at him in surprise, but he could see some pride in her eyes, too.

He started again, louder, for the whole of Jim's crowd to hear. "We can't stay on this ship. My friends and I have been fighting these aliens for days. I've seen these things kill everyone and everything in their path," Evan explained, glad to be covered in greenie guts and dirt and blood. "I took out the guards, but I don't know how much time we have before more arrive."

The crowd's rapt attention for Jim was shifting to him.

"We have to get off this ship, so we can destroy these things once and for all," he said.

"But we're chosen, Evan," Jim said, his milky eyes narrowing.

Evan shook his head and looked at the crowd. "You can either be saved, or you can be rescued," he said. "The choice is yours."

"We're not chosen—we're captured." His mother grabbed his hand, tears flowing from her eyes. "We're all going with you. Everyone is getting off this ship."

As the crowd fell in line behind him, Evan grinned. Even a guy playing the hero didn't mind a little motherly love.

35

UZI-LICIOUS

Teena McAuley, 6:08 A.M. Casimir Pulaski Day,
Aliens' Ship

In the ranking of improbable life events, invading a massive alien ship was pretty high up on Teena's list.

Invading said ship with Leo Starnick was up there, too.

Thinking about Evan Brighton this much was higher still.

"Do you think Evan's okay?" she asked Leo. They were walking back through the burned-out cavity of the ship where the alien nest had been. The aggressive odor, like fertilizer that had been soaked in bleach, singed her nostrils and brought tears to her eyes. She welcomed the excuse to cry and blame it on the smell.

Leo stopped and squinted at her in the darkness, as if trying to see inside her brain.

"I think he's okay, Teena," Leo said, stepping over a pile of alien guts. "But I'm an optimist."

Teena's jaw trembled a little. They shouldn't have split up. They should have stayed with Evan. Or at least *she* should have stayed with Evan.

"I'm sorry about being such a bitch the last few days," she said, her foot landing with a crunch on a singed alien tentacle. "I think you and Sarabeth are really good together."

Leo turned again and looked at her. "You're kind of unreal." He reached down to pull the sticky carcass of a greenie off his spandex pant leg.

"What do you mean?" Teena sidestepped a cluster of the mama aliens' green hair tendrils piled on the ground like intestines. She hadn't noticed before, but the floor in this room was smushy and soft, and made slurping noises when you stood on it. It really was, as Leo had said, like a big vagina. How disgusting.

"I mean, as much as I'd love to sit down with this sweet Teena and talk about our feelings . . ." He coughed as some alien dust clogged his throat. "Your timing is so fucked."

Teena laughed. "I know, I know. But end of the world and all."

They had made it back to the puckered door cavity that led out into the ship's corridor. From here, they could look back and see the totality of their wreckage. Every surface was charred, and even in the dim lights, you could make out splatters of greenie guts. The people Evan was evacuating were going to freak out. But at least they would be safe. That is, as long as Evan could kill the alien guards. She said a little prayer for him and couldn't wait to see him on the other side of this.

She wondered if Leo felt the same tremor of worry for

Sarabeth as she did for Evan. She reached out and grabbed Leo in a hug. Beneath their feet, the floor continued to wobble like a trembling Jell-O shot.

"Without a word, he hugged her back.

"Do you really think Sarabeth was right about this central hub? That she found it?" Teena asked, pulling away.

Leo nodded. "I kind of do," he said. "I know she doesn't rule the school McAuley-style, but she has all that stuff going on under the surface, you know?"

Teena blushed because she was thinking of someone else with a lot going on under the surface. "Yeah. I know. Evan, too. It was pretty cool, how he told us to go ahead without him back there."

"Cooler than anything I've ever done," Leo said. "I'm sorry, too, by the way. About the way I was."

Teena knew he meant the way he was before, over the summer. She waved him off. "You don't have to apologize. It's not like I gave you any reason to be nice to me."

Leo smirked with a twinkle in his eye. "I can think of several reasons." He turned serious. "But maybe we needed to go through all that to get us here."

Teena looked around. "You mean in a room of smoldering alien guts? With a floor that sounds like it's going to eat us?" She grinned. "What a way to make a girl feel special."

Leo stuck his hand in the door cavity, pulling it back slightly so that Teena could squeeze through. "You're right. Let's get out of here."

Back in the clean, comparatively well-lit hallway, Teena and Leo paused to get their bearings. Teena almost wanted to step out into another battle, just so she didn't have to worry about where the aliens were lying in wait for them.

Leo must have been thinking the same thing, because he stopped walking and pulled a little bottle of perfume from his backpack as if it were pepper spray. "It's weird, right? That we come out of there, after destroying, like, their wives and children, and they're not waiting for us."

Teena nodded. "Yeah," she said. "But maybe we're overthinking it."

It was a good thing, the lack of attackers. They needed the corridor as free of aliens as possible so that the captives could escape. And Evan, for that matter.

Leo loped forward, running a finger along one of the purple illumination strips in the wall like a little kid playing with the handrail of an escalator. "At some point, this hallway has to lead to the ship's chewy caramel center, where we find Sarabeth and shut this mother down."

"Totally," Teena said, feeling suddenly giddy. Maybe, finally, they'd actually kill all the bad guys. Which meant she could get on with her life. Maybe a kinder, gentler life. After a long shower, of course.

"Doesn't this floor remind you of a Tomorrowland ride?" Teena said, looking sideways at Leo.

"Never been to Disney, but it's definitely not what I expected from these guys," he said. "It's like a futuristic dance club or something."

"Yes!" Teena jokingly started moonwalking down the hallway. She hadn't been goofy like this in forever. Leo doubled over, laughing.

Leo pointed at her, a look of amazed wonder on his face. "You're such a nerd!"

"You would know!" She added some over-the-top Britney Spears-esque hand motions, trying to make them funny instead of sexy.

She rounded a bend, still moonwalking, when Teena felt a pair of skeletal yet strong arms close around her. They smelled distinctly of good coffee and were a purple color she'd never feature in her wardrobe again.

Leo's expression made it clear that this surprise was not of the pleasant variety.

"It's only one," Teena said, trying to remain calm. "Just spray it."

Leo robotically pointed his tiny bottle of perfume at the thing's squishy chest membrane just behind Teena's head. He sprayed. Teena felt the alien's skin go crusty, like a rapidly forming scab, and then it turned to dust. She spun around, dreading what she would see.

A few dozen more aliens were behind her. She backed away hurriedly and grabbed Leo's shoulder so she wouldn't fall. The hallway behind them was empty, but there were so many of the aliens, they'd be caught in no time if they ran.

"Booze," she said.

In a flash, Leo swung his backpack in front of him, and Teena reached into her purse. They pulled out bottles of Abe's liquor.

It was like a bar fight in an old Western. She smashed a bottle of vodka into an alien's chest, sending glass shards and alien dust to the floor. Leo twirled a bottle in each hand, hitting two aliens at once, the smell of Captain Morgan spicing the

262

air. They went through every bottle they had, killing most of the aliens.

Teena pointed down the empty hallway.

"Go," she told him. "I'll hold them off. You find Sarabeth."

"But you can't take them alone," Leo said.

"I have an Uzi," she yelled back, pulling it out of her pack. "I can do anything alone."

Leo shook his head, holding his ground. "The greenies," he said. "The greenies."

"I have an idea," Teena said, more harshly, as she pushed him in the other direction. "Just, you have to find Sarabeth."

She loaded a cartridge with a definitive click. "Go," she said. "Fast." Leo gave her one long, lingering look and took off running.

There was a not-so-small number of aliens left, and one ran after Leo. It ran without grace, but fast. Teena fired several bullets into its leg, and as the beast whipped its head around toward her, she said, "Forget him. Come and get me."

It did, barely limping despite the bullets she could see piercing its leg. She shot it, right in the throat, letting it retch up its greenie puke. The other aliens didn't like this and started to close in on Teena, as if realizing they needed to contain her.

"I can do this," she said to no one.

And she believed she could. She was a bitch, and bitches got stuff done. "Unleash hell," she said under her breath.

She fired into the alien army, her bullets riddling them with holes that made no difference. She fired more rounds, hitting some of them in their delicate throat and chest region, and they started to puke up the green slime from which greenies began to rise.

The greenies immediately swarmed around the aliens, and the large beasts jostled one another to get through the haze of little goblins. Teena unloaded two more cartridges into the frenzy, even as greenies attacked her, going right for her leg where she'd been cut yesterday.

But as she fired more and more, and as the greenies realized that by herself, Teena wasn't much to sink their teeth into, they began to turn on the purple aliens. The cutthroat greenies dug their pointy incisors into the aliens, just as Teena thought they would, after seeing them go all cannibal on one another in the nest.

Behind her, Teena heard a commotion. A human commotion. She peeked around the curve in the hallway and saw that captives were appearing down the corridor, emerging from the puckered doorway. Disoriented and tired, some trailed alien tentacles from the burned-out nest on the bottoms of their shoes like toilet paper.

Teena smiled. "Good job, Evan," she said.

She looked back at the aliens, fighting amongst themselves and smashing greenies to the ground. She was lightheaded with pride. She'd done it.

Now she could return to the holding bay, to find Evan, help him, and tell him how she felt.

Then she looked down. Her thigh wound had reopened, and blood gushed freely to the white floor. The purple and green lights swirled before her eyes.

She slid to the floor, her last thoughts of Evan as the white corridor went black.

36

LIKE A BAT OUT OF HELL

Evan Brighton, 6:22 A.M. Casimir Pulaski Day,
Aliens' Ship

People were leaving. He'd helped people escape.

He was a hero.

He watched with satisfaction as the room emptied. Even Godly Jim had shuffled out, muttering angrily.

He just needed to find Teena and the others, and the worst would be over. Maybe Sarabeth could shut down the freaky laser-shooting ship, and with all the captives free, the town could help fight the aliens, if there were any more left.

The room was down to a couple dozen people, younger guys who'd been helping round up people and get them out. One of them was Cameron Lewis, Teena's true object of affection.

But he wasn't jealous. He wanted Teena to be happy. Maybe someday, she'd pick him. If not, he'd live. *Obviously, I'll live,* he thought. At the very least, alien attacks put things in perspective. Even if sometimes, in his heart, falling for Teena felt bigger than life and death.

"I can't believe that you did all this," Cameron said, coming up and slapping him on the back. Cameron was one of those guys who never made Evan feel like a loser. "I mean, it was freaky, man."

"Pretty fucked-up," Evan said. "It wasn't just me, though. Leo and Teena helped, and your sister was with us, too."

Cameron's eyes grew watery. "Sarabeth? Do you know where she is now?"

Evan clasped his arm. "We think she's okay, and somewhere on the ship," he said, not wanting to say more because he really didn't know.

"She was lucky to have had you guys," Cameron said, smiling wanly. "*Is* lucky," he added, not seeming convinced.

"We were all lucky, I think. Really lucky." Lucky to have been trapped in a cellar with the best people you could ever be trapped in a cellar with, he thought.

"Pretty crazy shit, four high school students fend off an alien attack," Cameron said, discreetly wiping his eyes. The last few people trickled out the door. Cameron nodded his head toward the exit. "You coming?"

"I'll be there," Evan said. "I just want to do one thing."

"Okay, dude. Thanks again," he said casually, as if Evan had helped him move a couch.

As Cameron finally left, Evan contentedly took one last look around the empty room. The giant room that he'd helped evacuate. He marched up the ramp, ready to go. Ready to find his friends.

He was about to push his way into the burned nest when two claws locked around him and dragged him backward. Above him were the fly eyes of an alien.

The only weapon he had left was his bat. It had done him a lot of good against the greenies, but it wasn't going to do much good against a huge, indestructible foe.

The alien had Evan under his arms. He kicked his feet against the ground uselessly. The alien's grip was so strong, Evan could barely move.

The creature threw Evan onto the human juicer and fastened straps across his ankles, stomach, and chest. The juicer was like being in a coffin already. Its lid, which would soon close on him, was covered with hundreds of tiny needles, waiting to emerge and pierce his flesh. Beneath him, he felt hundreds of pinpricks against his back, next to his skin. In seconds, they'd be *in* his skin.

How could he have let this happen? He'd come so far, and he was still going to die. The hero wasn't supposed to die.

The alien pressed a button, and the machine started to close in on him.

"Cameron? You there?" he called. "Is anyone out there?"

The only answer he got was the machine's malicious hum.

He could barely move his hands, and he couldn't kick his feet high enough to keep the door from closing down on him. He felt the pinch of the pins as they penetrated the back of his spandex suit.

Wriggling his hands back and forth, he felt the familiar ash handle of his bat next to him. The alien had thrown it inside with him. He grabbed the handle. Somehow, he managed to stand the bat up, wedging it between the lid and the bottom of the juicer.

The bat prevented the lid from continuing to close. Evan was safe for now, but he wouldn't have long before the bat broke under the pressure of the lid's descent. If he could free himself from the straps soon, it would mean his trusty bat had come through again. If he couldn't . . . he didn't want to think about it.

He gritted his teeth and strained against the straps that held him down.

He couldn't die. He had a new life to live.

37

WHEN LIFE HANDS YOU ALIENS . . .

Sarabeth Lewis, 6:28 A.M. Casimir Pulaski Day,
Aliens' Ship

Sarabeth was one stubborn piece of protective alien glass away from shutting down this piece-of-shit ship. That glass was all that separated her from the big silver orb that she believed—no, *knew*—was the source of the ship's power.

The orb sat atop a helical pole, with green and purple tubes weaving around and around a silver cord that looked to be made from an organic material. The cord pulsed and pumped a fluid upward into the giant silver ball, which looked bigger than the one that dropped in Times Square on New Year's Eve. In the right light, the orb picked up the purple and green colors of the weaving cords beneath it. It jiggled and wobbled and radiated warmth, even from beneath the thick glass shield that protected it. And at its gelatinous center was a sparking, rattling red orb that looked like it was making all the heat.

Sarabeth was six feet off the ground, having managed to climb partway up the helix so she could reach the casing around the orb. It was split down the middle, like it could be pried apart, but probably only if you were a huge alien, not a teenage girl who sat out of gym class with regularity. She'd tried shooting it, with the .38 that was still tucked in her waistband, but the glass was impenetrable.

Sarabeth gritted her teeth, dug in her fingernails, and pulled. For a split second, she thought she finally had loosened the casing, but then she fell to the ground, landing hard on her butt.

If only her friends (Leo!) would get here, one of them (Leo!) could help her get to the core and shut down the ship. Even with the task of destroying the core before her, she couldn't stop thinking about Leo and how much she wanted to see him again. She was worried about Teena and Evan, too, of course. But Leo was the one who kept sneaking into her thoughts.

Part of her just wanted to share the story of how she'd gotten here: The jet-packed aliens that had stolen her from the bathroom had zipped her to the ship so fast, she'd felt like she'd been whirled around in a KitchenAid mixer. She'd been so disoriented, one of the aliens had to carry her onto the ship. Prone in the beast's arms, she became aware of the tiny travel-sized bottle of Otherworldly she'd put in the pocket of her jeans. Still playing dead, she'd slyly pulled the cologne out of her pocket, and with two quick spritzes to their chests, the aliens were dead, and she was on the ship. So she'd run for the center, eager to see if she'd been right about the core, and had wound up here.

There'd been two aliens on duty when she arrived, but they'd been equally easy to dispatch with the Otherworldly. She'd found it funny that—with all the aliens' technology—their top-secret room was less well protected than Teena's dad's wine cellar. But how long could she really have before one of the aliens found her?

From the entryway outside the chamber, she heard noises. Stumbling, fumbling noises. She rose quickly to her feet and held up the bottle of cologne tentatively. She thought the jellylike orb would dust up just like the aliens if she sprayed it. But she didn't have much choice if she wanted to survive. She'd have to find another way to take out the core. She pointed the cologne bottle at the door with a shaky, useless hand.

Planting her feet and closing her eyes, she steeled herself for the aliens as something pushed its way through the puckered door.

"Don't shoot!" The voice was familiar, and Sarabeth briefly wondered if the aliens had the skills to fake a human voice in an effort to trick her.

"At least, don't shoot until you see how douchey I look."

Nope. There was no way the aliens could replicate Leo's witty repartee.

She opened her eyes.

And then she burst out laughing.

"Is that spandex?" she asked, not knowing if they were at a point in their fledgling relationship where she could run into his arms. Plus, the sight of Leo wearing something so rigid and sartorially opposite to his usual holey jeans, black tee, and boots was almost more than she could handle.

"Yes," he said, blushing. "So, what's a nice girl like you doing in a place like this?" His flirty smile appeared. Even though his face was covered in alien guts and dirt, even though he was wearing spandex and a kids' superhero chest plate, Sarabeth really wanted to kiss him for dangerous lengths of time.

"Where are Teena and Evan?" she asked, biting her lip. She was an awful person to be so distracted by him that she hadn't asked yet. But he was so cute.

"They're okay," Leo said, then grimaced uncertainly. He expelled a quick, nervous breath. "Well, they were last I saw them. But—"

"But what . . . ?"

"Well, Teena hung back and sent me here. When I left, she was fighting off a huge cluster of them," Leo said, looking sheepish. "I was going to stay and help, but she wanted me to find you."

"Oh my god," Sarabeth said. "And Evan?"

"He was going to try to take out some aliens—who have a creepy human juicer, by the way—so he could get the captives outside."

"So you found the captives," she said, excitement for the accomplishment turning quickly to worry. "I hope Evan's okay."

"Me, too. He seemed sure of himself. So you never went to the holding bay?"

Sarabeth grinned. "Well, they popped up on me when I went to the bathroom. But as I screamed, I thought of something . . ."

She filled him in on the rest. Leo stared at her, and she couldn't read his face. She hoped he didn't regret what had happened between them.

"Did you know that booze works, too? Can you believe we

didn't think of that?" He laughed. "You have got to see Abe's trailer. It's nuts. We raided his bar."

"Is that why you smell like rum?"

Leo sniffed the air. "Probably." He smiled at her. "So, what is your plan now?"

"Well, I think the whole ship will come down with a single spritz." She pointed up at the orb as it rotated and pulsed. "I think that's made of the same kind of organic material that the aliens are, but in a much more delicate form. That's why it's sheathed under the glass. But I can't get that damn shield pried off. But maybe if we do it together?"

"I'd be honored." They climbed up the helix, and took positions on either side of the shield. Sarabeth wedged her fingers into the small groove, and Leo did the same. Their pinkies touched.

"Count of three," she said. Leo's eyes met hers over the orb, and his pupils caught the silvery light. Sarabeth was ready to be done with aliens once and for all.

She counted down and then pulled on the shield with all her might. Leo strained against the cover as well. The aliens hadn't been messing around when they'd built this protective casing. Sarabeth was about to give up, and then, when she thought she couldn't pull any harder, the case gave way. The orb was unprotected.

"We did it," she said, hearing the surprise in her voice.

"Of course we did," Leo said, gently squeezing her hand with his own. "So what now?"

Sarabeth was ready for this part. Still holding on to her side of the now-opened casing with her feet on the green tubing,

273

she reached a hand down and pulled the Otherworldly from her pants pocket. She sprayed everything that was left onto the pulsing silver ball.

Nothing happened. Nothing at all.

"It's not working," she said. She wasn't used to being wrong. It was not nearly as bad as she'd thought it could be, except for the pesky fact that now the aliens would take over the world.

"Wait, I have something that might work," Leo said. Now he reached down and pulled a small bottle from the waistband of his ridiculous spandex pants. He twisted off the cap one-handed and gave it to her. "It was Abe's," he said. "Smell it."

She uncapped it and took a whiff. It was strong, the scent practically singeing her nostrils. The label said PURPLE PEOPLE-EATER.

"The name's appropriate," she said. She splashed the pungent purple liquid onto the orb.

What she'd expected to happen with the cologne was happening now. The liquor started to eat a hole into the orb, slowly dissolving it. Leo returned her carefully to the floor and turned her so she was facing him.

"So, I just want to make sure of one thing," he said with his hands still lightly on her waist. "We're still going to go to prom, right?"

She smiled and nodded, her emotions whirling in a good way. Out of the corner of her eye, she saw the ball slowly dissolving, like a sugar cube in water, coming closer and closer to exposing the red orb, which looked like it was getting hotter and hotter as layers of the silver ball fell away. "Sure, but right now, I need you to do something else." She couldn't help the cockeyed grin that spread across her face. "I need you to kiss me like your life was hanging in the balance."

Leo looked from her to the glowing, disintegrating orb at the core of the ship. "Right now, it kind of is, isn't it?"

His lips hit hers electrically. It was even better kissing him now than it had been last night. Warmth spread through her body, and not just because of the undefined alien energy source that was melting a few feet away. Leo didn't seem to want it to end any more than she did.

They broke away at the same time and in unison said, "Let's get out of here."

38

IMAGINE ALL THE PEOPLE

Leo Starnick, 6:34 A.M. Casimir Pulaski Day,
Aliens' Ship on the Verge of Self-Destructing
(He Hopes)

Now this was the end-of-the-world scenario Leo had had in mind.

He was running down the corridor of an alien ship he'd invaded that hopefully was about to explode. But the best part, the absolute best, was that he was running while holding the hand of the girl he liked. A lot. Okay, maybe loved.

Wow, if he was thinking love, it really must have been the end of the world.

They sprinted, and behind them, they could hear footfalls. Big footfalls. Leo looked over his shoulder to see at least ten more purple aliens bearing down on them.

Sarabeth pulled the semi-automatic she'd used on the

greenies at IHOP from her waistband and took aim. Had she had that thing while they'd been kissing?

"Don't shoot!" Leo thought adding a swarm of greenies to their escape wouldn't be the most helpful thing right now.

Sarabeth fired, hitting one of the aliens in its leg. It fell to the floor in front of several other aliens, tripping some of them. She fired again, hitting the kneecap of another alien.

Okay, he definitely loved her.

"You're freaking me out with the sharpshooting," Leo said, pulling her along faster now. "We're almost there."

He'd had full faith in Sarabeth's theory at the execution stage, but now he was starting to get nervous. Shouldn't something be happening? The ship hadn't made a peep.

As if answering his thoughts, the ship began to vibrate and hum. He felt like he was leaning against a subwoofer as his heart thrummed.

The tremors beneath them freaked him out so much, he charged forward. Sarabeth's feet practically came off the ground as he pulled her along. He'd never run like this in his life.

He hoped Evan and the captives had made it out, and he hoped Teena was safe, because there was no turning back now.

Running down the exit ramp into the March morning, he inhaled a sharp, cold breath. He and Sarabeth looked back at the ship once. The metal structure was shaking so quickly, it was like seeing double.

"We need to get farther away!" Leo yelled over the din.

They raced over the Shoppoplex construction site and tore through the chain-link fence that separated it from Orland Ridge Mall. They turned past the doors to the Orland Ridge

277

food court, their feet beating against the parking lot in unison. Then up ahead, Leo saw the most welcome sight.

People.

Lots of people, standing at the farthest edge of the Orland Ridge parking lot several hundred feet away. Thousands of them. They were lined up and facing the ship, watching as it started to clatter like a pile of tin cans. Leo couldn't help but look for Teena and Evan and his father, but at the speed they were running, he couldn't make out anything very clearly. Everything was a big blur, and he didn't dare slow down, because he could sense that some of the aliens were still behind them.

He would not, could not, look back.

And then, the ship blew. The explosions in movies didn't ever pull your eardrums out of your head. They didn't make your feet lift off the ground and make your skin feel like it was being pulled away from your bones. Even Leo's hair felt like it was being yanked by individual strands from each follicle on his head.

The crowd was still about fifty feet away. Leo dove, half on purpose, half involuntarily, pulling Sarabeth with him. He hoped his face said to the unprotected masses, "Get on the ground now!" The crowd got it. Down they went, like they were doing a full-body version of the wave.

As Leo and Sarabeth flew through the air, he pressed her head next to his, and their arms wove together as they covered each other. They hit the pavement just as the explosion rocked the ground beneath them.

He didn't turn to look, but he could hear metal hitting pavement. The earth seemed to sink down beneath them.

Smoke filled his nostrils, along with the aroma of melting asphalt. A hot whoosh of air rolled over him and Sarabeth, like an ocean wave of ash. Then the world stopped swaying, and Leo dared to lift his head and peek behind him.

"Holy shit." What he saw brought him to his feet. The ship was burning, like a massive, self-contained bonfire. It lit the sky orange to the point he could almost believe the sun was out and had fallen to Earth. Sarabeth pulled up next to him, emitting a gasp.

Next to the burning ship was a giant hole where half of the Orland Ridge Mall had been. The food court, the movie theater, the whole water-feature wing had been taken out by the explosion, leaving behind a crater that sank deep into the earth.

"Guess I won't be going to work tomorrow," he said to Sarabeth.

They turned to face the cast of thousands behind them.

He barely had time to register any faces when Cameron Lewis came up and folded both him and Sarabeth into a massive bear hug. "You guys fucking did it," Cameron said as Leo looked over his shoulder and saw his father standing right at the front of the crowd. His dad, who had never shown up for any of Leo's string-ensemble concerts, who couldn't even remember Leo's birthday, was alive and smiling at Leo, like he could actually see him. Leo pulled away from Cameron with a nod of respect and made the last few steps to his dad.

"Dad, I'm glad you're okay," Leo said to his father, noticing the little lines that mapped his face.

"Me too, son," Ed Starnick said, offering his hand. They shook, like strangers. But maybe they wouldn't be for much longer.

Across from him, Sarabeth pulled out of the hug with Cameron and, still holding her brother's hand, rushed up to a tall woman Leo assumed was their mom. And who looked an awful lot like the woman in Abe's picture. Interesting.

"Mom!" With tears in her eyes, Sarabeth leaned into her mom, who grabbed Sarabeth tightly and stroked her hair protectively.

"You helped do this? Blow up the ship?" Ms. Lewis was now holding Sarabeth at arm's length and rubbing smudges of dirt off her daughter's face. Ms. Lewis's brow was furrowed like a question mark above her eyes.

"Yeah. I mean, yes," Sarabeth said, and then she took Leo's hand and squeezed it. "With Leo."

Ms. Lewis raised an eyebrow as high as it could go. "Interesting," she said, directing a slightly intimidating gaze at Leo. He smiled to himself. If Ms. Lewis disapproved of him and Sarabeth, he wondered what kind of leverage the picture of her and Abe, a man who'd lived in a trailer by IHOP, would get him.

"And with Teena and Evan," Sarabeth added, peering around. "Where are they?"

"I don't know," piped up a woman who was clearly Evan's mother. Her hair was the same sandy-blond color, and she had the same wide blue eyes.

"Probably taking all the glory for himself somewhere," said a man Leo recognized as Godly Jim, Evan's stepfather. Leo watched his crazy Bible-banging show late at night when he was stoned. He always thought the guy was acting, but maybe he was just a lunatic.

Sarabeth's face went pale in the late-afternoon glare as she urgently said to Leo, "What if they didn't make it?"

"He went back for Teena, I think," Cameron said, popping in next to them. He looked over his shoulder at Evan's mom, who was scanning the crowd nervously. "He got everyone out here, but he said there was one more thing he had to do."

Oh, no.

Leo clutched Sarabeth's hand tightly. "We have to go back." He remembered how easily he'd left Teena behind to go find Sarabeth. What if he had gotten both her and Evan killed?

Sarabeth nodded and started pulling him back toward what was left of the mall, and the smoking cavern and the still-burning ship, ignoring warnings from the crowd behind them. *They don't get it*, Leo thought. *We can't leave them behind*.

Doom settled over them as they moved closer to the massive bonfire and the adjacent crater. How could anyone have survived that? Leo bit his lip, trying to stay strong, when he spotted a figure emerging from the wreckage. Dust-covered, dirty, and glistening with what had to be man sweat came Evan, carrying Teena prone across his arms. She was unconscious, but as Leo ran closer to Evan, he could see the rise and fall of her chest. She was breathing.

Yup. Leo might have had his action-movie moment, but Evan was laying claim to the whole action-movie franchise.

"That guy better get some when all this is over," he said, a little louder than he'd meant to, as he made his way closer to Evan. A crowd of people, including Sarabeth, their parents, and Evan's mom, was following him, eager to help the ship's last survivors.

Sarabeth slapped him above the elbow, and behind them, he heard her mom give a little cough. "Thankfully, it *is* over," Sarabeth said.

Evan stopped in front of them, and his mom ran to him and pulled his head to her shoulder. "My boy," she said. Looking at Leo, Evan blushed.

"We need to get her some medical help," he said, nodding down at Teena.

"I'll take her," his mom said, and was joined by another woman, who helped carry Teena away.

"It's okay, she's a nurse," Evan said, looking from Leo to Sarabeth, who threw her arms around him. Leo did the same.

"Most-deserved group hug ever," Leo said, hardly believing they were all still alive and three of them were conscious.

"Do you think she's going to be okay?" Evan asked, looking down at Teena's pretty, peaceful face.

"I do," Leo said, looking to a grassy median in the parking lot where Evan's mom and several other people, probably nurses and doctors in their regular lives, were tending to Teena and a few other captives with minor wounds.

"What happened to you?" Sarabeth asked, pointing to Evan's arm, which was covered with tiny pinpricks.

"Leo tell you about the juicer?" Evan asked. Sarabeth nodded. "They tried to drain me."

He pulled the handle of his bat from under his arm. It was just a stump at this point, one end of it ragged and broken. "This thing saved my life, again. Broke their machine and everything." He glanced back at the burning ship. "Well, I think you guys did that."

"Group hug again," Sarabeth said, going for it. "Thank God you guys are all right."

"Forget God. Thank Evan," Leo said.

A small smile on his lips, Evan scanned the crowd behind them, looking at the thousands of people standing there.

"This isn't the whole town, is it?" Evan asked.

"I hate to say it, but doesn't look like it." Leo had been wondering the same thing.

"Yeah. If only a quarter of the town was captured, why haven't we seen anyone else in the last two days?" Sarabeth asked, reading his mind.

"They're at home. Asleep," came a strong voice from behind Leo. Leo turned and saw a very upright man in a black suit with such sharp edges Leo thought he could cut himself on them.

"Who are you?" Leo asked. "And what do you mean, asleep?"

The man extended a hand and said only, "The people you've been waiting for." His voice was so official, it worked better than a badge.

This guy was for real. Leo just knew. "*Now* the government gets here?"

"Ha. Government," the man said. "No. We're a private interest."

"Not interested enough," Leo said.

"And you still haven't told us what you mean by asleep," Evan said.

"The people who aren't here are asleep in their homes. The Veoisans have a technology—a gas—that allows them to bring on temporary paralysis in both humans and Veoisans," the suited man said, looking from Evan to Leo to Sarabeth. "You

283

probably saw it active in its more portable, short-term form."

Evan nodded. "Yeah, they used it on Leo and Teena."

"Interesting, we'll need to look into that." Mr. Private Interest checked the fact off in his head. "The Veoisans used their gas in all the homes with chimneys, where they could easily pipe it in. As those people slept, the Veosians captured all the people in their cars or houses without chimneys. The Veoisans were going to drain the people they had, then go back for the others."

"But why drain people?" Leo asked, piecing things together as the man spoke.

"Our bodies are a natural source of fluids that can keep their ecosystem healthy," Mr. Private Interest said. "They would have used our fluids to feed their planet."

"Ew," Sarabeth said. "And why stack the cars like that?" She pointed to the car towers off in the distance.

"A flair for the dramatic coupled with a slight fear of human technology," Mr. Private Interest said.

"Ah, that explains why our remote-control cars worked so well," Leo said, enjoying the agent's puzzled face. "So they stopped people from coming into town?"

"No," the man said. "We were keeping people out of the town while it was occupied by the aliens. But now there should be paramedics here, to help you."

Evan gave the man a dirty look. "Seriously? We could have had help all this time? What kind of assholes are you?"

"Yeah, why not help? And *why* keep people out of our town? And why did the Veoisans attack?" Leo asked.

"One question at a time. We knew. We just knew too late," the man said. "We've had cutbacks ourselves and failed to make our delivery for the last two months. The Veoisans—their planet isn't part of our galaxy—are normally a peaceful race. But when their planet began to dry out, they got desperate."

"What's this delivery? What do they need that we have?" Leo asked.

"Our group makes a special erythritol-based compound we supply them with to help keep their planet moist. The compound mimics the enzymes and moisture found in the human body, which is why they were harvesting people as a replacement."

"But what do you get out of these deliveries? Besides them not coming here to kill us all," Sarabeth asked.

"Let's just say they have resources equally valuable to us," the man said. "It's in our interest—our business interest—to be good intergalactic neighbors. That's actually in our mission statement at Intergalactic Hospitality for Other Planets."

"Wait . . . IHOP?" Leo squinted.

Mr. Private Interest nodded, seeming annoyed.

"For real? IHOP has something to do with this?" Leo sputtered.

"Yes," Mr. Private Interest said. "That's all I can say."

"So, explain to me again why you didn't help," Leo said, kind of annoyed. This guy was unreadable. It was like he was wearing dark sunglasses, even though his eyes were clearly visible.

"IHOP has agreements. Like I said, it's just business," he said. "Plus, once we realized most of the damage was done and several teenagers were controlling the threat, it became of interest to us to see how you would fare."

Leo felt his fists clench. "Even though we could have died?"

"Even though we didn't even know what we were up against?" Sarabeth asked, sounding equally pissed.

"Even though there were only four of us, and they're almost indestructible?" Evan was gripping what was left of his bat so tightly, it was shaking.

The man shrugged. "You're still alive, aren't you?"

"Barely." Leo wanted to send this tool back to wherever he came from.

"Mr. Starnick, you in particular caught our attention," Mr. Private Interest said, handing him an IHOP business card. All it contained was a logo and a three-digit number, 888. "You predicted that aliens would choose Tinley Hills, and you were right."

Leo squinted at the guy. "Maybe."

The man pulled a folded piece of paper from inside his suit jacket. "You posted on an online forum called Dangerous Skies last year that, quote, *when aliens decide to make the journey cross-galaxy or whatever, Tinley Hills will be the number-one target*, end quote."

"Dude, do you know how high I was when I wrote that?"

Sarabeth and Evan chortled.

"Our company doesn't care how you arrive at the answers, just that you arrive at them," Mr. Private Interest said, his impenetrable dark eyes lacking any humor whatsoever. "And, when you think about it, it makes sense. Plenty of people in a dry town means pure specimens."

"Clearly, they don't know my dad," Leo said. "Or Abe."

"Ah, they know Abe," Mr. Private Interest said, his jaw setting into a frown. "He used to work with IHOP, long ago."

Sarabeth's eyes widened. "Wait, are you talking about the same Abe who we met?" she asked. "Lived in a mobile home by the . . . IHOP?"

Mr. Private Interest nodded.

Leo remembered something. "He had squirt guns, filled with alcohol, just like us," he said, more to Sarabeth than to Mr. Private Interest. "They weren't just for drinking."

"That's kind of disappointing," Evan said jokingly.

"Yes, Abe made a few enemies in his day," Mr. Private Interest said, clearly not in on the joke. Then he morphed his serious expression into a salesman's smile and asked Leo, "Ever care to see Area Fifty-One, the world? Other worlds? We're looking for people like you."

Leo grinned and reached out for Sarabeth's hand.

"It's an interesting offer, and I'll keep it in mind," he said, flicking Mr. IHOP's card. "But for now, I've got a prom to catch."

39

HANGOVER

*Teena McAuley, 8:08 A.M. Casimir Pulaski Day,
Orland Ridge Mall Parking Lot*

Why did her head hurt so bad?

How much had she had to drink?

She must really have been mad about Cameron and Nina to have gotten so wasted.

Wait, why was she on the ground? Was this . . . the mall parking lot? She turned on her side.

Where was the mall?

"Breathe, honey," a woman's voice said. "You're gonna be okay."

Teena sucked in air, and it was like she'd swallowed back her memories. Her party. The dead people. The aliens. She wasn't hungover. She'd been hurt in the last battle. But where were Sarabeth and Leo? And Evan. She had to find them. She sat

288

bolt upright and tried to stand, but her nurse pushed her gently down. "Don't move too fast, sweetie. We just stitched you up."

"Yeah, your leg looked pretty awful," came a familiar voice.

She blinked and turned her head to the other side. There was Cameron Lewis, his teeth gleaming white in his perfect but ash-smudged face. Had Cameron saved her? How had he found her?

Teena smiled wanly in response.

"I've been waiting for you to come to," he said. "Are you okay?" There was worry in his eyes.

"I am, I think," Teena said. "Are you?"

Cameron nodded. She could barely pay attention to his handsome face because she couldn't stop herself from looking over his shoulder for Evan and her friends. Maybe Cameron had saved her. And if so, she was grateful. But the weird thing was, she didn't care the way she would have a few days ago. She just wanted to find everyone else.

"Have you seen your sister?" Teena asked, earning a quizzical look from Cameron.

"Yeah, she's back with my mom and that Leo guy," he said. "I can't believe you guys did what you did. And Evan Brighton. He's . . ."

"What about Evan? Is he okay?" She sat up again and this time didn't let the nurse urge her back down.

Cameron pointed to a cluster of people. "He was over there. People haven't stopped coming up to him since he brought you off the ship. It was pretty badass." Evan had saved her? Again? How many of her lives did she owe the guy?

She stood up. Her leg wasn't that bad. She started hobbling in the direction Cameron had pointed, even as the nurse protested.

What the nurse didn't understand was that, for Teena, finding Evan was a matter of life or death.

40

GIVE ME SOME (OUTER) SPACE

Evan Brighton, 8:13 A.M. Casimir Pulaski Day,
Mall Parking Lot

Evan was staring at the wreckage of the ship and the mall, or at least pretending to. He wanted to look like the stoic hero who'd be just fine on his own, even if he wasn't quite feeling it. He thought better of comparing his heart to the deep, empty pit in the asphalt where the mall had been. Instead, he just soaked it in, comforted by the realization that if he could survive an alien attack, he could certainly find a girlfriend. Someday, anyway.

"Evan." Teena's voice behind him was impossibly, annoyingly irresistible. He spun around without even thinking about it.

"Hey," he said, sounding cooler than he felt.

"What are you doing by yourself?" She was limping on her bad leg, and her tangled hair was pressed against her head in weird places. Yet she was more gorgeous than ever.

"You shouldn't be walking on that leg," he said automatically. He didn't know if he could ever fully stop worrying about Teena. Then, remembering the situation, he shrugged. "I was coming to check on you, but I saw you with Cameron. I didn't want to spoil your moment."

Teena hobbled closer to him. She was so much shorter than he was, he half wanted to lift her up so it would be easier to see into her eyes.

"What if I was hoping for a moment with you?" Teena asked, sounding kind of shy.

Evan smirked. "Look, you don't have to be all nice just because we got through some things together. I get it," he said.

"Oh, things like saving my life a shitload this weekend? Figuring out that I was not in the sea of people you freed from the ship? Coming back to get me?"

He shrugged again. "Seriously, it's no big deal."

"Just take some credit, already," Teena said, and now she grabbed his hand. Her little palm wrapped around his big one perfectly. "And maybe we can try a do-over of the Bed Bath & Beyond thing we started?"

Evan's blush rose so fast he whipped around so Teena wouldn't see it. With his eyes on the mall, he said, "Really, I don't want you to do me any favors. I know I'm not your type."

"Then I was choosing the wrong type." Teena was leaning into him. She tugged his arm, pulling him toward her, and then she kissed him.

She wasn't just doing this out of obligation. He touched her face, and he could feel her mouth lift into a smile beneath his fingertips. He almost wanted to jump in the air and pump his fists. Instead, he clutched her tighter, wanting to be as close to her as possible.

When they finally pulled apart, he grinned. "You know, we can do this thing, but I don't plan on taking any of your shit."

Teena smiled up at him in a way that made it clear he probably would take her shit. At least some of it. "I know," she said. "I was just wondering how you'd feel about a date."

He lifted her so they were face-to-face and kissed her again. "With you?" he said teasingly. "We'll see."

41

WHAT'S NEXT?

*Sarabeth Lewis, 6:09 P.M. Casimir Pulaski Day,
Orland Ridge Mall Parking Lot*

Sarabeth pulled a paramedic blanket tight around her shoulders. Now that night had fallen, the weather had grown colder. Still, she thought she felt a hint of spring's arrival in the air. She leaned her head back onto Leo's shoulder and sighed as he wrapped his arms around her. Next to them, Teena and Evan were huddled together beneath their own blanket. They were the last people in the mall parking lot, and in front of them, the gaping hole left by the mall was illuminated beneath streetlamps that had finally come back on.

Sarabeth was still in disbelief over everything that had happened, and the fact that she was standing here not just a survivor, but a survivor with a boyfriend. She looked from Leo to Tevan—Teena had already given herself and Evan a couple name.

"Should we take a walk?" Her friends agreed. Clearly they weren't ready to leave yet, either.

Everyone else had gone back to their homes and to check on loved ones who hadn't been captured and were waking up from weekend-long naps. The town went to work planning vigils for the victims. Seventy-one students had died at Teena's house, and the destruction at the stores on Route 33 and the killings on the ship added a few hundred more bodies to the dead.

It was a tragedy, but life was already going on. Sarabeth and her friends had been interviewed by every news station. Fan groups had already started on Facebook, and girls were arguing over who was hotter, Evan or Leo. Sarabeth was a little jealous and tempted to tell all of the groupies to keep their grubby hands off Leo. After saving the world, she wanted him all to herself.

Sarabeth and Leo held hands as they walked. Teena and Evan, right in front of them, were doing the same. For the first time in nearly three days, they had nowhere they needed to go, and no mission. The aimless walking was kind of nice, even if they did have to look out for debris. Suddenly, Teena stopped and pointed. They all stared disbelievingly at what stood in front of them.

"I can't believe it's still here," Teena said.

"It's indestructible," Evan said.

"It's incredible," Leo said, patting the Gussy Me Up van like it was an old and endearing horse that hadn't been ridden in a while. "Janie, we love you, too," he said to Abe's trailer.

295

Despite the blast that had taken out half the mall, the van and trailer still stood at the far corner of the parking lot, bruised but proud. The Gussy Me Up vehicle's dented pink surface kind of fit nicely with the dystopian landscape behind it.

Sarabeth surveyed the gaping wound left by the mall and the smoldering remains of the ship, which had been roped off by Mr. Private Interest's friends. Odd as it seemed, she was a little proud of the destruction.

It was going to be awfully weird to go back to her house and wake up tomorrow in her old life.

"Sarabeth, can I sleep over tonight?" Teena asked. "You know, since my house blew up and everything."

Sarabeth grinned. "Olivia Lewis would love to have you," she said. "Probably more than she'd like to have me."

Leo slung an arm around her waist. "Don't be ridiculous," he said, and, with a look at Teena, added, "No offense, Teena."

Teena cuddled into Evan, who looked down at her. "So, Sarabeth's house? Is Cameron going to be there?" He clearly was teasing her and not actually jealous.

"I don't see why you guys can't be there, too," Teena said. "Sarabeth has a basement with an outdoor entry, you know."

Leo raised an eyebrow. "That sounds tempting," he said. "But tonight I'm going to have a beer with my old man."

Sarabeth loved her boyfriend.

She loved her friends.

She loved her life.

Her next journal entry would be titled, *Today is the first day of the rest of my life and here is what I'm going to do with it*.

But she'd work on that later. For now, she looked at her

three friends and said, "So, what happens when we get back to school? Are we friends now, or what?"

Teena rolled her eyes.

"We'll have to see about that later," she said, clearly joking. "But give it a rest. Today's a holiday, remember?"

So, you're probably waiting for the inspirational song to kick in over the final credits. Sorry, soundtracks are just so pricey nowadays.

But how about a parting lesson? Everyone loves a good parting lesson.

It's like the old saying goes, "Be cool to people you don't think you need to be cool to, because one day that person might just save your ass."

And even if ass-saving never enters the picture, we're always looking for a few open-minded, able-bodied young people to keep the skies friendly. The coffee's free, twenty-four hours a day.

Don't call us, we'll call you.

Sincerely,

Your Friends at IHOP

ACKNOWLEDGMENTS

Funny thing about writing acknowledgments: You get to write them when you're all done writing the actual book. So, here I am, in victory-lap mode, and I'm so grateful and happy I sort of want to run down the most crowded street I can find, planting double-cheek kisses on everyone I meet. I guess it would be bad if you caught me on those couple of days somewhere toward the middle of writing the book, when I think every sentence I pen is utter drivel and I spend hours at my desk without typing a word worth keeping. Then, I'm an evil curmudgeon who just begrudges everyone in the universe for having more fun than me. "You called a plumber to fix your overflowing toilet? Grrrr. And I'm stuck here. Grrrr. Again." So, to anyone who may have been a victim of my scowly face, I'm sorry. I'm actually a very nice person.

I'm lucky to have worked with some really wonderful people who make awesome company, post-alien invasion or anytime. Thanks to everyone at Alloy Entertainment, especially Josh Bank and Sara Shandler for always believing in *The End of the World As We Know It*, and most especially two very special and lovely women: Joelle Hobeika, so instrumental in helping the book's unlikely heroes assemble, and Emilia Rhodes, who kept her mind on the mission, helped the funny bits be funnier, and made sure that saving the world felt like a really big deal.

My brother Bill Palmer makes spectacularly entertaining films, and I was lucky enough to have his thoughtful notes on an early draft of this book. My agent, Fonda Snyder, helps keep me sane when sanity isn't my natural state. My in-laws, Steve and Mary Stanis, are due thanks for headquartering the Chicago chapter of my unofficial fan club.

My parents, Bill and Debra Palmer, have always been the kind of parents teenagers in YA books wish they had (and never do). None of my crazy schemes and dreams ever sounded too crazy to them, and they instilled in me enough wherewithal to work hard and never give up. (And, when I was just nine years old—long before I ever thought someone would pay me to write—they actually did when they bought several of my original works for a dollar each. I definitely overcharged them.)

This book is dedicated to two of my favorite people in the universe. My son, Clark, is not quite two and laughs in the face of childproofing, and while his unique brand of chaos might seem counterproductive to the writing process, I love every anxiety-addled, sleep-deprived second of being his mom. Clark, you are without compare.

Finally, my husband, Steve Stanis, is the one I'd want by my side in any adventure (and who's already been by my side for so many.) He'd make one badass alien fighter—and a quippy one, too, which in my ranking rates higher even than badass. Steve, you are my ideal love on this or any other planet.

ABOUT THE AUTHOR

Iva-Marie Palmer grew up in Chicago's South Suburbs, and—despite her educators' best efforts—she could never remember what Casimir Pulaski did to get a holiday until she researched it for this book. Now she lives with her husband and son in Los Angeles, where there are no three-day weekends for Mr. Pulaski, but since there are also no –11-degree days (before wind chill), she makes do. She loves books, Disneyland, food sold off carts and trucks, John Hughes movies and Joss Whedon everything, books, old movie palaces, shiny shoes, crossword puzzles, drivers who do the little wave thing when you let them in your lane of traffic, vending machines that sell odd items, books, non-life-threatening adventures, and roadside attractions. You can find her online on Facebook, Twitter (follow @ivamarie), and http://ivamariepalmer.com. Come visit, and she'll wish you a happy Casimir Pulaski Day.

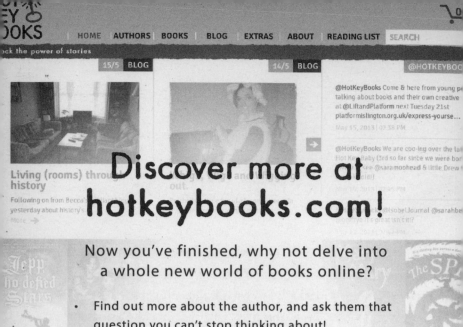

Discover more at hotkeybooks.com!

Now you've finished, why not delve into a whole new world of books online?

- Find out more about the author, and ask them that question you can't stop thinking about!

- Get recommendations for other brilliant books – you can even download excerpts and extra content!

- Make a reading list, or browse ours for inspiration – and look out for special guests' reading lists too…

- Follow our blog and sign up to our newsletter for sneak peeks into future Hot Key releases, tips for aspiring writers and exclusive cover reveals.

- Talk to us! We'd love to hear what you thought about the book.

And don't forget you can also find us online on Twitter, Facebook, Instagram, Pinterest and YouTube! Just search for Hot Key Books